My son
married to the author's
daughter this year
2024. nov.
Such a beautiful
family. enjoy this
and donate it on.
xx.

ISBN: 9798363788864

Names, characters and places throughout this book are products of the authors imagination.

Independently published and printed by KPD

Publisher: Independently published

Publication date: November 2022

Author: Johanna Cogbill

Ciao Cariad

By Johanna Cogbill

CHAPTER ONE

Alex chose a table in the shade, under a large red umbrella. Sitting down she crossed her legs to the side of the small bistro table, took out her laptop placing it on the table in front of her and lifted the screen open.

She had just over half an hour before she was due into work and took the opportunity to catch up on any emails before today's much anticipated meeting.

The waiter dressed smartly in a black shirt and cotton trousers approached her table,

"Buongiorno - The usual Signorina Alex?"

"Si! Luca, Buongiorno." Alex answered as she removed her Louis Vuitton sunglasses - her treat to herself from last month's bonus.

Luca quickly wiped the already clean table as Alex moved her laptop from side to side, allowing room for the unnecessary cleaning of the already spotless table.

"Ah, always working hard Signorina Alex, even when you are not at Rivolli's!" He inclined his head towards the left side of the street to the estate agents, where Alex had worked for the past almost 5 years.

"Just catching up on some emails" replied Alex smiling. Then added rather sheepishly, "well yes work emails".

"All work and no play will make Signorina Alex so sad and much too beautiful, to be sad!" said Luca dolefully.

"Oh, Luca I'm too busy to be sad, look I'm catching up on Facebook too!" Alex turned the screen slightly towards Luca to show him the Facebook page, just to prove she wasn't 'all work obsessed' at this time of the morning.

Luca smiled and nodded "all very well to watch everyone else's lives, but you need one too!"

He returned to the kitchen to get Alex's daily Americano coffee order, before Alex could protest that 'she had a nice life thank you very much'. Just because he didn't see her off on nights out with various suitors like Sofia - her work colleague who was always out and about on the town - no Alex was very happy as she was.

She clicked to refresh the Facebook home page and a photo of her mother appeared with the caption, 'Hell on wheels!'

Alex gave a small laugh - "oh mam!" she exclaimed.

Her Mam, Carole, had recently taken up rollerblading, her latest craze or was it a phase. When Alex had spoken to her last - when was that? Over a week ago Alex thought guiltily - she'd been going for her second roller-blading class having apparently loved her first exclaiming "Its fab babe. I'm probably the oldest there, but I don't care!"

"Be careful Mam you're not getting any younger, you don't want to go breaking your neck!"

"Oh babe" chided mam, "it's fun and it'll keep me fit, you know how I love my tai chi but it's hardly energetic!" Alex laughed at this, Mam – she had a hectic social life – Alex glanced at the lovely white gold modern watch on her slim wrist. 9.30am, 8.30 'back home' in Porthcawl, and as it was a Tuesday Mam was probably doing a beach clean with one of the many environmental social groups she had joined. Alex clicked the 'WOW' emoji under mam's photo and made a mental note to call her later. Scrolling down her Facebook page a photo of Connie appeared, 'an ice cream selfie' taken after Connie's shift at 'Nice Ice' had finished yesterday evening. Connie was Alex's oldest and 'bestest' friend. They had met on Connie's first day at the local primary school, when she had moved there with her mother to live with her doting grandparents when she was 7. They had been friends now for two decades. Connie looking suntanned with her dark hair piled on top of her head in an untidy knot, wearing her trademark sunshine yellow 'NICE ICE' polo shirt, happily licking a multi coloured ice cream. "Nice advertising Con" laughed Alex to herself as she clicked the 'love' emoji under the photo 'always bellissimo gelato at Nice Ice!' she commented and posted. 'Nice Ice'- The girls had gone there whenever they had enough pocket money saved for a special treat and then later on, girly evenings or teenage dates with local lads - Alex thought back - the first date she'd had with Jared had been there, September 2004, "my goodness" Alex shook her head - over a decade ago!

Where had the years gone - Jared - Alex thought of him, tall and athletic with his wavy dark hair and friendly green eyes. Had it really been five years since she'd last laid eyes on him? Last kissed him? Last said "arevedici" to him? When he had returned to university to continue his studies, but she had wanted an adventure – a change, a new life abroad - after a wonderful extended trip around Italy that summer, drinking vino, eating pizzas, visiting so many beautiful cities, Rome, Florence, Luca, Siena and then finally Naples and romantic exciting Sorrento. When the time had come to return home back to Wales - back to University in Cardiff – Jared was ready, but Alex wasn't, she couldn't go back, wouldn't go back. She'd finished her Media degree, was pleased she'd passed with a 2:1 and wasn't interested in continuing her studies. She'd enjoyed being a student whilst it lasted but wanted a change now. She wanted fun and a career, and where else better than in beautiful, vibrant Sorrento. They argued, they cried and then they parted going their separate ways. Jared booked his flight home and Alex had stayed - and that's where she still was, aged 27 single and contently so, had a job she loved in an estate agent 'Rivolli's', selling and renting everything from small city apartments to amazing villas with views across the bay of Naples, to local working-class people to the rich and famous. Everyday there was something different, it was her dream job. Mam missed her obviously but with a busy social life and the promise of visits to Italy, she soon came around, and that was it really - Alex hadn't returned to Porthcawl in all those years and had never wanted to.

She clicked off Facebook and clicked onto her emails whilst sipping her Americano.

Emails regarding new properties, people making enquiries about properties that Rivolli's had advertised and a few looking for properties that might come up for sale or rent in the future.

Alex scrolled down until she saw the email she had been looking for,

Dolanp@27yahoo.co.uk

She clicked it 'open'

Hi Alex,

Wyatt is coming to Italy late next week to view the villa. Not sure what day yet - as you know he's got such a busy schedule. I know I don't need to mention this again, but confidentiality is paramount at all times - I'll be in touch as soon as I can confirm

Regards Pete Dolan.

"Great!" Alex said out loud.

"Good news?" asked Luca with an inquisitive smile.

"Er only work."

"Oh oh, work again Signorina Alex, I, as they say, despair of you!"

Luca gave a small sigh.

'Only work,' thought Alex. But very exciting work, a real bona fide rock star was coming to Sorrento to meet her and to hopefully buy a beautiful cliff top villa from her - well not 'her' exactly - but still this was a biggy for 'Rivolli's' and definitely a 'biggy' for her!

Alex finished her Americano and left the money by the side of the cup,

"Arrivedici Luca- see you tomorrow!" she called to Luca who was wiping the bar.

"Ciao Alex and don't let them work you too hard!" He called back wagging the cloth he was wiping the bar within the direction of 'Rivolli's.'

Alex waved in reply.

She was excited to get to work, to the meeting which was an update on the villa and the rock star.

Sofia arrived at the entrance of Rivolli's the same time as Alex,

"Hi Alex, oh how do you always look so fresh and lovely in the morning?" Sofia moaned in a playful manner.

"Hi Sofia, try staying in for a change one evening and not drink so much wine!" chided Alex just as playfully.

"Oh no, where's the fun in that?!" laughed Sofia.

Alex had the key to open up and after opening the shutters and pressing the lever to higher them; she opened the office door, holding it open for Sofia to enter.

Rivolli's didn't have a uniform, but the girls generally wore smart skirts and shirts in whites or creams. Alex smoothed down her cream linen skirt and checked her honey blonde hair was still fixed tightly in the band that was holding her sleek shoulder length ponytail.

Sofia sighed, "Oh Alex how I wish I had your lovely, neat hair, it always looks so smart" she touched her own wild curly brown hair, "I give up with mine!!"

Alex laughed "believe it or not this takes a lot of work, don't know where I'd be without my faithful old straighteners!"

Sofia sighed again "come out with us tonight Alex, a gang of us are going to Romero's for cocktails, oh come on, and after today's meeting you may even have something to celebrate!"

"I hope so 'he's' coming over next week to see the villa! I had an email off Pete Dolan this morning!"

The girls referred to Wyatt Morgan as "He"- he was in fact a singer and guitarist - for want of a better word 'a rock star.' He was pretty famous in Britain and America, but not so much so in Europe, although the girls were aware of his popularity. He wanted a place to chill when he wasn't working or touring, and Sorrento had ticked the boxes for him.

No one at Rivolli's had met Wyatt yet, only Pete Dolan his manager, a portly man who was not just short in stature but short in attitude. He could be quite abrupt and abrasive at times and would only deal with Alex, as he didn't think the others at Rivolli's would understand him fully or he them as Sofia and Ricardo were Italian nationals. This undoubtedly annoyed them as they obviously spoke perfect English – much better than Alex's Italian - but as they say the customer is always right, even if he's a narrow-minded bigot! Something Ricardo would mutter when the office had no customers!

"Buon giorno signore!"

Ricardo arrived 5 minutes later, biding the girl's good morning.

"Morning Ric. I've had an email; 'He' is coming next week!" Exclaimed Alex excitedly, she couldn't wait for Ricardo to take his seat behind his desk in the corner.

"Ah 'HE'- at last, we will meet him! I hope he is better than that, that MAN!!" Ricardo removed his beige linen jacket, before sitting down, making a slightly unpleasant face as always when there was a mention of Pete Dolan.

"Well at least he's more handsome!" laughed Sofia, turning her laptop screen towards Ricardo showing a photo of Wyatt Morgan at a recent concert in London, dark hair and beard, sporting a white t-shirt and ripped jeans, brandishing a guitar, the others turned to look at the screen.

"Ok" continued Ricardo, "I know I said we would be meeting this morning regarding Mr. Morgan and his villa, but I think now there is no need, other than to say Signora Canale has given permission for Mr. Morgan to visit the villa at any time, I have the key here, she is in Naples visiting her brother for the next couple of weeks, so we do not need to make arrangements, whenever Mr. Morgan is ready we are ready, Si Alex?" Ricardo nodded at Alex.

"Si Ricardo, I have all the paperwork up to date, so I am ready when he is ready!" Agreed Alex enthusiastically.

Signora Canale was selling the villa and moving back to Naples to be closer to her brother, since her husband had passed away, she had no interest in being there anymore and wanted a quick sale.

"Romero's?" Sofia enquired, as she slipped back behind her desk in the opposite side of the room to Ricardo.

"Maybe" replied Alex as she moved around the office with some filing.

Sofia tutted and tossed her curls back "we'll be there from 7."

Alex smiled to herself, maybe she'd go, she hadn't been out in the evening for weeks. She preferred to sit on the small veranda of her tiny apartment usually reading or catching up on social media, but what to wear? Smart casual was probably best.

The office telephone rang making her jump slightly,

"Buongiorno Rivolli's - come posso aiutarti!" (Good Morning Rivollis, how may I help you), answered Sofia in her usual efficient manner.

"Si! Si!" Sofia's voice became sotto and she spoke quickly, she took the hand piece from her ear,

"Alex! There's been an accident - it's your Mama!"

CHAPTER 2

Connie wrapped her anorak around her and tried to hold up the hood against the cool morning breeze, as she walked quickly along the promenade to her place of work 'Nice Ice.' It was her turn to open up the ice cream parlour today. It had been her dream since being a 10-year-old, to work in 'Nice Ice' when she and her best friend Alex would imagine and discuss mad and adventurous flavours if they ever owned an ice cream shop - and now here she was 17 years later. She had started working there as a weekend helper on her fifteenth birthday and had basically worked there ever since. Connie enjoyed the early mornings when it was her turn to open up – she had barely passed a soul on her way to work, but she didn't mind as there would be plenty here later, especially if the weather forecast was right, as a bright and sunny day had been promised. After getting the cafe area prepared, returning to the kitchen, Connie glanced at the shell shaped clock that adorned the wall "Ooh that was quick. Fifteen minutes to kill!" She had attended to all the preliminaries quicker than anticipated, so she poured herself a welcome cup of tea and sat at the counter to enjoy it in case there was a mad rush later, and a cuppa would be out of the question. She clicked onto the Facebook app on her phone, scrolling down and smiling at the photo of her friend Alex's Mam rollerblading "Go Carole!" she commented.

Scrolling down she abruptly stopped, a photo glared back at her of her 'supposedly' boyfriend 'Matt' wrapped around a girl she didn't know - both looking 'very friendly'. After a few seconds of investigation, it appeared that Matt was at a party last night in town after telling Connie,

"Sorry Con won't be seeing you tonight. Having an early night - busy week in work. Love ya!"

"Early night!" Connie said indignantly out loud even though there was no one there to hear her.

"Lying swine!" she added.

Connie was just about to ring him and give him a piece of her mind when she heard a screech of tyres and then a bang.

She rushed to the window and opened the blinds to see what had happened - her eyes darted up and down the prom, but she couldn't see anything other than an old gent walking his dog in the opposite direction.

She rushed to the shop door and clicked it open so she could see down the side street.

Connie locked the door behind her and walked around the far side of the building. There she was greeted with three cars stopped in different directions, people milling around and there lying on the road was a woman.

Connie ran over towards the scene "oh my god what's happened?"

A man in his early thirties, still in shock, quivered "I-I don't know. I was just driving into the street, and she came from nowhere. I couldn't stop I didn't mean it I just..." his voice trailed away as he rubbed his forehead and looked in anguish at the poor woman lying in the road.

Another man approached them, it was Wal from the hot dog stall. "Ambulance on its way" he shouted, before noticing that Connie had joined the group "Connie, hello love, you know who it is don't you?"

Connie, wide eyed, shook her head.

"Carole Stevens! Your old mate Alex's Mum"

"Oh no, Wal! Is she... is she..." Connie couldn't finish her sentence, clearly shocked. Carole was like an auntie to her, she had always been there for her since Mum had died and even before, when she and Alex were children.

"She's unconscious love, the medics will know what to do when they get here - don't worry"

The next hour passed in a bit of a whirl; the ambulance arrived and took Carole, the police arrived and spoke to everyone, and Connie was accompanied back to 'Nice Ice' by Wal, who had called Mario the proprietor to come in early after explaining what had happened.

"She's in shock Mario, a sugary cuppa might help" Wal pulled up a chair for Connie.

Mario bustled around and brought Connie a drink, "oh my lovely. Drink this and I will take you home."

Connie sipped the tea slowly "do you think she'll be ok?" her worried eyes went from Mario to Wal.

"She's in the best place now Con, we'll call in a while and see what's what!" answered Wal sincerely, patting her gently on the shoulder.

Connie nodded, then suddenly she jumped up "oh no Alex! I'll have to call her!" she slowly sat back down "but what do I say?" She put her hands to her head.

After finding out from the hospital that Carole had regained consciousness but was suffering with a broken leg, wrist and bruised ribs - Connie felt a little easier calling Alex. She tried her mobile first, but it was switched off, so she scrolled down her contact list until she found Rivolli's' Alex's place of work in Sorrento, Italy. Once through Connie hastily explained to the female voice at the other end of the phone - probably Sofia - Alex had spoken about her before. Alex came on the phone,

"Alex! It's Connie,"

"Con! What has happened, is she ok?" asked a stunned Alex.

"She's been hit by a car, but she's ok Al, luckily, but she's got a few broken bones"

"Oh no! Poor mam."

"It was a total accident the bloke couldn't stop, Carole was on her roller skates, he said she just came out of nowhere! She's got a broken leg and wrist and a couple of other minor bumps and bruises."

"Oh no! Those bloody skates! Have you seen her Con?"

"No, not since she was taken to hospital. I'm going to phone Granddad now to ask him to take me there so Gran and I can see her."

"Please let me know as soon as you've seen her, and how she is – and tell her I love her and I'm thinking of her - I can't believe my phone is off I never switch it off I..."

"Don't worry Al, I'll phone you straight away, I'll phone granddad now. Take care and I'll call a bit later."

"Ok, thanks Con! She'll be glad you are there and your Gran, thank you, thank you" Alex was in shock.

"Bye."

Alex hung up. Sofia and Ricardo were waiting in anticipation.

"She's been hit by a car and has a broken leg and arm!"

Saying the words out loud, Alex started to shake and tears ran down her face.

"Oh, poor mam and she's all alone, I know Connie and her Gran Mary will be there for her but, but..."

"Alex you must go to her!" demanded Sofia.

Alex looked up and then at Ricardo "Si Si Alex, it's your Mama! It is important to go to her, family is everything at a time like this"

"But Wyatt Morgan is coming to see me next week – I suppose I could get a flight now and be back before he comes"

"Don't worry Alex first get a flight home, see how your Mama is and then we will worry about Mr. Morgan!" Soothed Ricardo.

Sofia was already back behind her desk looking for suitable flights, "Alex there's a flight this evening to Birmingham? Shall I book you on? The next one isn't until the end of the week to Bristol and of course nothing to Cardiff unless you want to fly to Milan and then on to Cardiff, but I think this is better and you'll be able to see her in the morning."

"Birmingham yes ok – are you sure this is ok Ricardo? I hate to leave you in the lurch at a time like this"

"Do not think about it for another second! Book it and go! Gianni will take you to Naples airport he owes me a few favours (Gianni was Ricardo's younger and more feckless brother-although very charming and very handsome) now go home and pack" said Ricardo taking charge.

Sofia printed the boarding pass and handed it to Alex with a hug, "take care Alex and give your Mama our love"

Alex walked back to her apartment in a daze. She let herself in and pulled out her case from under her bed.

She started packing and then sat down on the edge of her bed "home!" she hadn't really thought about home for a long time - to be honest she thought of Sorrento as her home now, well it had been for the past 5 years. It was where she lived and worked, and she loved it. She had avoided returning home for all these years. Mam had been more than happy to spend long weekends and even a few Christmases in Italy. Was 'avoided' the right word - yes probably – Alex felt that apart from Mam there was nothing in Porthcawl for her. She missed her girly times with Connie, but they were always on social media or texting or phoning, so that was ok, and then there was Jared. What she thought about him now she didn't know. He wasn't on Facebook, she didn't have his number and Connie had said that once he returned to Cardiff after leaving Alex alone in Italy, he had never come back to Porthcawl, so Connie didn't know anything about him either. So, he wasn't the reason she hadn't returned. Or was he? She just didn't know. She supposed that she just didn't think that there was any reason to return, until now. Gianni whisked her to the airport in Naples in record time travelling in his old but smart Lamborghini. Connie had called, as promised with a progress report on Mam. She was in a lot of pain, but able to speak to them briefly and Connie imparted that she definitely perked up when she was told that Alex was on her way back home.

Alex smiled to herself ruefully, was that what Mam had really wanted all these years but had never said? For Alex to come home once in a while? Alex felt like the world's most selfish daughter. She voiced her thoughts to Gianni,

"You are going home now though Alex, now when it matters. You'll be there for her"

"Thanks Gianni- you make me feel slightly less of a selfish cow now!"

Gianni flashed a gleaming smile at her, his eyes crinkling at the corners.

"Don't forget to come back to us though Alex. I'm still waiting on that date you have been promising me for the last few years!"

"Oh, Gianni I'm too boring for you"

He winked "I'm always ready for a challenge!"

She kissed him goodbye on both cheeks and entered the airport terminal, heading for her check in desk, before going home.

CHAPTER THREE

Following a delayed flight to Birmingham, a long wait in the train station for a train to Cardiff, another to Bridgend, an 'around the houses' bus ride to Porthcawl and a taxi to Mam's apartment, a very exhausted Alex practically fell through Carole's front door at 6am. Sleep had now deserted her, so she made herself a strong black coffee and jumped in the shower. Once dressed in a pair of cream chino type trousers and a crisp white shirt, she tied her hair up in a bun - not bothering with the usual straightening daily procedure – and then slipped her feet into a pair of comfortable tan Italian leather loafers, picked up Mam's car keys, locked the front door behind her and jumped into Mam's little red Vauxhall Adam. Alex started the car engine and then panicked. After five years of living in Italy she hadn't driven a right-hand drive since last living in Porthcawl. "Right girl think!" She urged herself. "Take it slow and you'll be fine!" She pulled onto the street where Mam lived and indicated left, entering the main road. So far so good!

Alex arrived at the hospital in one piece, twenty minutes later. She parked the car and entered the building. The last time she'd been here was when she was 12 and had sprained her wrist playing netball, after all these years nothing had changed, it all looked the same. Within a few minutes she found herself sitting next to Mam's hospital bed holding her 'good hand'.

"Oh, Alex babe you came" whispered mam hoarsely.

"Of course, I came Mam, as if I wouldn't"

Alex looked down at Mam, she was so pale and had a massive purple bruise on her cheek. Her right leg was plastered and slightly suspended, her left wrist was covered in plaster too, and her middle area was bandaged up. Alexis hugged her, conscious of not hurting her.

"Are you in pain mam?"

"They've filled me full of drugs babe so I'm ok" Mam tried to laugh, then grimaced "oohh my bloody ribs - don't think I'll be roller-blading for a while!"

"Bloody roller skating! That's what landed you in here!"

"Well, I didn't fall off them, I just miscalculated my speed against the side street gradient" Mam still defiant and defending her newfound, if somewhat dangerous new hobby.

Alex shook her head "oh mam!"

Later that day after leaving Carole to rest and finishing unpacking her case, Alex called into 'Nice Ice' where Connie was working a shift. Connie was busy serving a customer when Alex entered the shop and stood by the counter waiting for Connie to notice her. When Connie spotted her she shrieked, "ALEX!!!!!!!"

She ran from behind the counter as the two flung themselves into each other's arms. They hugged and shrieked and hugged again to the bemusement of the Nice Ice customers.

"Alex! Welcome home!" called Mario from behind the ice cream counter, which served the outside customers "How is your Mama?"

"Bruised and battered, but I think she's going to be ok thanks Mario."

The two girls looked each other up and down "I can't believe you're here! Back home in Porthcawl oh Al, I've missed you!" exclaimed Connie.

"Yes, back home" answered Alex rather subdued "I've seen Mam, she's had quite a knock hasn't she."

"Yes, but she's a fighter Al. She'll be back on them roller skates before you know it!"

"Ha, over my dead body! They'll be going in the bloody bin as soon as I get my hands on them!" answered Alex indignantly.

"Sit down Al and I'll get you one of our specials" said Connie pressing Alex into a seat at the nearest table "I'm on my break soon."

"Take your break now Con, I'm fine. It's getting quieter now" called Mario.

Connie brought two Nice Ice 'specials' over to the table where Alex was sitting and joined her, sitting opposite.

"Just like old times" Connie smiled.

"Yes" Alex nodded "It's good to see you Con"

"How does it feel coming back?"

"Well, I only got back this morning so I don't know really, but I do feel a bit cold "Alex laughed "it was 30 degrees when I left and it's, what, 15 today?"

Connie laughed too "rain promised for the rest of the week too. Welcome back to the British Summer!"

Alex looked around the parlour, nothing had changed over the years, same peppermint-coloured walls, shell clock ticking away, and the picture painted by Connie's mother Laura of Nice Ice still adorned the wall behind the counter. The two continued to spoon the delicious ice cream special into their mouths. "As good as Italian Gelato?" asked Connie, breaking into Alex's thoughts.

"Mmm" Alex thought for a second or two, then sampled another spoon full "well Mario is Italian!" the two laughed again.

"What do you think Al, that bloody Matt. I think he's messing around with someone else!" Connie announced, imparting the news on her so-called boyfriend.

"You are too good for him Connie!" called Mario from behind the counter "I always said it, he's a wide boy!" Mario being old enough to be Connie's Dad, had always been fiercely protective towards her.

"With whom, Con what makes you think this?" asked Alex concerned for her friend.

Connie showed Alex the photo on Facebook.

"Hmm looks like he lied, stopping in, but this doesn't really prove anything Con, have you confronted him?" Alex said after Connie filled her in about the supposedly 'early night'

"No to be honest, what with your mother's accident and everything I totally forgot until now!"

"Maybe it's best to ask and then see what he has to say"

"Arghh that boy is no good!" said Mario with a stern look and a tilt of his chin.

"Why's that Mario?" asked Alex.

"He got a too confident way of him! Always got an eye for all the ladies!" Mario muttered something under his breath in Italian. Connie looked at him "What's that Mario?"

"He said if he was a dog then he'd be neutered!" laughed Alex.

"Oh Al, I forget you can speak Italian; you are so clever!"

Alex laughed again, "not fluent though. But I'm too bad"

"Not bad at all" Mario was laughing now too.

"Confront him Con and let's see what this "dog!" she emphasised the word dog "has to say for himself!"

The next few days flew by with visits to the hospital, talks with the doctor and arrangements for Carole to return home. Alex was in constant communications with Ricardo and Sofia, she'd had an email to say Wyatt Morgan would be flying out to Italy on 12th and was hoping to meet and view the property on 13th or 14th.

It was now the 9th of the month, and Alex was hoping to get Mam settled back home, organise home care in the next few days, and then hopefully fly into Naples on the morning of 13th June. That gave her a whole 3 1/2 days to get organised.

Alex cleaned Carole's flat from top to bottom - luckily it was on the ground floor so at least there were no stairs to worry about. The hospital was going to supply Carole with both a wheelchair and crutches, so Alex tried to make the flat as easy as possible to move around, moving small tables, stools etc. She had an hour before she was collecting Mam from hospital; the doctors had been very pleased with her progress and had agreed for her to return home. Alex waited in the side room next to Carole's hospital room to meet the consultant who had been looking after her.

"Miss Stevens?" Alex looked up as a woman entered the room. Dr Meadows was around Alex's age. She was tall and slim with dark hair pulled back from her face, her glasses were perched on the end of her nose, and she had an air of authority about her. "I have spoken with the home care team today and your mother is entitled to visits, but as you are here to look after her and there are several other more urgent cases, they won't be able to start their visits until the second week of July,"

"What! No, that's not what I was led to believe" Alex panicked, that was no good to her, no good at all. "I'm returning to Italy next week, well in 4 days, I have a job I can't stay, I just can't"

"I'm very sorry Miss Stevens but that's the best we can do. You'll have to alter your plans, I would say your mother can stay here a bit longer, but even if it was agreed there'd still be a wait for home care, and from what your mother has said she thinks that you are going to be there for her, and she is very keen to return home" Doctor Meadows stared at her over her glasses.

Alex opened her mouth to argue but there was something about Doctor Meadows that silenced her, she felt that she was back in school being chastised by her head mistress Miss Black when she and Connie had been caught swearing (nothing too bad!) at the boys in the yard when they were ten - she felt the same now as she felt then - guilty and not wanting to upset or disappoint Mam.

"No that's fine" answered Alex subdued by the conversation "I'll be there for my mother for as long as she needs me"

An auxiliary nurse entered the room pushing a wheelchair with Carole sitting it in looking bruised and battered, but happy to be going home.

Alex got up out of the seat she was occupying, "Come on Mam let's get you home!" she said brightly, for Mam's benefit. As she took the handles of the chair from the nurse she smiled in thanks, but felt torn, her mind was on the Wyatt Morgan deal, her head was in Sorrento, but her heart was here with Carol. The wheelchair took a bit of negotiating and after a few false starts Alex managed to push the chair and Carole safely through the hospital and out to the car park, "Come on Mam lets go home" said Alex brightly.

That evening Connie came over to the flat with a bottle of wine and some chocolates.

"Oh, it's so lovely seeing you two back together again it's just like old times" smiled Carole, as Connie bent to kiss her on the cheek. The three chatted for a while before Carole decided she needed to go to bed as she was understandably shattered. The girls helped her into bed and returned to the lounge.

"I'm not going back to Italy Con, at least not for a good while" said Alex as she took a sip from her glass of co-ops best Chardonnay that she had just poured. She went on, "I can't Con, Mam needs me and there's no care available until next month, so looks like I'm here for the foreseeable."

"What about your important meeting?" Connie knew a bit about the deal, but not who it actually was.

"Don't know yet Con, I was thinking of flying over just for the meeting and then flying back. But that will mean having to fly from Manchester to Naples, and then back to Edinburgh, which sounds crazy! But they are the only available flights, and the client wants to meet and view the property on June 14th, but then this morning..." Alex took another gulp of wine, "...Mam had a letter from the fracture clinic in Swansea, and they want to see her on the 14th, can you believe that!"

"Oh Al, can I do anything to help? I know I can't drive, but there's Granddad and..."

Alex interrupted, "Thanks Con but it's about time I did something for Mam instead of relying on everyone else, it has been great just having you listen to me and my moans, anyway what about the Matt situation?"

"I think this calls for another bottle of wine!" announced Connie. The girls settled down with a bottle of Lidl's Italian Red that Mam had taken a fancy to on one of her visits to Italy- it wasn't the same but close enough mam had told Alex over the phone a few days after returning home following a fabulous new year celebrated in Sorrento, seems like another lifetime ago now, sighed Alex reminiscing, anyway she thought, back to the present and this unpleasant character Matt!

"Well apparently he was all set for an early night when Bazza and Evans texted him about this party!" Connie paused took a sip of the red nodded in approval and continued, "the 'GIRL' in the photo is apparently Evans sister it was her birthday party, and "Honest Con" Connie adopted a smarmy male voice "there's nothing going on hun" She went back to her own voice "like there was nothing going on with Zoe Turner when I caught them a bit too close in The Globe corridor or Keely Smith when she passed me in the hall outside his flat early one Saturday morning or bloody Emma Williams who told everyone he was the father of her baby."

30

Connie sighed and looked at Alex, "I've been a blind stupid fool haven't I Alex" this was more of a statement than a question because Connie obviously knew the answer.

"No Con you're just a romantic at heart and always see the best in people you always have, do you love him?"

Connie thought for a few seconds and shrugged her shoulders, "well I suppose I liked him, oh I don't know Al, it was hardly Romeo and Juliet!" she laughed and so did Alex.

"Well babe you're better off without him, I don't even know him, well not really, I sort of remember him in school a couple of years above us and a bit of a lothario!"

They both laughed again, "oh Alex why do I always pick a wrong 'un?"

"You know what they say Con you gotta kiss a few frogs before you find your prince"

"I'd be better off with a bloody frog!! Remember Stuart Pugh he two, no, three timed me, then Ben Summers he moved to the other side of the bloody world and Chris Samuels, he came out as gay!"

Connie spluttered on her wine indignantly laughing out loud

"Oh, Con I haven't laughed this much in years, I know we should probably be sad, you with a loser boyfriend and me with poor mam and my Italian life out of reach for the foreseeable"

"Maybe I should've come to Italy to see you and met a nice Italian Stallion who'd take me home to his mama!"

"You should have Con it's so, so, beautiful and the men are so charming you'd love it- they'd love you! Look at you with your lovely figure and boobs to die for" Alex looked down at her own lack of voluptuousness! "You're beautiful Con and you'd fit in so well with your Mediterranean looks."

Connie laughed "thanks Al, I've missed you!"

The girls refilled their glasses when Alex turned to Connie and said," Con this is only an idea but it would be wonderful, how would you feel about going to Sorrento and stepping into my shoes, well not literally as we're not the same size" Alex giggled whilst Connie stared at her perplexed, Alex went on, " Dolan only likes dealing with someone British damn cheek when he's conducting business in Italy, anyway, you could meet them and take them to see the villa I can fill you in on everything we could be in constant touch by phone and email so you wouldn't have to worry about anything, and you could have a little holiday too."

Connie still stared at Alex, "have you gone mad? Me go to Sorrento and pretend I'm you?"

"No, not pretend to be me just someone like me, someone British who he can 'Understand' as he so 'quaintly' puts it!"

"I don't know Al that's like, well, massive, its mad" Connie took a large gulp of wine and sat back, "And what about Nice Ice and gran and granddad?"

"Surely you're owed holidays? And when I saw your grandparents yesterday, they looked fine, so well and well able to cope without you for a couple of weeks, so what do you say Con, obviously I'll have to run it by Ricardo my boss first, but I can't really see a problem, as he was a bit gutted, I can't return for the 14th"

"Yes, I say Si! Si! Why not? I am well overdue holidays, like you say my grandparents," she tapped the top of the coffee table "touch wood, are fit and well, my love life is in tatters- so what have I got to lose?"

"Fantastic I'll speak to Ricardo in the morning, and we'll get your flights booked! Oh my God Con you'll love it!"

The two hugged.

"I hope so!" Connie said, and then thought "what on earth have I agreed too!!!!!!!!"

CHAPTER 4

Connie opened her eyes and looked around slowly as she focused on an empty bottle of wine on the table in front of her. Rubbing her eyes, it suddenly dawned on her that she wasn't in fact tucked up in her own comfy bed, at 'Sea Breeze' cottage, but lying on Carole Steven's settee covered in a pink and blue patchwork quilt.

"Morning!" Alex appeared in the doorway carrying two mugs of steaming coffee "thought this might bring us around- before we start all our organising and planning!" announced Alex brightly, far brighter and livelier than Connie felt, as she lay back onto the cushions that had served as last night's pillow.

Alex placed one of the mugs in front of Connie, "Well Con, I thought I'd get a head start so I phoned Ricardo and ran through what me and you discussed last night!" Alex took a sip of her own coffee and pulled a face, "Urghh Instant! I will never get used to this after 'real' coffee- never mind Con you'll be drinking the real stuff very soon!"

Connie sighed, her head ached, she didn't know if it was the effects of too much wine last night or the memories of the Italian plans they had discussed excitedly fueled by the said wine and now seemed crazy in the cold light of day.

"Anyway" went on Alex putting her mug down, "Ricardo wasn't totally against the idea, I told him you had ok Italian and..."

"Ok Italian?" Connie spluttered on a mouthful of coffee,

"Well, you know, GCSE Italian is not to be sniffed at Con, and I told him you were in PR" Alex glanced down at Connie warily "well it is sort of in Nice Ice, I mean, well, you know you deal with the public and..."

"Alex what the hell was you thinking! I know basic greetings in Italian and I work in an ice-cream parlour! P bloody R my foot- so what did he say?"

"Well basically, he said OK as long as I get back when I can, he said that he couldn't see the harm in you covering and we'd say that you were my PA and that I'd been called away on urgent family business- which I have" said Alex quickly defending her idea, then added brightly, "so see Con –all sorted!"

Connie took a long sip of coffee then put her mug back down, "oh I don't know Al- this is like – well massive- I mean – well – I don't know if I can, I ..." She looked up at Alex hopelessly.

"But Con you were all for it last night!" Alex sat down next to her

"I know but with the wine and Matt and everything it seemed like a good idea."

"Oh, Con it is a good idea, you'll be helping me so sooo much, if I know you are there to schmooze the client and his bloody manager, you are fab with people, much better than me, you are a people's person" Alex took Connie's right hand and held in between both of hers in a persuasive gesture,

"And Con you need a change from here and all the Matt crap" She lowered her head and looked at Connie in a sad pleading way" pleeeeeeeaaaaase, pretty pleeeeeaaasssssseeee!!!!!!!!!!"

Connie smiled, then Alex smiled, then they both laughed,

"Oh, you rat bag! Don't make me feel bad!" Laughed Connie

"You know it makes sense! You'll love it there!"

"Right talk me through it again, then when I've had a shower, taken some paracetamol for this headache, and spoken to Mario, and obviously my grandparents, I'll give you my answer!"

"...But..." Alex wheedled, but Connie stopped her," No Alex! in that order, then and only then I'll give you my decision!"

An hour later Connie felt more human after a shower and the paracetamol began to take effect, she had to pass Nice Ice on her way from Carole's flat to Sea Breeze cottage, so it was easier to see Mario first. Today she wasn't due in until the afternoon, so when she walked into the cafe at 11am Mario looked up at the shell shaped clock frowning.

"Hi Mario" can I have a word?" Connie had approached the counter

"Sure, I thought either the clock had stopped or you had changed your shift, what's up?"

"I know its short notice but is there any chance I can take a few weeks off?" well she'd bitten the bullet; this was the first step towards her Italian adventure.

"Uh well when were you thinking?" Mario put down the ice cream dishes he had been putting away.

"In a day or two, it's Alex, she needs me to go to Italy to help with a deal she is putting together in work" Connie laughed at this "Makes her sound like some kind of gangster!"

"So, she's going back now, so soon" asked Mario.

"No, she has to stay here Carole needs her, so I'll be going instead of her, I know it sounds mad but she said she'll sort everything, my flight, someone to meet me in Naples, I'm to stay in her apartment and then go to work in her office, saying it out loud now did sound a bit mad to Connie, but something else too, a bit frightening and a lot exciting!

"Well!!" Mario scratched the side of his balding head, "Alex sounds like she's got it all covered, but are 'you' sure Connie?" he looked at her concerned.

"It's all happened so quick Mario, but yes I think I want to go, yes I'm sure I do, and it won't be for long but only if you can spare me?" Connie looked expectantly at Mario, hoping that he could spare her "OK, yes, you are due holidays it's a good month before the schools break up for the summer and even though you'll always be my little Connie, you are a grown woman now and it will be good for you to go to Italy!" he nodded in a sage like way "yes very good"

Connie hugged him tightly, "I know you miss Italy even after all the years you've been here, thank you Mario thank you so much"

"It will be wonderful for you, my lovely girl, and hopefully meet a nice Italian man to sweep you off your feet!"

Connie laughed, "With my luck with fella's Mario, he'll sweep me off my feet and I'll end up with a broken ankle!"

"You wait and see" Mario nodded again sagely, "yes don't worry about it here, Nicola is always asking for extra shifts now that her boy is away in University, think she needs the money and the company."

Nicola had worked at Nice Ice for the past 2 years, she was a divorcee and her son had gone to Leeds to study and was missing his company, even though she said he spent more time on his x box than talking to her, she felt lonely, and the house was now too quiet, so she'd be glad of more hours at Nice Ice.

After telling Mario she'd be in for her shift later, Connie left, and made her way home to see her grandparents.

"I'm home!" she called as she let herself in through the front door; she slipped off her jacket and hung it over the newel post at the bottom of the stairs. The cottage decor hadn't changed much since she and her mother had moved in with her grandparents two decades earlier, the hall way painted a sky blue with white skirting boards a painting of the harbour hung on the wall adjacent to the stairs, Connie smiled as she looked at it, it was signed 'L Devereux' Her mother Laura had painted that picture the first year they had come to live with Gran and Granddad.

Laura had been an artist, Connie loved telling people this when she was growing up, everyone else's mums were housewives or worked in the local supermarket, or some, like Alex's mum Carole, worked in offices, but nobody else's mum was an artist- Connie was so proud of her. She was younger and prettier, or she was to Connie anyway, than anyone else's mum and when she died Connie felt a part of her had died too. Mum always had had a weak heart and Connie knew that mum was always ill, which was the prime reason that they had moved from London back to Porthcawl. When she finally passed away, Connie was 15 and Laura herself was just 38, it was still a very hard and sad time. Connie remembered how wonderful Alex and Carole had been helping her through the most difficult of times before and after mum had died. That was part of the reason Connie would be there for Alex now and hopefully be a help and not a hinder, in Sorrento.

"Oh, hello my love, good night with Alex? How's poor Carole I must pop around there, do you want something to eat, or have you eaten?" Typical gran, thought Connie always ten questions and statements in one sentence without giving you a chance to answer any of them.

"Morning gran" Connie kissed Mary on the cheek, "yes nice night, is granddad around I want to speak to you both"

"Ohh that sounds ominous" Mary turned away from Connie and yelled towards the garden "Sid, Sid, come in for a minute!"

A few moments later Sid Connie's granddad appeared in the kitchen doorway stamping his feet to dispel any muck and dirt from the garden off his shoes before he entered the house

"Oh, Connie hello love, do you want a cuppa, I'm parched getting too old for this bending lark!" He rubbed his lower back "I love gardening but it's not loving my back!"

"Here I'll put the kettle on" Mary handed Connie an opened packet of rich tea biscuits and bustled around the kitchen as Sid swilled his hands in the sink in the corner and sat at the little pine table next to it, "well then our Con what is it you want to talk to us about" asked Mary.

"I'm going to go on a bit of a holiday" announced Connie.

"Oh lovely, well tell us more then our Con" said Sid as he wiped his spectacles in the bottom of his tattered old gardening jersey, as Mary tutted and frowned at him.

"Er Italy well Sorrento to be exact, I'm going over to help in Alex s office for a bit as she's here and looking after Carole, so I'm going, er, over there" explained Connie suddenly feeling like a nervous kid, as Sid and Mary looked at her startled,

Sid and Mary exchanged glances "Italy!!! When?" Sid asked raising his voice in surprise.

"Um in a day or two" Connie looked at one to the other and fidgeted with the edge of her sweater, what was wrong with her, she felt as if she was doing something wrong.

"Well, I never!! What about your job here?" questioned Mary

"It's only for a couple of week's gran and Mario doesn't mind!" defended Connie.

Sid mumbled incoherently under his breath.

Connie turned to look at her grandfather, "granddad?"

"Nothing love" said Mary glaring at Sid, "well we can't stop you so I guess we should say good luck and bon voyage!"

"Stop me?" questioned Connie feeling a bit braver now, "why would you want to stop me, it's not like I'm going to the moon or anything gran! And I am twenty-seven!"

"Ignore us love, it's just that to us you are still a little girl, and you've always been here, safe with us, you know what I mean, never went away to college, always happy to be here with us and in Porthcawl" gran caught her hand now, "not like that Alex, buggered off and left poor Carole high and dry, oh well that's none of our business and she's back now at least when she's needed!"

"So, you are ok about this?" even though Connie was a grown woman of 27 she still liked to have her grandparent's approval, Mary squeezed her hand, "as long as you don't go marrying an Italian fella and move over there permanently, then I expect it'll be alright, Mary turned to look at Sid "won't it granddad?" She said more of a statement than a question.

"Yes" Sid muttered and stared into the distance, not wanting to meet Mary or Connie's eyes.

The next day passed by in a blur and it was time for Connie to pack, she looked through her wardrobe, her clothes consisted of dozens of pairs of jeans, hoodies and a couple of Nice Ice polo shirts she wore to work.

"What about this?" Alex held up a long pink and white lace dress with Bardot top and a flowing skirt.

"I had that for my second Cousin Danielle's wedding last summer, never worn it since, like where am I going to wear something like that again?"

"Sorrento! Pack it you never know when you might need it, it's lovely, said Alex, gently folding it over her arm.

"If you say so" Connie pulled an unsure face.

"I've got a skirt somewhere" Connie pulled a few things from her wardrobe.

Alex laughed, "Somewhere!" She joined in the search, "put this white blouse in and these" holding up a pair of plain black trousers

"Here it is, "announced Connie triumphantly holding up a denim skirt, "oh" she sounded crest fallen, "do you think it will be smart enough? "All your clothes are so smart, casual but so chic, mine are not casual chic more awful shit!" Moaned Connie.

They both laughed, "They are fine Con, you only need a few shirts and trousers for the office as long as they are clean and tidy, you'll be fine!"

Connie looked doubtfully at the meagre pile of suitable office clothing she possessed, "I suppose so, I don't want to look like a frump though!"

"A frump" Alex laughed "one look at you with your flowing locks and lovely figure everyone in Sorrento will be putty in your hands!"

"I wish!" laughed Connie, throwing her underwear, pjs and a couple of pairs of shoes into her old and much underused suitcase.

"Thanks for this Con" said Alex suddenly, "I know it's a big deal for you to go, but thank you so much, I know you will love it, but thank you for agreeing to go."

"I'm really looking forward to it now, I'm crapping myself mind you," Connie laughed nervously, "but yeah I'm thinking opportunities like this don't come along much, and I'm 27 now so I think I'm overdue an adventure, I just hope I'll do you proud Al," The girls hugged.

"You'll be great Con" not too great mind, they might not want me back!" they laughed, "And I'm missing Italy like crazy- the weather, the food, the way of life" Alex looked out and slightly shivered as she looked at the drizzly rain spotting Connie's bedroom window, "Everything!" She added sadly.

CHAPTER 5

Connie took her seat on the plane, 20C next to the aisle, a couple in their 50's were already seated in seats A and B, they smiled at her politely in greeting, and Connie smiled back looking more confident than she felt! Her heart started to beat rapidly, she could hardly believe it, here she was aged twenty-seven and this was the first time she'd actually been on a plane, how had that happened? Where had all the years gone? Well, now here she was, on her way to Naples for her first ever adventure "No turning back now Con" she told herself.

She had a passport and had been to Europe before, she had been to Euro Disney and Paris for her second cousin Danielle's hen weekend last year, but then the gaggle of ten hens had gone on the bus or luxury coach as it had been advertised – not so luxurious after a couple of bottles of vodka and 14 hours travel!! So here she was only a few years shy of thirty having her first taste of air travel! She wasn't scared, more pleased that she had finally done it- Alex had asked her over to Sorrento but for one reason or another, usually some hopeless romance she had been caught up in had stopped her going, or was that just an excuse. True she and Alex hadn't been so close once Connie had stayed at the local Comprehensive School to do her A Levels whilst Alex had taken hers at the college in Bridgend, then moving to Cardiff with her boyfriend Jared when they both had gone to university.

Connie hadn't really fancied studying anything at university enough to get herself into debt, so she just stayed in Porthcawl, working more and more shifts at 'Nice Ice' drifting from one romantic disaster to another, and before she knew it, she was coming up to thirty! Thirty! Oh my God! Where did the years go! And what had she achieved? There was Alex with a life and a career in Italy and there was her, yes where? Still where she had been a decade ago- still living at home, still working in an ice cream shop, still unlucky in love! "This is going to be a turning point for me Al" Connie had announced to Alex on their way to Bristol Airport, just before Alex had dropped her off at Departures, "I need to get a life before I'm thirty!"

"Thirty though Alex, remember when we would plan that by the time, we were thirty we'd be rich or famous, or at least be happily married with a family of our own and a fantastic career- thirty seemed so old!!"

Alex laughed, "Well look at me Con, ok I love my life in Italy, but I'm not rich or famous and there's no relationship" then quickly added, "not that I want one! I am more than happy being just me!"

"But surely there's been someone or you must think about being with someone" Connie turned to look at Alex, who was concentrating on the road, "No Con, no one, like I've been out a few times in groups with some very nice, charming even good-looking guys, but no romance I'm not interested."

Answered Alex firmly her eyes focused on the road ahead

"But you must think about Jared, Al, you two were so much in love, I would have done anything to have a relationship like you two had"

Alex touched the breaks suddenly as a white Audi pulled out in front of her.

"Bloody idiot!"

"Who, Jared?" asked Connie who hadn't noticed the Audi

"What? No."

"You then?" went on Connie not realising Alex had been aiming her comment at the Audi driver.

Alex thought for a moment, "Yeah Con, maybe we were both idiots, but that's in the past now" briefly wondering if things could have been so different.

"Do you wonder where he is now, what he's doing? If he's married even."

"NO!" Alex" answered sharply more sharply than she had meant, Connie shot a look at her, "Sorry Con" she spoke softer now "I try not to, what would be the point, and it's too late now."

Always the eternal romantic optimist, Connie touched Alex's arm gently "It's never too late" Connie flicked through the airline magazine, Thailand, New York, St Petersburg, Dubai, every page adorned shiny luxurious photos of different destinations all over the world. Connie felt that she had been missing out on so much, tucked away in her small corner of Wales.

Well, Italy was a wonderful way to start this new chapter of her life; maybe she would become the new jet setting Connie, Connie smiled to herself, and relaxed back into her seat.

Alex was deep in concentration driving back to Porthcawl from Bristol Airport. She'd been back now for several days and those days had flown by, she hadn't really had time to think about anything other than mam and sorting out arrangements for Connie to go to Italy. Her days had been so busy that she hadn't had time to really miss Italy until now. Dropping Connie off at the airport made Alex's heart ache for Italy, as much as she was glad that she could be here for mam now Connie had gone Alex started to wonder when she'd get back to her little apartment, the morning Americano coffees served by Luca overlooking the square, going into the office chasing deals and setting up new ones, weekend visits to the coast and monthly visits to shop in Naples, and the beautiful long hot sunny days. And now Connie bringing up the subject of Jared- she had tried so hard over the past few years to push all thoughts of him from her head and heart and had succeeded, until now the mention of him and being back in Porthcawl brought it all back to the forefront of her mind. Yes- she would be a liar if she said she hadn't at least wondered if she'd bump into him, but as mam and Connie had both said his family had moved away it was highly unlikely- still though, last week when she walked past his old home she had felt nervous and goose pimples came up on her arms even though it was an unusually sunny day. Alex pulled up in front of Carole's apartment block , mam had definitely been improving, but was still getting tired very easily, Alex thought that she'd offer her a walk on the front today as the weather was looking quite promising, she had mastered the wheelchair without tipping mam out or crashing into anything so a bit of fresh air would do both of them good, a change of scenery for mam and a breath of fresh air to clear Alex's head and all her mixed thoughts and emotions about being back home and about Jared!

Alex let herself into the flat and could hear women's voices coming from the lounge.

"Oh, hello Alex love just popped into see your mam in case she needed anything, I didn't know how long you'd be at the airport, did our Connie get off ok?" the other voice had belonged to Mary, Connie's gran.

"Hiya Mary, yeah dropped off safe and sound and at this moment she should be just about taking off" Alex answered glancing at her wristwatch.

Mary nodded, "Good right ok, well now you are back I'll be getting on, she turned to Carole "see you soon Carole take care lovey"

"You too Mary, and try not to worry, she'll be fine"

Mary left then the flat.

"Alright mam, I didn't expect to see Mary here, is she ok?"

"Hmm, this and that on her mind you know with it being Italy and everything."

"Italy?" Alex sat down next to Carole.

"Well, you know, what with Connie's father, and things"

Alex frowned, "you mean because he was Italian, but mam what's that got to do with Connie going to Sorrento?"

It suddenly dawned on Alex, "does she think that Connie might want to see him if she's in Italy then mam? Con has never even mentioned him or anything."

"Well, you know how it is love, I suppose that Mary and Sid thought that if Connie had never wanted to find out about him when Laura was alive or even after she had died, then that was that, but with her going to Italy it might stir up some thoughts of him."

"But no one even knows where he is, for all we know he could be living in Bridgend."

Carole frowned at her, "I wouldn't have thought so babe."

"Oh well you know what I mean, just because he came from Italy it doesn't mean that he's gone back there, he lived here and London and he could be anywhere, and Italy is a very big country!"

"I know babe, but well Mary can't help worrying, and Sid's not too happy either about her going."

"Bet my names mud over in the Devereux house!"

"Why, Alex."

"Well, it's my fault she's gone to Italy,"

"Oh well like you say, babe, she probably hasn't given him a second thought and he could be anywhere."

Alex pushed Carole's wheelchair from the flat up to the promenade, the beach was packed with holiday makers and day-trippers, a strong mixture of fried onions from Wal's stall and candy floss filled the air, deep in concentration, Alex thought back to days gone by when first she and Connie would 'hang out' on the prom and beech and then to times when she and Jared would stroll hand in hand walking the same route as she and mam were now. She shook her head sharply as if to throw off all thoughts of Jared.

"Shall we call in at Nice Ice for a frothy coffee, and let Mario know that Connie got off ok?" Alex suggested to Carole, trying to forget the past, the two turned to go through the open doorway of Nice Ice.

"I feel like the queen in here" announced Carole to Mario indicating to her wheelchair, "everyone getting out of my way and me giving orders where to go."

"Ah Carole it is so good to see you out and about" Mario kissed her on both cheeks.

"Can't wait to get back to normal though Mario, you know me I like to be active."

"Yes Carole, too bloomin' active! I hope you have thrown those skates away Alex" he said turning to Alex.

"Oh, don't worry Mario, they are long gone!" announced Alex sighing and shaking her head.

Carole scowled, "I was just getting the hang of them"

"Tough! They are gone and don't ever think of replacing them" threatened Alex.

Mario brought the coffees over to the table.

"Glad to be back home Alex?" He asked.

"Yes and no" Alex answered as truthfully as she could, "glad to be here with mam, but missing Italy like mad, I don't know how you do it Mario."

"Oh, after all these years I still miss home" answered Mario sadly, "but my wife was here, God rest her soul" Mario made the sign of the cross on himself, "and now my children and grandchildren, they are all here in too, but a big bit of my heart will always be in Italy, and who knows what the future will bring."

Alex smiled, and wondered if Mario was thinking of going back to Italy.

When she went to the counter to pay, she thought she'd make a casual enquiry about Connie's father.

"Mario, do you remember Connie's father?"

Mario looked up his eyes round in surprise "Giacomo, yes of course I remember him, what on earth made you mention him?"

"Nothing really, I was just thinking as he is Italian too"

"Has Connie said something?" Mario was frowning now.

"No, no not at all, it was me, er you know, I mean, I never met him, and I was just sort er wondering where he was now", stuttered Alex looking a bit guilty at being just a bit nosey.

"Oh, I haven't seen or heard from Giacomo in what ..." Mario silently counted "twenty-seven years, I have no idea if he is alive or dead, my dear."

Alex nodded, "oh right" she said quietly wishing she had kept quiet now and feeling a right nosey cow.

"What you talking to Mario about?" asked Carole when Alex returned to their table.

"Oh, nothing really mam, just passing the time of day, come on let's go and have a look around the shops, well whichever ones I can get you in without running anyone over."

"Yes, come on then let's buy something nice for tea."

CHAPTER 6

Connie and Alex had been in constant communication from when Connie touched down in Naples-She had hurriedly texted Alex "landed- got case- feels like I've walked into an inferno- shouldn't have worn my jeans!"

Alex had arranged for Gianni to meet Connie at the airport, and when Connie had exited to arrivals, she saw first the sign held aloft saying "CONNIE DEVEREUX" then second, she saw the very dishy man holding it.

She waved dragging her case behind her and made a bee line towards 'dishy man'.

"Boun giorno Connie?" enquired the dish.

"Yes, si Boun giorno Hi I'm Connie" flustered Connie under the sultry gaze of Ricardo's younger brother, she held out her free hand Gianni took it and held it up to his lips and kissed her hand gently "Oh my God! No wonder Alex never wanted to come back home, if this is what I'm to expect!!!!" thought Connie smiling and feeling suddenly hotter than just the beautiful weather was making her "Come, I'm parked just over there" Gianni indicated with a flick of his head, whilst taking her case from her.

Connie followed Gianni through arrivals and out into where he had parked up, admiring the way he opened the passenger door for her, put her case in the boot and swagger around to the driver's seat nonchalantly giving her a winning smile.

"Welcome to Italy!" and with that he sped off making Connie feel that she had entered some sort of movie set where she was the glamorous femme fatale being whisked away by the sexy suave hero!

"This place is Heaven!" Connie texted Alex.

"Yes, yes it is!" replied Alex.

After an exhilarating ride through Naples and onto Sorrento through exquisite villages with tantalising views of Mount Vesuvius, with Gianni pointing out points of interest, they at last pulled up in the busy main street of Sorrento. Gianni climbed out of the car and opened the passenger door for Connie.

"Welcome to Sorrento!" he said flashing her a sexy smile

Connie got out of the car and looked up at the sign on the building in front of her,

"RIVOLLI'S" in bold black letters, well here she was here at last

Gianni held open the office door, Connie entered hesitantly, she instantly recognised Ricardo and Sofia, as she had heard so much about them and the office from Alex, she felt at home as soon as she had entered.

"Welcome Connie" Ricardo rose from his desk and came around to greet Connie shaking her hand, "I am Ricardo Rivolli as you have no doubt guessed and this is Sofia Rossi," Sofia had already come over and hugged Connie kissing her on both cheeks.

"Oh hello, hello" gushed Connie "I feel that I know you both already I've heard so much about you from Alex."

"Did you have a good journey and did Gianni drive carefully?

"Questioned Ricardo shooting a look at his brother.

"Yes, fine thanks it was my first time on a plane, but it was lovely and the ride here with Gianni was magical" enthused Connie

"Magical, well I've heard my brothers driving described as lots over the years but never magical, no!"

Said Ricardo holding out his hands and shaking his head.

"The scenery, the drive, everything, oh it's glorious" said Connie smiling.

Ricardo shook his head again and thought to himself, "Gianni you have this one under your spell already! I will have to speak to you at another time to tell you to behave and not seduce this impressionable young lady!!!"

Later Sofia took Connie to Alex's apartment, which was just along the street, they entered a side door and climbed the stairs to another door, which was the entrance to Alex's apartment on the first floor.

"It's fabulous the view is wonderful no wonder Alex loves it here so much!" exclaimed Connie stepping out onto Alex's bijou balcony overlooking the city, she closed her eyes drinking in the sounds and smells so unfamiliar but so intoxicating.

"Yes, she spends too much time here alone though, sitting up here, I am always trying to get her to come out, but 'No' she says, I like my own company!" sighed Sofia.

"I can't blame her it's so lovely "said Connie looking around and stepping back into the compact apartment admiring it all over again, "Alex used to be the life and soul back home always ready for fun and adventure, well that's why she came to Italy and stayed because she wanted an adventure."

Sofia shrugged, Connie went on "guess she found what she was looking for and stopped Adventuring."

"Huh" said Sofia indignantly, "If you believe that then you are dafter than her, no man no romance, I think that she has stopped looking because there is someone she cannot forget or move on from."

"maybe" answered Connie cautiously not wanting to betray her friend, but secretly agreeing with Sofia that Alex had definitely not moved on romantically because no matter how much Alex shrugged it off or denied it her heart would always belong to Jared Jones!

Alex smiled as she read Connie's latest e-mail "Your apartment is amazing Al, I'll take good care of it for you and your job- met everyone at Rivolli's they are lovely, Sofia took me to your apartment after I had a quick briefing at the office, I'm starting tomorrow, gives me a whole day before I meet Mr. Big YIKES!!!!!!!!!!

Gianni collected me from the airport in his sports car he is HOT!!!!!!-

Just getting a shower now meeting Sofia later for cocktails! OMG Al can't believe I'm here- your life is A M A Z I N G!!!!!!!- love you xx"

Alex sighed "Yes my life in Italy is pretty amazing" she thought to herself, she typed back: -

"Glad you're enjoying yourself- but don't forget you are there to work Mrs, LOL, only kidding, watch Gianni though he's a one for the ladies!!! Have fun with Sofia she's lovely like an Italian version of you really! Good luck for tomorrow I'll ring you first thing just to double check details- love you too xx"

Alex smiled ruefully, it should be her there meeting Wyatt Morgan she'd done all the leg work he would be her biggest client since she'd started at Rivolli's, oh well she'd done the groundwork so it was still her 'baby' so to speak, but still she would have loved to have finally met him and 'sealed the deal'!

She closed her laptop and went to check on Carole.

"Hi mam, fancy a cuppa"

"Oh yes please babe I'm parched" answered Carole.

Just as Alex was leaving the room to put the kettle on the doorbell rang, she jumped a little startled still deep in thought about Italy and Wyatt Morgan.

Alex answered the door and standing there was a balding, greying man dressed younger than his 58 years holding an ostentatious bunch of flowers.

"Dad!" Alex exclaimed in surprise.

"Alexandra! What a surprise! Just heard about your mothers' accident and came to see how she is" announced 'dad' trying to push past Alex.

"She's resting I'll see if it's ok" answered Alex bluntly, half closing the door on him.

She turned and went back into the lounge, what was he doing here? Him-her father-John Stevens- yes it was a big surprise, no 'hello Alex how are you?' What's it been, seven years or more? Oh well typical dad- she never expected anything else or more and had learned from a very young age not to expect anything except disappointment and let downs from him, "Mam, you've got a visitor, my father has..." she didn't have change to finish

"Carole oh my love I had to come when I heard!" he was in the room behind Alex, brushing her aside with the giant bloody flowers and cooing and crooning toward mam, he knelt down beside the settee.

"Oh well, come in why don't you!" muttered Alex under her breath, as he pushed the bouquet towards her, she snatched them from him and stomped into the kitchen to find a vase, "nothing ever changes" she muttered mutinously dumping the flowers into an old vase she found at the back of the cleaning cupboard.

"Alex darling" cooed mam in that sickly voice she always used when 'dad' decided to grace them with his presence, "be a love and make a cup of tea for your dad too, there's some lovely Marks and Spencer's biscuits in the cupboard"

"I bloody know! "Thought Alex, "Because I bloody bought them!!!"

After simmering down to not quite boiling point Alex carried the teas and biscuits into the lounge on Carole's art deco tray she kept for visitors.

"Well, I didn't expect to see you home Alexandra" said John pointedly, sipping his tea.

"Why, you haven't seen me for years so how would you know what I am doing or where I am, and anyway I definitely didn't expect to see YOU!!! Answered Alex stirring her tea like her life depended on it.

"Oh, now now let's be friends it isn't very often I have you both here together" cooed mam.

"Thank God!" thought Alex.

"Darling, I didn't mean anything I just was surprised that's all" said John, then turning back to Carole, "now then my other darling how are you?"

Alex got up and went back into the kitchen, that was enough of 'dad' for her, she'd leave them coo at each other in peace before she was sick!!

John had never really been on the scene as a dad for Alex or a husband to Carole come to that, they had divorced when Alex was two and he had flittered in and out of their lives since then. Always with a roving eye Carole had finally had enough of being married to him after eight years of unfaithful marriage, unfortunately she still carried a torch for him and between 'ladies' he normally came back with a bunch of bloody flowers and some claptrap, and they would be together again for a short while until he got bored and found a new love interest or a job in some other town or city. This went on until Alex was 14 and then he met Michelle, twenty years his junior – thinking he wasn't getting any younger or now becoming less attractive to the opposite sex, he thought he'd better hold onto this one, and did the unthinkable for John Stevens- he married her and they went on to have two sons Simon and Joseph, and basically that was the end of the very fragile relationship between Alex and John. He lavished all his time and money on Michelle and the boys, whilst Carole was working all the hour's god sent in the solicitor's office just to make ends meet. Carole always tried to encourage good relations between Alex and John, but after being let down so many times, he wouldn't turn up to school concerts or sports days saying he was too busy in work, cancelled tea at his new house at a moment's notice- as apparently one of the boys would be 'ill' and then finally promising to pay for Alex's driving lessons then after dodging the subject for months, announced he couldn't afford it as he and Michelle were taking the boys to Florida! How Carole could bear to look at him let alone be civil and 'cooing' Alex would never know even if she lived to be 200!!

"I bet bloody Michelle has chucked him out and he's around here all smarmy and charming looking for somewhere to stay!" thought Alex angrily, "as if he gives a damn about mam and her accident!!"

John left after about an hour and Alex put the clip on the door behind him.

"Well, what's he after this time?" she asked.

"Oh, babe he heard about my accident and came to see if I was ok"

"And?"

"Well, nothing really, he and Michelle have been going through a bit of a rough patch, and..."

Alex laughed bitterly, "Oh right, and he's looking for somewhere to stay"

"No babe no he's staying with your Uncle Dave, no he was only concerned about me after the accident" defended Carole

"Yeah right" answered Alex knowing her father of old and not believing a word of it.

CHAPTER 7

The alarm on her phone woke Connie, she checked the time, 'seven thirty' she stretched out her arms then her legs, she had been having a lovely dream reliving the previous day and night.

Sofia had taken her to 'Romero's' yesterday evening, after a long soak in Alex's bath and a call which turned into an inquisition with her grandparents, she'd applied her makeup carefully, piled her hair up fastening it with a sequined clip and slipped on a red sundress that she'd had for years but had barely worn, finishing the look with silver sling back sandals and matching clutch bag that she'd bought to go on a works Christmas doo the year before. She had checked her reflection in the full-length mirror in Alex's bedroom, "not bad Con, you'll do"

Sofia arrived at eight thirty to collect Connie, dressed in a shimmering sheath of coral Connie looked down at her plain dress, "you look fantastic" greeted Sofia kissing her on both cheeks and propelling her out of the apartment and down the stairs, "not compared to you- you look like a movie star!" exclaimed Connie admiring Sofia's designer look.

"Ah this old thing" laughed Sofia "it's comfortable" "Comfortable?" thought Connie, "only if you were a size 6," Looking down at her 36e bust and size 12 figure If she was to wear such a dress, by the time she'd finished with tight pants and industrial strength foundation garments she wouldn't be able to breathe let alone be comfortable.

The two linked arms and walked across the square to 'Romero's' where they were met by Gianni, who Connie had met and been escorted to Sorrento by earlier, Maria and Gabriella, Sofia's friends since forever and Antonio an ex of Maria's but who was obviously still on good terms with. After kisses all around Gianni came back from the bar with a bottle of prosecco, "a toast to our new and very beautiful new friend" he announced "To Connie" everyone raised their glasses, "to Connie" they chorused. Connie beamed, even though she felt slightly embarrassed, she secretly enjoyed being referred to as "beautiful", whispering to Sofia "I think I'm going to like it here"

The evening went by in a whir, when Sofia excused herself and Connie at eleven O'clock, giving the explanation of "very big day tomorrow and Connie's had quite an adventure for one day!"

Even though Connie was shattered she couldn't get off to sleep, she didn't know if it was excitement of being here in Italy, the charming attentive and totally gorgeous Gianni and Antonio, or the anticipation of the following day.

She drifted off eventually and now climbed out of bed wrapping Alex's kimono around her she opened the French doors and stepped out onto the balcony. The city below her was wide awake the road teamed with endless traffic with vespa's buzzing in and out of the line of traffic, people called to one another in Italian, the smell of fresh warm bread and brewed coffee drifted up to her and she realised how hungry she was, only snacking on tapas and prosecco the previous evening.

She showered and got ready quickly, dressing in the white shirt and black trousers that Alex had suggested she bring for the office, a slick of eyeliner and lip-gloss, hair piled up, she slipped her feet into her comfortable scholls, and picking up her handbag she left the apartment in search of food.

Her phone buzzed as she entered the street below, taking it out of her bag she could see it was Alex ringing, "Hi Alex"

"Morning Con, all ready for later?" asked Alex

"Yes, he's due in the office at ten thirty, I'm so nervous Al, but don't worry I won't let you down"

"I know you won't babe, anyway, how did your first night go"

Connie told Alex all about her evening out at Romero's which took her until she arrived at Luca's bar and cafe, telling Alex about this fact.

"Oh Luca's- I'm missing his coffee soooooo much, tell him I'm asking after him and of course his coffee" said Alex longingly

"I will" hey it's your mothers hospital appointment today isn't it" said Connie, then putting her hand over the mouthpiece as she was greeted by Luca "a table for one please" she said to him smiling, he ushered her to a table close to the bar handing her a menu, nodding pleasantly.

"Sorry Al, just sitting down in Lucas"

"Oh, Con you are making me feel so homesick!" groaned Alex, "Yes she has her appointment at eleven in Swansea so I'm getting going soon in case of traffic"

"Talk about traffic, its mad here isn't it Al, last night was lovely, as you know they close the main street from traffic but this morning oh my goodness it was like Porthcawl prom on bank holiday-bonkers!" Connie laughed,

"I know, you'll get used to it though Con, just be careful, when you think it's ok to cross the road and there's no cars coming a vesper will appear from nowhere and they don't like stopping!" warned Alex, "I nearly got run over every day of the first month I lived there!"

"I can imagine, hey I'd better go Al, Luca's looking in my direction to order, better not upset the locals" Connie laughed

"You're a local now Con, good luck for later and ring me as soon as you can"

"You know I will, good luck at the hospital too Al,

Connie beckoned Luca over, introducing herself as Alex's friend

Luca beamed all over his face, "Oh Signorina Alex she is lovely works too hard mind you, how is she I heard her mama is not good"

"She's fine Luca and her ma, er, mother is getting stronger thank you, she is missing your coffee though"

Luca laughed, "Ah always enjoys her daily Americano"

After a delicious 'Luca special' breakfast Connie felt ready to face the world or the office anyway, wondering what the day would bring and hoping and praying that everything would go well with Wyatt Morgan.

The morning flew by with Connie being briefed to an inch of her life on the Wyatt Morgan deal. At ten past ten the office door opened and in walked a short stout chap rather dour looking and wiping his brow muttering about the heat, followed by a taller, slimmer, younger guy dressed in a white t shirt and ripped jeans with a baseball cap pulled low on his brow, and a dark beard covering the lower half of his face.

Connie looked up, but before she could say anything, the younger guy said rather awkwardly, "Buongiorno, una riunione, a meeting?"

"Er, buongiorno" said Connie smiling" "Can I help you"

"Oh you're English!" answered the guy in a strong 'black country' accent clearly relieved, "sorry its just that my Italian isn't very good" he pushed the peak of his cap back and smiled back at Connie,

"Yes, well, erm, Welsh I am actually" gabbled Connie suddenly realising who was standing in front of her, twenty minutes earlier than expected, she looked behind her helplessly into the office, Sofia was on the telephone and there was no sign of Ricardo, she turned back to the guests, smiling her most confident smile, bellying her nervousness.

"I'm Connie" she shot her hand out suddenly, Wyatt Morgan shook it firmly, "Hi I'm Wyatt sorry we're slightly early,"

"Where's Alex?" interrupted the other man glowering around the office

"Erm I'm Connie Devereux her PA" Said Connie offering her hand now to Pete Dolan, he ignored it, Connie went on, suddenly feeling more authorotive at Dolan's poinedly rudeness, "Alex is unable to meet with you today sir, which I understand she has informed you of, so, I'm here to help you in anyway I can,"

She smiled sweetly at Dolan whilst thinking what a positively unpleasant man he was!

At that moment Ricardo returned to the office, "ah Mr. Morgan, so pleased to meet you at last" he swept around the office shaking Wyatt Morgan's hand and then reluctantly Dolan's "I see you have met Connie, right then whenever you are ready to see the villa" he indicated his arm towards the door,

"Yes, I'm ready to go if that's ok with you" said Wyatt pleasantly

"Course its ok, that's what you're paying them for" growled Dolan. Wyatt, Ricardo and Connie exchanged glances, Ricardo regained his composure, "Right then Mr. Morgan if you'd like to follow me," he smiled at Connie, "ready Miss Devereux, "then slightly losing his smile, "Mr. Dolan "he opened the office door as they all went outside, where Gianni was waiting holding open the back door of a smart hired people carrier, dressed in a smart grey suit shirt and tie, he nodded to Wyatt and Dolan "Good Morning Sirs," he ushered them towards the open car door, for them to enter, "Miss Devereux" he winked saucily at Connie, whilst admiring her as she climbed into the vehicle.

Ricardo chatted to Wyatt as the vehicle sped through Sorrento and out and up into the hills, Dolan wiped his brow and muttered about the heat again before finally settling into his seat and closing his eyes as the air conditioning swept over him.

Connie was sat directly behind Gianni who was smiling at her whenever she caught his eye in the rear mirror; she tried to avoid his glances so he would hopefully keep his eyes on the road and not on her as they climbed steep winding narrow roads. She looked out at the breathtaking view of the Amalfi coast, Wyatt mirrored her thoughts, "It's even more beautiful than I imagined!" he exclaimed, "oh it's amazing" he beamed all over his handsome face, he looked just like a little boy who had just opened a coveted birthday present, as he gazed out of the car window in amazement, a picture of pure happiness.

Connie was gazing out too, "how absolutely beautiful" she said, Wyatt caught her eye and they both smiled at each other in appreciation of the beautiful landscape. "Oh my god it doesn't get better than this" thought Connie dreamily, "fantastic views both through the window and in the car!" stealing a look at Wyatt and then at Gianni who winked at her in the mirror.

They came to a stop in front of a pair of tall white metal gates, Ricardo jumped out and pressed some digits on a metal keypad set into the wall adjoining the gates, the gates swung open slowly and Gianni turned to drive through them and up towards a magnificent mansion basking in the sun. The russet red paved driveway was edged with lemon trees, Gianni parked the car outside the villa, and they all got out and climbed the five steps leading to the large white arched front door which was festooned with fauna. Ricardo had the keys and opened it ushering Wyatt, Dolan and Connie inside.

The hallway was painted in pale Mediterranean hues with a beautiful sweeping marble staircase standing some way in front of them; the high ornate ceiling adorned a large crystal chandelier. Doors led from the hallway to a magnificent lounge, a smaller lounge, which, Connie suspected was probably the same size as the whole of the ground floor of 'Sea Breeze' cottage, a dining room, big enough to seat all of Nice Ices Cafe customers and more, a kitchen you could hold a dance in it was so big and a utility room. Wyatt nodded and smiled in appreciation at each room, the kitchen led onto an orangery which led out to a large, covered patio area, which then led onto a beautiful, manicured lawn edged with the most exquisite flowers that Connie had ever seen, "eat your heart out Alan Titchmarsh" she thought as she looked around the garden in awe.

"Yeah, I can see me chilling in my hammock out here" nodded Wyatt looking around, "strumming my guitar"

"Mmm" I can too" thought Connie dreamily looking at Wyatt, and imaging him, stretched out, possibly shirtless, she silently shook herself, "behave yourself Con you're here to work girl!!"

"And there's more" announced Ricardo leading the way around the side of the villa. There in front of them was a Roman bath styled swimming pool, tiled with the most exquisite paintings of cherubs" Connie gasped at the sheer perfection of it, even Dolan nodded in complete approval.

"Amazing!" said Wyatt "what more can I say- Heaven on earth" Next Ricardo led them all upstairs, they ascended the beautiful marble staircase which led first to the master four poster bedroom with an en-suite bigger that most family bathrooms, four more bedrooms two with smaller en-suites and a huge bathroom complete with a Jacuzzi big enough to sit two very comfortably, thought Connie stealing a look at Wyatt's impressed face. Each of the bedrooms led out onto quaint Juliet balconies, with the master suite leading onto a large ornate balcony. Ricardo was beaming from ear to ear, "Well Mr. Morgan is it to your liking?"

Wyatt was standing out on the balcony that led off from the master bedroom he had thrown open the French doors to the most fantastic view of the city below, the blue ocean and Mount Vesuvius in the distance.

"Oh yes Mr. Rivolli, it's wonderful, the photos on the web site didn't do it justice, yes, I want it! Where do I sign?" Wyatt was smiling then laughing, he turned around and whisked Connie up in his arms, spinning her around excitedly, Connie was laughing now so was Ricardo, even Dolan managed a smile, he put Connie down, "I'm so sorry it's just that I'm so happy!" he apologised

"No problem" laughed Connie, "Here to help!"

They all laughed again.

"We have all the paperwork ready for you and your solicitor when you are ready to sign" said Connie regaining her composure and adopting a professional stance.

After making some quick phone calls Dolan nodded to Wyatt, "well that's all the important bits sorted, "announced Wyatt jubilantly, hands were shaken and the party all returned to Rivolli's office, Sofia was collected, and the office closed early as Wyatt Morgan insisted on taking them all out to celebrate Gianni included.

Connie sent Alex a quick text" "He loved it- deal going through asap-speak later xx"

Alex helped mam into the car, the front seat was moved right back so she had room for her leg cast and the back seat was down flat to accommodate her wheelchair, "It's like taking you out first time as a baby in our old fiesta babe, pram in the boot, baby seat in the front and no room for any shopping!" said Carole.

Alex smiled, "don't know about that mam, you always managed to shop till you dropped and find room somewhere!"

"Oh, I miss getting out and about I'm so fed up with having to rely on you for every little move I need to make" sighed Carole

"I know mam, but I don't mind, we're spending quality time together- isn't that what all these magazines are full of"

"Quality time my foot, poor you having to help me bath and get to the toilet!"

"Is that your good foot or your broken one mam?" Alex cast a wicked glance at Carole.

Carole laughed, "you are a tonic for me babe, you really are, you manage to make me laugh even when I'm so cheesed off"

Alex clasped Carole's hand, "hopefully the doctor will have good news today"

Carole nodded, "Yes babe let's hope"

Alex was glad she chose to leave early as the traffic was quite slow and bumper to bumper as they approached Port Talbot" she switched on the radio, to help while their time away

"Oh Elvis" exclaimed Carole as 'Love me tender' came on, "I won't be jiving in this year's Elvis Festival"

Porthcawl was famous for holding an Elvis music festival every September which attracted thousands of people. "we'll see you might be ok to go as long as you don't do anything daft" said Alex, "well anything else daft" referring to her roller-skating

Misdemeanor.

"I hope so, I'm missing all my dance girls, fair play they've all been around to see me or have phoned me, but it's not the same as going out for a good old dance" said Carole slightly sadly

"Dance girls" Alex laughed "There's not one of them under fifty, more like dance grans"

"Cheeky devil I'll have you know that we are first up on the dance floor and last to leave young lady!" chastised Carole, defending her Friday night pals, a group of fifty and sixty something's who had formed a friendship through their mutual love of dancing and made Friday night a regular dance hall visit.

"I know I'm only teasing, oh looks like the traffics moving a bit now" said Alex changing up a gear.

They arrived at the hospital twenty minutes before Carole's appointment, after driving around the car park twice Alex eventually found a parking space, once Carole was in her wheelchair the two entered the main building and followed the signs to the fracture clinic.

Alex parked Carole's wheelchair next to a free chair and sat down next to her and waited to be called.

"Have you heard anything from Connie, yet I know it was an important day today for you" Carole touched Alex's hand. "No, I spoke to her this morning so I guess it's all systems go now" Alex looked at her wristwatch,

"They should be meeting just around now; I hope it all goes well"

"If it wasn't for me you'd be there now, I'm so sorry babe"

"Don't be silly mam..." before Alex could finish her sentence
Carole's name was called.

"Carole Stevens to Room 3 for Doctor Jones"

Alex got up and pushed mam in the direction of the nurse who had
called her name.

"Come through I just need to check a few details and then Doctor
Jones is ready for you"

After asking Carole a few questions and checking some personal
details they were shown into another room, "Doctor Jones, Mrs
Stevens for you"

As Alex pushed Carole's chair through the door of the adjoining
room the Doctor looked up from his desk.

Alex's eyes rounded and her jaw dropped as she looked into those
green eyes she had known and loved so well.

Carole spoke first, "oh my god Jared Jones as I live and breathe!"

Jared jumped out of his chair and came around his desk, "Carole!...
and Alex!"

He rushed up to them and shook Carole's (good) hand and then
looked into Alex's eyes, he held out his hand to her, but she just
froze, and then all around her went kind of fuzzy, then nothing...

"Alex! Alex!" Alex heard a familiar voice, what had happened?

"Alex oh good you're alright, you had us worried for a minute" the concerned voice belonged to Jared, he was bending over her holding her hand and propping up her head.

"You fainted, here, drink this" he held a glass of ice cool water to her lips, as she sipped it slowly.

"Are you alright babe?" this time it was Carole, "no bloody wonder seeing this one here" nodding her head towards Jared, "after all this time"

Jared helped Alex up and into a chair, the smell of him as he held her close, was still the same, same tangy aftershave, same zesty body spray, she closed her eyes for a second, was this really happening, Jared, who would have guessed he was Doctor Jones and here in Swansea.

"I didn't think really when they gave me the files and I saw the name C Stevens, I'm so sorry I gave you a shock, but I had a hell of a shock too, I never expected to see you here in Swansea, I thought you were still in Italy!" said Jared rubbing his forehead and looking at Alex, the first time properly since she had entered his office, still the same Alex, a bit more tailored and chic but still the same pretty face and big blue eyes staring back at him.

"I am er I was, I came back when Mam had her accident" said Alex still bewildered.

"Sorry Carole it's you we are meant to be discussing," he looked down at the notes on his desk in a bid to get back to business

Carole shot a wide-eyed look at Alex and mouthed "OMG Jared!"

"Er I've looked at your x-rays and everything looks fine Carole, both were clean breaks and should heal well," he smiled up at Carole," We'll get them both reset in lighter casts and then see you back here in a month."

He got back out of his chair and shook Carole's hand again" It's been nice to see you Carole take care."

"You too babe" said Carole still bemused at seeing him.

"Alex, are you ok now, or do you need a few more minutes, I'm due my break now so I can accompany you both to the plaster room, er, if that's ok?" said Jared a little uncertain.

"I think I'm ok thanks" answered Alex regaining some if not all of her composure after seeing her ex- boyfriend for the first time in five years.

"But we'd love you to accompany us, though, wouldn't we, Alex?" Added Carole quickly, hoping to give the young couple time to talk The trio left Jared's office and walked through the hospital with Jared pushing Carole,

"How have you been?" he asked Alex, glancing at her as he negotiated the foyer with Carole's chair

"Good thanks, Sorrento is lovely"

"I remember" He answered solemnly.

"And you?" enquired Alex,

"Well, yeah ok, I went back to Uni, and my parents moved to Llanelli, and I got a job here."

"I heard you moved away from Porthcawl" said Alex quietly.

"Yeah, nothing to keep me there, after" answered Jared, meaning after Alex had stayed in Italy.

Alex nodded; they were at the plaster room now,

"Well thanks" said Alex, taking back control of the wheelchair

"Part of the service" Jared gave a little bow, "See you soon Carole" he touched Carole on the shoulder in a friendly gesture,

"Yes, darling see you soon" Carole touched his hand on her shoulder

"See you" said Alex, wishing part of her was a million miles away but the other part wishing she could stay here with him and talk and ask him what he'd been doing for the last five years and gaze into 'those eyes'

"So good to see you again, I mean that" he said to Alex and touched her arm gently.

"You too" answered Alex, then turned away from him, who was she kidding she thought as she pushed Carole with purpose through the entrance to the plaster room, one look at Jared Jones and she had passed out, she wasn't over him and never would be!

CHAPTER 8

Connie reached for her phone tucked away in her new bag she'd treated herself to, purchased from a little boutique just off the harbour, "Just going to call Alex to let her know everything's gone through ok and to see how her mother got off in the hospital" she said to Sofia and Ricardo who were sat next to her in the bar overlooking Sorrento harbour sipping champagne.

"Give her our love and tell her she's done well!" said Ricardo lifting his glass in a toasting gesture.

"Yes, send her my love and tell her I will speak to her soon!" said Sofia.

Connie got up and went to a quiet part of the bar and dialed Alex's mobile number.

"Hello?" Alex answered" "Connie?"

"Hi yes, it's me just ringing to say everything's gone well, you done good girl! Everyone sends their love."

"That's great Con I knew you'd do it."

"You had done all the work I was just going along for the ride, so to speak, nice ride it was too the views, the house, how the other half live, it's beautiful Al."

"Great."

"Everything ok Al with Carole? You sound a bit I don't know...down?"

"Mam's fine thanks Con, it's just that I feel a bit out of it here, I bet you are all celebrating and on cloud nine there."

"Oh, I'm so glad she's ok, yeah we're celebrating, Wyatt insisted on taking us all out he's over the moon with the house" Connie laughed," House, I should say mansion, palace even, oh Al it's amazing!"

"Hey, Con I'd better go we only just got home and my bloody father's here, don't want to get into that now, speak later, ciao, give my love and congratulations to everyone."

"I will, bye" Connie looked at the blank screen on her phone as Alex had ended the call, she couldn't put her finger on it, but Alex didn't sound right. Was it because she felt a bit down because she wasn't here in Sorrento? Was it her dad making a re- appearance? Or was it something else? Connie decided she'd ring her in the morning and hopefully get to the bottom of it. She rejoined the others in the bar; Wyatt had just opened another bottle and was pouring it into everyone's glasses.

"Alex ok?" asked Sofia as Connie sat back down.

"I don't know "answered Connie truthfully, "She said everything was ok with the hospital visit but she seemed down, not herself really."

"Oh no, missing Italy maybe?" said Sofia concerned.

"Yes maybe" Connie took a sip of champagne.

After an hour or so of general chit chat and more champagne being drank, Wyatt declared that he had a 'few days off' and wanted to see more of the Amalfi coast. It was somehow decided that as it was the weekend and Sofia had a day off and that as Connie hadn't seen any of the beautiful little villages there about that Sofia would act as their tourist guide and take them off to see the sights in the morning.

"Righto I'm turning in for the night, see you outside Rivolli's at nine tomorrow morning" announced Wyatt getting up from his seat and bidding everyone good night, Dolan was already stood and followed Wyatt in the direction of the exit.

"Well, I think we'd all better think of making a move" said Ricardo getting up too.

"Maybe another drink? Huh?" suggested Gianni to the girls.

"Oh, why not, come on Connie the night is still young and so are we!" laughed Sofia.

Connie nodded, "ok just the one."

Alex didn't want to go into the flat with her father there, she needed time to think and time on her own, so he was a good excuse really for her to go for a walk.

She walked and walked her mind in a buzz and found herself on the sand dunes overlooking the calm blue sea, she sat down and took off her sandals feeling the sand creep between her toes, she closed her eyes and took in the scent of the sea, then lay back onto the sand, "Jared!" her mind and body was in turmoil even after all these years seeing him again had had such a profound effect on her. They would walk in these sand dunes hand in hand, lie in them laughing, kissing and sometimes they would just lie there not saying anything just content curled up together with her head on his chest. She sat up again, should she try to contact him? Or was the past best left in the past? Why hadn't she mentioned anything to Connie? Connie knew that there was something up with her- was it because she knew Connie would guess she still loved him still wanted him? Alex didn't know- yes only one look at him had made her pass out- it was a shock –yes, but more than that- he was still drop dead gorgeous, even more so now- just thinking of him again- something she'd stopped herself from doing over these past years- made her stomach flutter and her heart ache- had she been a fool all those years ago to let him go! There had been no one since, a few dates and that was it- she loved her life in Sorrento- her man free life- her love free life- it was all she wanted, needed- or was it?

Now she'd set eyes on Jared Jones again everything was confused, mixed up, crazy- was her life so perfect or was it missing love? And not just any love but the love of her life?

Connie awoke next morning early but not bright! Her head was still muzzy from too much Champagne the previous night and worse when she came too, she remembered a drunken kiss with Gianni when he had walked her home!

"Oh no!" she sighed to herself "Gianni of all people", Alex had warned her, Sofia had warned her even his own bother had, but damn, he was so bloody charming and good looking! He had tried his best to be invited in, but Connie had heeded the warnings and had managed to get rid of him with talk of headaches and jet lag-jet lag she laughed to herself the excuses you could come up with after a few drinks! Ah well it got rid of him even though like a fool she had kissed him first!

After a quick shower to revive herself, she sat on the balcony and pressed 'Alex's on her contact list on her phone whilst sipping a 'medicinal' coffee.

"Hello Al, are you ok? I was worried after talking to you yesterday you seemed, I don't know, not you!"

"Hiya Con, I'm sorry yeah I suppose you're right"

"What's up hun" asked Connie concerned "is it your dad? I know he never had a good effect on you!" "Oh, him yeah I could do without the addition of him, Michelle has binned him, and he's been sniffing around mam again, but no it's not really him, I suppose I'm feeling a bit down with all the excitement going on with work and I'm not there and I'm missing out, silly really"

"Not silly at all Al we're all missing you loads" answered Connie, "hey you'll love this, I sort of copped off with Gianni last night"

"Oh, Con how did you manage that?"

"Quite easy really with a bit of help from Mr. Champagne and Mrs Prosecco" Connie laughed.

"And?" enquired Alex temporarily forgetting about her woes

"Nothing really a kiss and a cuddle, I know you warned me but Al he's so bloody gorgeous and so bloody seductive!"

It was Alex's turn to laugh now, "just be careful as long as you know it's just a bit of fun and don't get hurt"

"Don't worry Al my integrity is still intact, and I managed to get in and into bed alone!!"

"You've been there, what, 4 days, not bad going for your first bit of romance!!!" said Alex teasingly.

"Oh, Al I'm not that bad, I know I'm an incurable romantic, how the hell you didn't fall for anyone here I'll never know!" laughed Connie

Alex didn't answer, "Oh my god I'm so sorry, I didn't mean to sound horrible, Al, are you ok?"

"I saw Jared yesterday!" there she'd said it now, Alex exhaled

"What? Where? Oh, Al I knew there was something wrong! Are you ok?" Connie put her cup down suddenly surprised by this revelation

"He was the Doctor Jones mam went to see yesterday, Oh Con I saw him and fainted, I felt so stupid!" "Oh, hun that's unbelievable, Jared! Are you ok now?" asked Connie concerned.

"I don't know Con and that's the truth, I haven't slept, my heads a mess, I thought Jared was in the past but seeing him yesterday, I just don't know any more everything is just..." she trailed off

"Will you see him again? Do you want to?"

"I, I, oh Con what am I to do?" asked Alex helplessly

"What do you want to do Al?"

"I want to come back to Sorrento and hide in my work I can't deal with all this right now!" cried Alex

"Oh, Al don't be upset I feel so helpless here, come back Al even if it's just for a few days gran will look out for your mam I'm sure, come back and relax and think about what you want to do, you will be able to think clearer here"

"I don't know Con, that's just me running away again I need to face up to this once and for all and the only place I can do that is here in Porthcawl."

"If you are sure, please ring me if you need to talk any time of the day."

"I will thanks Con, you take care over there."

"I will, you take care too."

Connie deep in thought about the surprise return of Jared Jones was brought suddenly out of her thoughts by a shout from the street below.

"Connie, are you ready? I'm just picking up some supplies for our day out and I'll meet you in ten."

It was Sofia, was it time to meet already? Connie glanced at her phone 8.50am they were meeting at Rivolli's in ten minutes for their day out with Wyatt Morgan touring the Amalfi coast.

"Be with you now" called back Connie casually, then running back into the apartment and throwing on her clothes like a mad woman grabbing her bag whilst frantically fighting her hair into a quick chic style raced down the stairs and out onto the street to their meeting place.

"Good night last night?" enquired Sofia eyeing Connie saucily

"Er yeah great wasn't it" answered Connie trying not to catch her eye.

"Hmm, and after?" Continued Sofia.

"Er yeah" muttered Connie.

"And? You and Mr. Rivolli junior?" Sofia nudged her.

"And nothing nosey! he walked me back to the apartment like a gentleman!"

"Ha Gianni Rivolli behaving like a gentleman now I know you are lying!" laughed Sofia. At that moment Wyatt Morgan arrived, wearing a white t shirt, cream Bermuda shorts and a dark baseball hat, expensive looking sunglasses coverer his eyes and a bag pack on his back, looking like an eager tourist, "Morning ladies I'm ready for an adventure!" he announced excitedly that reminded Connie of a little boy just like yesterday when they were travelling up to see the house.

Glad of the sudden distraction from her interrogation by Sofia, Connie answered just as excitedly, "great let's go, Sofia lead the way!"

CHAPTER 9

After voicing her thoughts and fears out loud to Connie, Alex felt a bit better, even though she still didn't have a clue what she was going to do.

She joined Carole in the lounge taking her in a cup of tea

"Morning babe, are you ok, we didn't get a chance to talk yesterday with dad coming over and you going out, where did you go?" asked Carole concerned.

"Just for a walk to clear my head"

"And did it? Clear your head I mean?"

Alex shrugged her shoulders.

"It was a big shock seeing Jared again after all this time, I know, how do you feel about it?"

Alex shrugged again, "strange, it was such a shock mam, well you know, you saw me make a fool of myself."

"Fool nothing, if I hadn't been sitting down, I think I would have fallen down myself, it was a hell of a shock!" Carole caught hold of Alex's hand, "how do you feel about him though babe?"

Alex turned her big sad blue eyes to look at Carole, "I think I still love him mam!"

"Oh, come here my sweetheart" Carole held Alex close, and Alex burst into tears for the second time that morning," no, no my sweetheart" soothed Carole as she cradled Alex like she was a little girl again. "I don't know what to do mam" sniffed Alex.

"Follow your heart baby that's all you can do" soothed Carole kissing her on top of her head.

Connie and Wyatt walked along after Sofia as she ushered them onto a local bus, she was in charge of their 'outing' and was basking in the pleasure of the job like a schoolteacher taking excited children on their first-class trip.

"First stop along the drive will be Positano" she announced "we'll have a picnic there in a little area I know overlooking the sea" she held up her bags containing fresh bread rolls filled with various delicious fillings and a carton of orange juice, "when we call in Amalfi later, we will call into my Aunt Francesca's restaurant for a special Italian meal"

Connie sat back in her seat and admired the beautiful scenery as they drove along, the bus drove through Sorrento and out onto the narrow winding coastal road that snaked out of city overlooking the azure blue sea below and on towards the villages along the Amalfi coast. The views were breathtaking Connie marveled at the way the bus driver maneuvered the vehicle along the drive keeping her fingers crossed that they'd get to Positano in one piece as the road appeared to get narrower and steeper, she took her mind off this fact by thinking about Alex and Jared. She hoped Alex would be ok she couldn't begin to imagine the shock poor Alex must have had and she supposed the shock Jared had had too- she hoped they would be able to resolve things as in her heart of heart Connie always believed they should be together. Even though she hadn't seen Jared for over 5 years and not a lot of Alex either in the past 5 years when they had been together in Porthcawl they were obviously made for each other, and Connie always thought they'd be together and get married and have a family and had felt so sad for them both when they had parted.

Sofia was pointing out landmarks and seamarks such as Capri as they drove along, Wyatt was constantly out with his iPhone taking photos as they drove along, soon they had arrived at Positano, and Sofia ushered them off the bus. As soon as she alighted from the bus a mixed aroma of leather and lemon hit Connie she breathed in deeply, "Ohh that smell it's divine."

"They hand make shoes here, don't they" said Wyatt leafing through his Amalfi coast tourist book, "I was reading about it on the plane over here."

"Yes, there are many small family businesses here that hand make shoes, clothes, soaps you name it not to mention the delicious local foods" said Sofia in tourist guide mode

"Mmm lemon soaps, I am loving all the lemon groves in Sorrento there's one just opposite Alex's apartment, absolutely beautiful" Connie smiled at the sheer loveliness of Positano, "I think I've died and gone to Heaven!"

Sofia laughed "Yes, it is very beautiful here; I suppose I am just used to it being born here."

"Imagine being born somewhere like this!" exclaimed Wyatt in his strong midlands accent, "I was born in a council house looking out at, well, more council houses!" Wyatt reminisced about the house he had grown up in with his parents and his two brothers

"I lived in London for the first few years of my life and when we moved to Porthcawl I couldn't believe it, right by the sea I only ever saw the sea side when I had visited my grandparents so to actually live there and to walk on the beach and go swimming was amazing" said Connie remembering how she felt as a little girl seeing the sea side for the first time remembering the smell of the sea at high tide and the excitement of having ice cream even in winter

"I know what you mean we only saw the sea when we went on our annual holidays and then it meant a couple of hours drive, we went to Porthcawl one year think I was about ten, stayed in a caravan," said Wyatt.

"Trecco Bay I expect that's just minutes from where I live with my grandparents, in the summer holidays me and Alex always met new friends there who were on holidays, how old are you, Wyatt?"

"Twenty-eight, coming up twenty-nine soon, yeah Trecco Bay that rings a bell, we had a great week, me, my parents and my brothers, happy times" Wyatt smiled to himself remembering the holiday

"Maybe you met me and Alex there."

"Oh, I think I'd remember if I had met you" said Wyatt smiling in a way that made Connie's heartbeat fast and her stomach do a little flip.

"You live with your grandparents, not your parents?" enquired Sofia

"Yes, my mum is dead, she was ill, so we came back to live with my grandparents, and well I'm still there at the grand old age of 27!"

"I'm sorry I didn't mean to pry" said Sofia apologetically.

"Its ok mums been gone twelve years now, but I still miss her so much" said Connie sadly thinking about her mum Laura as she did often if not quite as often as she did.

Wyatt and Sofia both uttered all the right sentiments and Wyatt added, "my dad's gone too, ten years now, his lungs, I still miss him like mad, he never got to see any of me doing my stuff," Wyatt sounded bitter, not like his usual happy go lucky self, he continued, "I was still playing around the pubs and busking when he died, without a pot to piss in and now look where I am I would have loved dad to have had a bit of this high life, he died from asbestos, worked seven days a week for peanuts..." Wyatt shook his head sadly, "life's a bitch!" It was Connie's turn to utter sentiments now, "oh I'm so sorry, but your right life can be a bitch, he would have been so proud of you though," she caught hold of his arm, it just felt like the natural thing to do and gently squeezed it, "bet your mum and brothers are so proud of you" He nodded "yeah, I guess they are, it's great to be able to help them out, I think my dad would have liked that" Wyatt returned Connie's smile and she gave him an impulsive hug, he put his arms around her, and they stayed like that until Sofia spoke, "Come on you two let's have a bite to eat" said Sofia gently stroking both their backs as Connie and Wyatt slowly broke away from their impromptu embrace, Connie didn't know what urged her to hold him, she would never normally be so bold and forward with someone she had only just met, but there was just something about him...something vulnerable, and something else she couldn't put her finger on.

As they ate and drank and chatted Connie stole a look at Wyatt, on stage he radiated such confidence and energy and when she remembered seeing him on TV live from some festival or other, Connie wasn't sure which, (she was never really one for the latest music, stuck in the eighties an ex of hers would always tease her, her mums influence when she was a little girl and she would still tune into Radio 2 in 'Nice Ice' to "enjoy the old stuff"), there Wyatt held the entire field of adoring fans in the palm of his hand. Seeing him just now so vulnerable and yesterday so excited like a child she wanted to hug him again and hold him tight and tell him that everything would be ok, she watched him as he lay back on the grass hands under his head and felt her heart doing a little somersault, she said to herself "Connie Devereux, what's happening to you girl- snogging Gianni yesterday, now hugging Wyatt today- must be the Mediterranean heat and atmosphere" but as she looked at Wyatt again, she thought, "no girl it's more than that with this one here, but he's not going to give you a second thought being a famous rock star- so stop daydreaming!!"

The rest of the day was spent browsing both designer and small local shops in Positano whilst Connie and Wyatt marveled at the local shoemakers making sandals in their tiny shops, the smell of leather here was something Connie thought she would remember forever, she felt she would just have to close her eyes and the smell would return to her no matter where she would be! They re-boarded a local bus and drove along to Amalfi, when they arrived Connie and Wyatt looked up at the magnificent cathedral at the top of what seemed like a million steps presiding over the village,

"Oh, look there, it's a wedding!" exclaimed Connie excitedly looking up at the bride and groom as they exited the church

"Duomo di Amalfi Cattedrale di Saint 'Andrea," Sofia informed them, "My cousin Arianna married her husband Louis here, yes, it is very lovely!"

"How wonderful and romantic!" said Connie dreamily.

She caught Wyatt's eye who smiled in agreement.

"Imagine getting married there" she thought romantically

They all had an ice cream from a gelateria close to Amalfi's town fountain and sat down to enjoy them in the shadiest area they could find.

"We're always looking to sit in the sun back home and now we are here it's so hot all we do is look for the shade," laughed Connie

"That's true!" agreed Wyatt" it is bloody hot though!"

The three decided to have a quick dip in the sea to cool down, even the sea was warm, Sofia got out and went for a lie down whilst Connie and Wyatt enjoyed the sea gently lapping around them

"I love it here I knew as soon as I saw a photo the house that I had to come here!" said Wyatt looking around him in amazement

"It sure is beautiful, do you feel that you can be yourself here?" asked Connie.

"Definitely! I put on my old faithful" said Wyatt indicating to his ever-present baseball hat," and no one knows me."

"It must be nice; you can just relax then."

"Yeah, I don't think that I'm known so much over in Europe as I am back home, but yeah, I love the fans, but it is nice just to do my thing and go about just like anyone else" he smiled ruefully, "Dolan has a bit of business in Rome so I feel as if I can chill and enjoy myself, just being me for a bit."

"I'll bet, everyone needs time out!" said Connie, "It'll do you good to have a bit of fun."

He smiled at her melting her heart again, as they looked at each other in mutual understanding.

Their day was topped off by a visit to Auntie Francesca's restaurant, tucked into a back street, looking like just another house from the outside, but inside it had about a dozen tables covered in red and white check cloths with wine bottles holding a lit candle in the middle of each one, a rustic bar in one corner had dozens and dozens of bottles of wine behind it and where a woman in her late forties with dark wild curly hair, bearing an uncanny resemblance to Sofia, called out to them, "Sofia, welcome and welcome to your friends, come in and try our special."

"This is my Aunt Francesca" Sofia introduced them, "and these are my friends Connie and Wyatt from the UK!" they were guided to a table in the corner, where specials were ordered all around

"I'm stuffed!" announced Connie sitting back on her chair "that was absolutely delicious, but I couldn't eat another thing!"

"Me neither" agreed Wyatt, "mind you those ice creams look nice" he said looking past the girls to the cold counter in the distance

Connie laughed, "I work in an ice cream parlour ask me anything about them."

They all chatted about Ice Cream and Connie told them about Nice Ice, then Sofia left the table to see her aunt at the counter

"You never mentioned your father earlier when we were talking," said Wyatt.

"No, I suppose I never really think about him, I don't really remember him" answered Connie truthfully.

"I'm sorry I didn't realise, has he passed away too?"

"Oh no, no, well I don't think so anyway, he and my mum parted when I was a little girl before we left London and I have never seen him since."

"Oh, I'm sorry Connie I didn't mean to bring back bad memories for you" Wyatt touched her hand gently; Connie felt her skin burn beneath his soft touch the warmth travelled straight to her cheeks as she felt herself blushing.

"No, it's ok I haven't really got any memories, to be honest I don't even know where he is, he could even be here."

"Here?" enquired Wyatt.

"Yes, he is, Italian."

"Who's Italian?" asked Sofia rejoining them.

"My father, Giacomo Santini" announced Connie it felt strange to her saying her father's name out loud.

"Where in Italy does he come from?" enquired Sofia.

"Er the Tuscany area I think, ooh it's so strange talking about him like this no one has mentioned him in years, definitely not since my mum passed away."

"And you haven't seen or heard from him?" asked Sofia.

"No and I was never bothered, but now discussing him and being here in Italy I am starting to wonder about him, I think that's why I was nervous about telling my grandparents I was coming over here and why my grandfather in particular was a bit 'well' funny about it," explained Connie.

"Yeah, I guess it stirred up memories long forgotten by you all" said

Wyatt, he smiled at Connie such a caring smile it made her heart melt.

"Do you think you'd like to see him again?" asked Sofia

Connie shrugged her shoulders," I really don't know Sof," Connie honestly didn't know, but it was now definitely in her thoughts, and she thought that it would stay there until she heard about or saw him again!

Alex had drifted off to sleep watching the TV soaps when the sound of the doorbell of Carole's flat woke her suddenly; she looked across at mam who had also drifted off on the settee and was still sleeping soundly. She got up and pushed her feet into her slippers straightened her hair back into its bobble and padded to the front door.

Standing there was Jared, Alex jumped back a little, truth be told she had drifted off to a dream about Jared they were back in the hospital she hadn't fainted this time but he was there with a very attractive dark-haired woman who turned out to be his wife- Alex had tried to run away so he didn't see her but she couldn't move – she hated dreams like this – then the doorbell had woken her and here she was face to face with him!

"Sorry I didn't mean to startle you" said Jared a little apprehensively.

"Oh no, no you didn't I was just, er you know" Alex fished around for an answer which didn't make her look stupid but was failing miserably.

They looked at each other for a few seconds, "do you want to come in?" at last Alex asked.

"Only if it's convenient."

Alex ushered him in, Carole had woken up now too," oh hello Jared love, doing house calls now is it?" joked Carole.

For a minute Jared looked confused then remembering Carole's sense of humor he smiled and answered, "yes if it's good enough for the Queen its good enough for you!"

The ice was broken or slightly thawed as they all laughed

"I'll go and have a lie down on my bed, no good on this old settee do me more harm than good" announced Carole wanting to give the young couple privacy to discuss whatever they needed to, "can you help me up and in there Jared my love?"

Jared obliged as Alex went to put the kettle on, "thank you love" said Carole as Jared helped her onto her bed, she caught hold of his hand, "I hope you two can sort things out"

Jared smiled and nodded, and then he left Carole to return to the lounge and to Alex.

"Tea or coffee?" asked Alex as he re-entered the room.

"Tea please" and then they both said together, "milk and one sugar!"

They both laughed, "you remember?" said Jared.

"of course," answered Alex smiling, as she returned to the kitchen, "as if I'd ever forget" she added to herself, she poured the freshly boiled water onto the tea bags and stirred in the milk before adding some sugar to one of the mugs, she felt nervous now, stalling for time looking for biscuits as she wondered what Jared wanted. She eventually brought out the steaming mugs and placed them on the coffee table "sit down "she indicated with her head towards the settee to Jared, who sat down beckoning to Alex to sit next to him "Well, this is a surprise" she said looking down at the mugs and trying to avoid his stare.

"I wanted to come over sooner, but I only had time off today you know how it is junior doctor working all the hours God sends," Jared smiled as he tried to make a joke.

"Yes, I expect you are busy" answered Alex.

They sat in awkward silence "Alex" said Jared suddenly breaking the silence," I couldn't believe it when you walked into my room, I really thought I'd never see you again."

Alex turned to look at him, then blurted out "Me too I never thought I'd come back to Porthcawl let alone see you again I did wonder once I got back if our paths would ever cross, but no one had seen you for years, so I didn't expect to see you either"

"I'm glad you did though I felt that when we parted in Italy it wasn't under happy circumstances and this now gives us a chance to put that right," said Jared.

"Right?" Asked Alex.

"Yes, I thought we could be friends again."

"Friends? We were much more than that Jared" said Alex quietly.

"Oh yeah I know that but well you know what I mean, is there anyone, you know in Italy a boyfriend, a husband?"

Alex laughed shortly, "no, no one I have a job that I love and lots of friends and a nice little apartment that's enough for me" she dreaded the answer, but asked the question anyway, "what about you is there anyone?"

Jared eyes met hers, "well yes, yes there is someone."

CHAPTER 10

As they travelled back to Sorrento Connie, Wyatt and Sofia relaxed back into their seats on the bus, it had been a magical day and all three were tired.

"Thank you Sofia that was a wonderful day the best day I've had since I don't know when, thank you for inviting me along too Wyatt" Connie turned to each of them

"It was my pleasure I love showing off my beautiful homeland," said Sofia.

"Thank you for coming and yes thank you Sofia for an amazing day" agreed Wyatt, "Are you girls' free tomorrow? I'm not leaving until Tuesday, so I'm ready for another road trip!"

"Sorry darling but we are back in work tomorrow, and then I'm going to see my family tomorrow evening it's my sister Lucia's birthday" answered Sofia.

"I'm free tomorrow evening if you want to hang out" Connie suggested as casual as she could even though her heart was hammering a frantic beat in her chest as she thought "are you crazy Connie Devereux asking a famous rock star out on a date!!!!"

"Cool! I'll pick you up at six" answered Wyatt smiling enthusiastically at Connie.

"Cool!" answered Connie but feeling everything but cool, as she fiddled with the air con button above her head in a bid to look and feel chilled out!

They were soon back at their stop and all three alighted from the bus, the evening air was still balmy, and the smell of garlic met them wafting from a nearby open-air restaurant, Connie closed her eyes and breathed in deeply, "mmm smells heavenly!"

Sofia laughed, "Oh Connie you are such a tourist!"

"I know and I love it" answered Connie smiling a wide sleepy smile" and this tourist is knackered!"

Wyatt agreed, "me too, bella food and wine and lots of sun is a sure-fire way of getting me to bed!"

Not realising what he'd said until the girls both laughed, "Ah Wyatt Morgan please do not say that to the wrong person!" said Sofia, "or there will be scores of women lining up to wine and dine you"

Wyatt laughed" sorry but you know what I mean!"

He caught Connie's eye, she was glad it had gone dark as she blushed profusely, they all bid each other good night and Connie returned to Alex's apartment very tired but still on cloud nine and decided to phone Alex.

"Hello" answered a tearful voice on the other end of the call

"Alex? Are you ok?" asked Connie suddenly feeling more awake hearing the sad voice of her best friend.

"No Con, no I'm not! Jared came around tonight to the flat"

"And?" asked Connie.

"And basically, he said that he wanted us to be friends"

"Is that not good? You know? A start?"

"Then he asked me if there is anyone special" sniffed Alex.

"Well, there's not, is there, so what did you say?"

"I said there wasn't obviously, but then when I asked him Con, he said, he said..." she chocked back her tears "that, yes, yes there is!"

Any sleepiness had now totally eluded Connie who was now wide awake, "Oh Alex I'm so sorry hun, did he say who?"

"No, his buzzer went then; you know he was on call, and he rushed off to the hospital and that was it."

"So, he didn't say anything more?" asked Connie sympathetically

"No, he just left."

"Oh, Al I don't know what to say, I'm sorry to hear that, I really thought that, well you know..." she trailed off awkwardly

"So did I Con, I thought that fate had brought us back together, the stupid cow as I am, oh God I wish I'd never come back!"

"Oh love!"

Connie had phoned Alex to tell her about the wonderful day she had had, the butterflies she felt when she looked at Wyatt Morgan and the pending date tomorrow evening, well yes it was a date, even if it wasn't going to be a romantic one, it was still going out somewhere with a very eligible drop-dead gorgeous guy, but now she couldn't say, not after what Alex had just told her-poor heartbroken Alex!

The two finished their conversation with Connie making Alex promise that she would ring her no matter what time of day or night it was if she needed to talk.

The following morning Alex got out of bed aching all over, due to a lack of sleep, she looked at her swollen red eyes in the bedroom mirror and shook her head, "what's happened to you girl, you've only been here a few weeks and you are a mess! You look a mess you're heads a mess, what happened to that confident happy career girl you left in Sorrento?"

She pulled back the curtains and squinted as the light hit her eyes, another rainy day! The leaves on the palm trees outside in the house opposite s garden hung down sadly as Alex thought, "they look like I feel!!!"

Last night she had briefly filled Carole in with the details of Jared's visit who had called her into her bedroom when she heard him suddenly leave. She hated for mam to see her sad as she had said if it wasn't for her and her accident Alex wouldn't have had to come back and been hurt all over again- Alex had tried to reassure her that she probably would have found out sooner or later, but both Alex and Carole knew that it was much harder suddenly seeing Jared and now this!

Alex went through the next few days in a dream world picking at her food and barely leaving the flat unless Carole needed anything, she had blocked Jared's number from her phone after she ignored several calls from him. She had felt like a poor excuse for a best friend when she had rung Rivolli's for a catch up, as she was missing work and Italy so much, Sofia had told her that Connie had been spending the remainder of Wyatt Morgan's time in Sorrento with him when she wasn't at work. Sofia said that she had felt that there was romance in the air and Alex had felt rotten that Connie hadn't been able to confide in her because of her own shambles of a nonexistent love life!

"Babe now I've been meaning to mention this to you" said Carole cautiously as the two sat at the table one morning

Alex looked up from where she was looking at the daily newspaper, looking not reading as the words just didn't make sense to her tired eyes and muzzy head due to lack of food and sleep

Carole went on, "as you know your dad and Michelle are having a few difficulties"

Alex rolled her eyes at the mention of her father and took a sip of tea.

"So, I said he could move in here," Alex visually stiffened, "just temporarily, don't worry,"

Alex opened her mouth to voice her objections, but Carole shushed her, "it's decided, and I want you to go back to Italy!"

"You don't you want me?" asked Alex sadly.

"More than anything I've loved having you here with me, but I'm being selfish to keep you here, your dad is at a loose end and let's be honest he owes me, big time!" Carole nodded, "He can help around here and help me out until I'm back on my feet, don't worry he knows the score, nothing romantic and only short term"

Alex frowned at Carole,

"Please babe I hate to see you like this even if you only go back for a while, you need to go back and find your mojo, you need sun and fun with Connie" she pointed her finger at Alex "I'm your mother and I'm the boss! I'm ordering you!" she smiled at Alex, "I'll be fine here, and it'll do your dad a bit of good to think of someone else for a change, I'm not taking no for an answer, go and book your flights and pack."

"But mam, are you sure, I can come straight back if you need me"

"Go and sort out that flight missy!"

Alex got up and hugged Carole, "Thank you mam I think I do need to go back even if it's only for a while, just to get my head straight, thank you."

"You and your happiness are more important to me than anything, all I want is for you to be back to yourself again and I think going back is only going to help" Carole squeezed Alex's hand, "go on go and get sorted."

Alex managed to get a seat on a flight leaving the end of the week she phoned Connie to let her know, the two agreed that Connie would stay too for them to catch up and until she got sorted to return home, then Alex phoned Rivolli's to say she'd be back at her desk on Monday morning if that was ok.

Connie had loved her time in Sorrento and wasn't really surprised to hear that Alex would be returning sooner rather than later as during all their conversations she had sounded so down, she would be sad to leave though, and would miss everyone, maybe not Gianni though, she had managed to avoid him since their drunken tryst and since Wyatt had left for his extensive music tour of America, she hadn't really wanted to go out much socially so she was looking forward to seeing Alex again.

She thought back to that evening date with Wyatt, he had met her from work at six on a bright red vespa, "look Con I've hired this, jump on" he called excitedly.

"What, on that!" laughed Connie wondering how the hell she'd hike up her tight-fitting skirt to get on the back of it, not to mention the sheer fright of negotiating the heavy erratic traffic,

"Come on" beckoned Wyatt, something about his handsome eager face and boyish enthusiasm made Connie throw caution to the wind as she dragged up her skirt as much as modesty would allow, climbing on the back of the bike she grabbed around Wyatt's waist, and they sped off.

She didn't know if it was the thrill of the ride or the proximity to Wyatt, but she whooped as they zig-zagged the traffic and down to the port.

They came to a stop, Wyatt turned to Connie who was still gripping tightly around his waist "well that was great, what did you think

Con, did you enjoy that?"

"Very exhilarating!" she answered through chattering teeth, as she loosened her grip on him and tried to straighten her clothes and tidy her hair whilst wondering if she looked like she felt, very windswept!

"Come on" Wyatt caught her hand and dragged her towards a fancy looking yacht moored at the port with "Princess of Capri" emblazed on the side.

Connie went with him as he greeted the 'captain' who in turn greeted them with a tray carrying two filled champagne glasses "welcome Mr. Morgan, Miss Devereux to the Princess of Capri"

Connie gasped "for us?"

"Yeah I hired this to take us for an evening ride to Capri, got a table booked in some restaurant that Sofia said is top notch , come on Con, let's get on and enjoy this fizz" said Wyatt happily as he took the two glasses, proffering one to Connie and motioning towards the top of the yacht where the remainder of the bottle of fizz stood in an ice bucket in the middle of a fixed table surrounded by sumptuous cream leather seats, there was little bowls of aperitifs, Wyatt sat down and Connie joined him, "Cheers Connie here's to us!" he clinked his glass to hers as he beamed all over his handsome face, "cheers!" replied Connie happily as the yachts engine started up and started to move across the port and out into the sea.

The young couple had a lovely evening exploring the enchanting isle of Capri and found themselves so naturally walking hand in hand around the designer shops, as Connie helped Wyatt choose gifts for his family, they posed for selfies as they meandered their way around, finally finishing up in a tiny authentic restaurant enjoying a supper of creamy pasta, warm crusty rolls and tiramisu washed down with ice cold house wine, before making their way back to The Princess of Capri being met once again by the Captain.

The yacht rose and dipped in the swell of the sea as the breeze still warm blew on their faces they laughed like excited children as Wyatt put his arm around Connie and held her close, "thanks for coming out tonight I've had a wonderful time," said Wyatt

"Thank you for asking me I've loved every minute, even the vesper ride!" laughed Connie.

"It's my last day tomorrow will you come out again?" asked Wyatt as he looked intently at her.

"I'd love to" answered Connie breathlessly.

Wyatt leaned forward and gently brushed her lips with his, Connie returned his kiss, and the two stayed like that for a few seconds, Wyatt moved back slightly, "I really like you Connie, I have from the first moment I saw you In Rivolli's, I feel that we've got a real connection, but I'm leaving tomorrow for a pretty extensive tour, so I'll understand if you don't want to take it any further."

Connie couldn't believe it, here she was with this adorable guy who was telling her he liked her, but he was leaving, oh well, that was the story of her life when it came to guys and romance.

"Let's just enjoy whatever time we have together" she answered, and then kissed him again, a long slow kiss.

Chapter 11

The morning after their date to Capri Connie felt like she floated to work on an invisible carpet of heady romance, "My my, someone has had a nice evening!" remarked Sofia when they met just outside Rivolli's, Connie smiled happily, "even I can see that glow of love through my poor, tired, party worn eyes" Sofia yawned

"Did your sister enjoy her party?" asked Connie holding the door open for Sofia as they entered the office.

"Yes, and me a little too much" answered Sofia ruefully, "and you Signorina Devereux looks radiant at this time of the morning, do tell"

"Oh, Sofia it was magical from start to finish" answered Connie dreamily.

Ricardo looked up from behind his desk surveying the girls "oh no a hangover and a romantic, looks like there won't be much work being done here today!"

"Don't worry Ricardo we are ready for work" smiled Connie, "aren't we Sof?" Sofia grunted a reply whilst making herself a strong black coffee.

Ricardo tutted and the girls exchanged meaningful glances.

The day dragged on for Sofia as all she wanted to do was go home and go to sleep as she was still tired after her sisters' party and for Connie because she couldn't wait to see Wyatt again. He had arranged to have her picked up at7.30pm by the chauffer at the

5-star hotel he was staying at. Connie had decided to wear her pink bardot dress that Alex had persuaded her to pack, she was glad now that she had brought it. When she eventually finished work for the day she rushed back to the apartment and jumped in the shower. When she had dried herself, she sprayed herself liberally with the Marc Jacobs perfume she had bought in the Duty-Free shop in Bristol Airport. She blew dried her hair and clipped the right side back with a diamante slide which she had bought from a quaint boutique on her visit to Positano with Wyatt and Sofia, her thick brunette hair curled and cascaded down over her left shoulder. She applied her makeup carefully, with lashings of mascara to finish off her kohl rimmed eyes and a lick of peony pink lipstick that she only wore on special occasions- and tonight she thought was definitely a special occasion! She slipped on her new strapless bra and matching knickers, M & S specials, zipped up her dress and stepped into her silver beaded strappy sandals, which she had purchased with a matching clutch bag from a boutique in the winding pedestrianised street in Sorrento one evening after work last week. Most evenings she would walk to this area and spend hours perusing the myriad of tourist shops and boutiques and had purchased a few pairs of sandals and one or two new items of clothing, she loved the continental way of life where the shops were open in the evenings, and you could sit outside a bar alone sipping a glass of wine without looking like a sad 'alcy' like she felt she would if she did it at home in Wales!

Connie checked her reflection in the mirror she turned this way and that to make sure she looked ok- back home she would never have been daring enough to wear her hair like this, but being here in Sorrento had made her more confident to experiment with different hair styles and to wear sexier more feminine clothes, not to mention 'heels' but all the girls she went out with, Sofia especially always wore exquisite shoes and sandals and always with a high heel. "Ready!" she said to herself as she checked the time "7.25pm" she locked the apartment door behind her and went down into the street where the Chauffeur, Wyatt had sent, was there to meet her, "Buena Sera, Signorina Devereux, I am Al your driver, I am her to take you to meet Mr. Morgan, the limousine is parked just around to the left" a man in his, Connie guessed early 50s dressed in a smart uniform of navy blue topped off with a shiny peak capped hat indicated to the area where her transport for this evening was parked, they turned the corner and he opened the door of a sleek black limo and ushered Connie inside. Connie entered the car and sat in the middle of the back seat; the upholstery was similar to that of the yacht 'the princess of Capri' but it was like no other car she'd ever ridden in before. In front of her to the left-hand side was a mini bar lit up by tiny spotlights, the chauffeur lent forward and took a bottle of iced prosecco from the ice bucket on the bar, he popped the cork and poured Connie a glass, "Signorina, please" he proffered the fizz filled flute to her, "thank you" she breathed, he closed the door and reentered the car by the driver's door stared the engine, music drifted through the vehicle, slow and melodic, that Connie recognised as one of her granddad's favourites 'Dean Martin' Connie took a sip of the iced cold fizz as they sped off with her looking and feeling like a celebrity or a member of the Royal family!

They drove a short distance through the back streets of Sorrento and took the coast road out overlooking the Bay of Naples, until they came to a halt outside a pair of ten-foot-high gold ornate gates, the chauffeur opened his window and spoke into the intercom, the huge gates opened slowly in front of them as he drove slowly up the tree lined drive way and stopped outside the most magnificent building Connie had ever seen in her life.

It was like a baroque palace and Connie wondered if it had been a palace in days gone by. It was painted white with embellished gold leaves around the windows and main entrance into the hotel, the lawns at the front of the hotel were beautifully manicured, edged with an abundance of fauna with ornate tables and chairs strategically placed for the residents to enjoy the breathtaking views over the Bay of Naples. Connie's door was opened by Al the chauffeur, "Sigorina" he said as she gathered up her bag and elegantly (as elegant as her high heels would allow) stepped out of the car. Two well-dressed older couples were sat at the tables sipping drinks, the couple closest to Connie nodded in acknowledgement Connie smiled and nodded back, as she was greeted by a man dressed in a black tuxedo suit and bow tie, crisp white shirt and shoes so shiny you could almost see your reflection in them.

"Sigorina Devereux welcome to the Grande Sorrento Palace please follows me" Connie climbed the steps outside and followed the hotel manager into the 'palace'!

If the outside was magnificent then Connie couldn't even think of an adjective to describe the inside! Her cousin Danielle had got married last year and they had gone to a local hotel for the reception, but it was nothing like where she stood now, looking around her in awe and amazement!

The beige carpets were so thick and sumptuous that her sandals sank into the pile as she entered the hotel, gold and cream velvet chairs and sofas adorned either side of the reception area with high ceilings depicting paintings that put Connie in mind of pictures she had seen in books of the Sistine Chapel, by Michelangelo that she had studied for her Art GCSE, festooned with cherubs.

"Please" the Manager said indicating to her to follow him towards another glorious room, Connie followed him looking up and marveling at the chandelier hanging from the ceiling of this great hall, that was possibly the size of the whole of Alex's apartment!

Its crystals glistened as the evening light streamed through the huge stained-glass windows at each side of the hall making each dropper change colour as if by magic. As Connie's eyes were drawn back in front of her, there stood another magnificent vision, Wyatt Morgan, he walked towards her and caught her gently in his embrace kissing her on both cheeks, "Connie you look beautiful" he said appreciatively standing back to admire her, Connie smiled back at him, this was a Wyatt she hadn't seen before- he wasn't wearing his usual combat shorts ,T shirt and baseball hat- this Wyatt was dressed in a smart silver grey suit, crisp white open neck shirt and grey leather loafers, his hair was swept back and he smelt of very expensive aftershave , Connie eyed him back appreciatively thinking "eat your heart out Christian Grey- this is the real deal!"

Wyatt took her by the hand and led her off through a doorway at the end of the room, they walked through a passage way no less as luxurious and magnificent as the rest of the hotel and then came to another doorway "My suite" announced Wyatt opening the door, all the time the hotel manager had accompanied them and he now stopped at the entrance to the room and said "we shall serve dinner at eight thirty sir" did a quick bow of his head then left leaving Connie and Wyatt alone.

"This is your room?" asked Connie looking around her in awe, "it's amazing, and it's bigger than my grandparent's whole house!"

"It's called a suite, but yeah, it's pretty amazing, think it's one of the best I've been lucky enough to stay in, come and see the view Con" the old Wyatt was back, dragging her by the arm, with boyish enthusiasm towards the open French doors at the far end of the room, Connie quickly took in the beautiful decor this too was mainly gold and cream, everything was exquisitely ornate, from the table and chairs to the chandeliers and standard lamps, cherubs painted gold hugged and adorned every piece of furniture, the carpet was as sumptuous as the ones she had already walked on if not more so, the sofas were more like gold ornate thrones and on every wall hung a renaissance themed painting , the ceilings were high and delicately painted with more cherubs, and half naked people, strewn this way and that, "Look Con! look at the view!" exclaimed Wyatt, Connie walked out through the French doors and out onto a huge balcony with the most magnificent views of the Bay of Naples and Mount Vesuvius, the sea was so blue and calm and there was a gigantic Cruise liner moored out in the distance, "Amazing isn't it!" "Amazing" breathed Connie, and not just the views out there, Wyatt Morgan was an amazing sight too!

The meal was served in his suite, a cream of mushroom soup, followed by salmon in a white wine sauce with baby potatoes and green beans with lemon cheesecake to finish; they had prosecco and white wine to wash it down with.

They talked and talked about everything it was like they had known each other for ever not just a few days, they had so much in common and Connie marveled at how down to earth he was even though he was rich and famous he was so grateful and thankful for everything he had.

"Wyatt is an unusual name, is it your real name?" Asked Connie taking a sip of wine.

"Yeah, I hated it when I was growing up in Dudley, I mean what sort of name is that for anyone who doesn't ride a horse and wear a cowboy hat!" he laughed, "I had loads of stick, my dad was a big fan of the Westerns, so I was named after Wyatt Earp, my eldest brother is Jessie after Jessie James and my younger brother Wayne after John Wayne, I ask you...! What about you Connie Devereux, are you named after anyone?"

"Oh, that's cool being named after cowboys, I'm named after my granddads sister Constance Devereux, Aunt Con, she was close to my mum, we lived with her in London for a bit, she passed away a few months ago, I hadn't seen her for ages though" Connie took another sip of wine and looked down sadly as she remembered her aunt.

"Oh Con, I'm sorry I didn't mean to make you sad!" Wyatt held her hand and squeezed it gently. "No! No of course you didn't silly, it's just, well you know" and he did, he was the same with his dad, it was that they just understood one another, like Wyatt had said, they had a connection

"Now then 'Morgan' there must definitely be a Welsh connection there somewhere!" said Connie on a brighter note

"Yeah, my granddad Dai Morgan was from Swansea, my dad's dad, moved to the midlands in the 50's, something to do with work and then he met my Nan and the rest as they say is history!" Wyatt sipped his wine, eyes twinkling at Connie, "see Con another connection"

Connie laughed "oh definitely, I have Welsh, French and Italian blood running through these veins" said Connie holding up her arm tilting it over, "I could play for any of those sides in the Six nations!" she laughed

Wyatt frowned for a second, "Ah rugby" he laughed, "I forgot how passionate you Welsh are about your rugby.

"It's the law!" Connie laughed too, "I will take you to a match one day."

"Football's my game Con,"

"Well, we'll have to do something about that" replied Connie playfully.

He leaned forward and stoked her arm, "I'm going to miss this Con" he said now more seriously.

"What, me teasing you?"

"Yeah, and just this, being together, "he looked sad for a moment, but the added winking, "and you're a lot prettier than Pete Dolan too"

"Oh you" laughed Connie, "But you are looking forward to your tour?"

Wyatt looked into her eyes "I was, but I'm not looking forward to leaving Sorrento, or You!"

In a second, he was at her side kissing her at first gently then more urgently, Connie felt her stomach do a somersault as he held her close and then lifted her into his arms, as if she weighed nothing, he carried her through the room and laid her down on the biggest bed she had ever seen adorned with dozens of pillows and cushions he kissed her again, "I think I'm falling for you Connie Devereux" "I think I'm falling for you too Wyatt Morgan!" Connie replied but knew that she had already fallen for him, completely and utterly!

Chapter 12

Every morning when she woke, Connie thought back to that last morning spent with Wyatt, when on waking she rolled over to see him smiling down at her, propped up on one arm, "Good Morning" he said and leaned down to kiss her.

"Good morning" she replied.

He stoked her hair," Thank you for a wonderful evening and night" Connie felt herself blushing, here she was lying naked in a sumptuous bed the size of a boat, being kissed by a rock star, after spending an amazing night with him after knowing him for just a few days, what must he think of her.

As if reading her mind Wyatt said," I know we've only known each other a short while, but it feels like forever, it's been so wonderful Con."

"Yes, it has, but I hope you don't think I'm the sort of girl who does this, you know, regularly."

"I'm glad you are" teased Wyatt and put his arms around her and pulled her close.

"My flight goes in four hours Con, help me make the most of my time until Dolan drags me away" he kissed her again and any good intentions Connie had to get showered and go to work were lost.

Connie had felt like it had been weeks not days since Wyatt had left, she sipped the Americano that Luca had just brought her, having slipped into Alex's routine of calling for a coffee on the way to work. It was to be her last day at Rivolli's as Alex would be back in Sorrento later today.

"Ah sad face today Signorina!" said Luca concerned

Connie deep in thought was brought back to earth, "Sorry Luca, I was far away then."

"Somewhere not very nice?" he asked.

"Oh no, just thinking it's my last day at Rivolli's today, Alex is coming back, I've loved it here"

"Oh! So, you are leaving?" Luca stopped wiping the table and looked at Connie for a moment.

"Not straight away, but soon."

"I will be sorry to see you go, but if you change your mind, we are always looking for staff here."

"Ah thanks Luca I shall definitely keep that in mind," Connie smiled thanks, as Luca went back to his meticulous cleaning.

She wondered what Wyatt was doing now, he was touring around the USA and was due back to the UK at some point to play several festivals too, she hadn't heard from him since he had left, probably too busy she told herself, probably even forgot about her in his busy, crazy, exciting rock star existence, why would he want to contact her? On this depressive note she collected her things and walked the short distance to Rivolli's for the last time. She busied herself with a mountain of filing until she heard the office doorbell tinkle as someone had entered, she looked up from where she was kneeling on the floor surrounded by open files to see Gianni Rivolli smiling down at her,

"Connie, I'm glad you are here!" he said eyes twinkling.

"Uh oh" thought Connie, "what's he after"

"Would you like to accompany me to Naples Airport later to collect Alex?"

Connie looked at him doubtfully.

"No strings, just pleasant company" he said picking up on Connie's expression.

"I thought you'd be eager to see Alex" he added

Connie thought for a minute, she wasn't doing anything else this evening, and it would be lovely to see Alex and give her a hug, and not just for Alex's benefit, she too felt she needed a friendly hug, now she was missing Wyatt more than she thought she would

"Ok, yes thanks I will Gianni."

"Fantatico I'll pick you up from here when you finish, ciao" he winked then covered his eyes with his sunglasses that he had pushed up onto the top of his head and stalked out of the office, with the others watching his departing figure.

"That was quick, what did my 'darling' brother want?" asked Ricardo emphasising 'darling', as he walked across the office to where Connie was filing, armed with several buff folders.

"Only to see if I wanted to go to the airport with him to collect Alex"

"Oh right yes, I forgot I asked him to collect her, ah it'll do you good to see Alex again, I have noticed you have lost your sparkle since our Mr Morgan has left town" said Ricardo sympathetically as he handed Connie some paperwork to file.

She smiled, but the smile didn't reach her eyes, as she looked down to sort the latest lot of files, glad that she was busy, and trying, but failing, to think of anything other than Wyatt Morgan

As they left work for the evening and the last time for Connie, Ricardo locked the Office door and operated the shutters, Sofia lit a cigarette,

"I didn't know you smoked?" said Connie looking at Sofia's actions in surprise.

"Ah I didn't, not for a while and here I am again!" tutted Sofia, "Gino and me, finito!"

"Oh no I am sorry!" Gino was the latest in a long line of suitors that Sofia had been dating; Connie has only thought it had been casual Ricardo rolled his eyes," Gino, who is this one now Sofia I can't keep up with you!"

"Oh, shut up Ricardo, just because you have no love life!" snapped Sofia.

"Better no love life than looking at your two sad faces!" answered Ricardo gesturing to Sofia and Connie.

The girls looked at each other and agreed, "Si Ricardo maybe you're right," said Sofia sadly.

Just then Gianni pulled up in his old but still impressive Lamborghini

"Ciao!" he called through the open car window.

"See you later" said Connie to Ricardo and Sofia.

"Romero's at eight you must have leaving drinks!" called Sofia suddenly forgetting her melancholy and replacing it with a party planning mood.

"Ok" called back Connie as she got into the passenger's seat and Gianni sped off.

They sat listening to music as they drove through and out of Sorrento.

"So, Connie" said Gianni shooting her a gleaming toothed sideways look, "Haven't see you around for a while hope you haven't been avoiding me"

"Er no just been busy that's all" answered Connie keeping her eyes staring firmly ahead

Gianni laughed, "Only joking, maybe now Mr Rockstar has gone you'll give me another chance, eh?"

Connie didn't answer.

He went on, "I might not be rich and famous, but I can give you a good time, if you know what I mean!" she knew he was looking at her winking and smiling like a wolf eyeing up some poor defenseless lamb, but still stared straight on, wishing now she had said No when he asked her to accompany him to the airport.

After realising his words were falling on deaf ears, he turned up the radio and they continued the rest journey without any further conversation.

Connie sighed in relief when they finally turned off to the airport, crossing her fingers and hoping that Alex's plane wouldn't be delayed.

Gianni parked up and said "you go and meet her I'll stay here" she didn't know if she was imagining things, but he sounded a bit 'off' not his usual confident full of bravado self, "let's hope he's got the message" she thought as she got out of the car, "ok see you soon" she called as she closed the car door, Gianni grunted in reply.

Connie entered the airport terminal and looked up at the screen BRISOL EASYJET LANDED- "Great" thought Connie, she glanced at her watch, Alex should be going through passport control about now, or even waiting for her suitcase to come off the carousel if it wasn't too busy. Connie looked up again at the screen PISA, MILAN, ROME, she started to wonder again about her father and if he could be somewhere in Italy.

"Connie!" the sound of her name being called jolted her back to reality.

There, coming towards her dragging her Louis Vuitton case and waving madly was Alex.

"Alex!" the two rushed towards each other and embraced

"How are you?" they both said together, then laughed.

"It's so good to see you Con, and sooo good to be back!"

The two linked arms as they made their way towards the exit

"Gianni's just over there."

"You came alone with him; thought you had been avoiding him" teased Alex.

"Oh, don't ask, I was that desperate to see my best friend that I risked my reputation riding with Signor Rivolli" Connie squeezed Alex arm and they giggled.

"How are you though? I can't believe what's happened in just a few weeks" said Connie thinking about what had happened between her and Wyatt in such a short time as well as Alex and Jared

"I'm just trying to block the last few weeks from my mind, to be honest Con, what a bloody mess!"

"And you didn't see or hear from him again after he dropped that bombshell?" asked Connie referring to the last time Alex had seen Jared and he had confessed that there was someone special in his life.

Alex shook her head, "No he tried to ring me a few times, but I didn't answer and then I blocked his number, I know it sounds childish, but I honestly don't think I can hear him say that he loves someone else, I know it's been years and I've got a nerve to even think or hope there was no one else let alone he still wanted me, but, oh Con, it's awful!"

Connie put her arm around her, "I know love it's hard, come on you are home now, and Sofia's planning something tonight, I think we both need a distraction."

"Oh God love, there's me all self again, bet you're missing Wyatt Morgan too."

"Yes Al, more than I could have ever imagined!" Answered Connie.

Gianni hugged and kissed Alex when the girls returned to his car, "missed you Alex, missed me too?" he asked hopefully, as he put her case into the car boot.

"Always Gianni, and Ricardo and Sofia and my lovely apartment and especially a decent cup of coffee!" Answered Alex tartly

The three got into the car with the girls huddled in the back, chatting about Carole, and the return of John Steven's, Sid and Mary Connie's grandparents, about Nice Ice and Mario.

"It feels like I haven't been home for ages, you know what Al, I feel so at home here now."

"I told you that you'd love it didn't I."

"I do too, I'm missing Nice Ice and all the customers and obviously gran, granddad and Mario, but I've enjoyed being here so much"

"Yes, and a certain Mr Morgan had something to do with that too I bet" Alex lowered her voice as Gianni was looking at her in his rear mirror.

Connie nodded, "Oh Al, I've fallen for him big time, and it's not the rock star thing, like he said we had a real connection, he's lovely so down to earth,"

"Gorgeous, sexy..." Alex teased.

"Yeah, those too, and now he's gone!" said Connie sadly.

"But he'll be back Con, he lives here now!"

"Yes, but unfortunately, I don't!"

Chapter 13

Alex was so pleased to return to her little apartment; Connie had changed the beds and put a bottle of wine in the fridge to welcome Alex home.

"Home sweet home, I've looked after it for you don't worry!" said Connie.

"I can see, are you sure you'll be ok in the guest room?"

"Of course, thanks for letting me stay on."

"Thanks nothing, you did me the biggest favour ever coming over here for me and sealing the deal with Wyatt Morgan."

"I definitely did that Al!" Connie laughed.

"Yes, you did too" joined in Alex, they both knew that Connie had 'sealed the deal' with Wyatt in more ways than one.

"I know it's been crap, poor mam and her accident and then that fiasco with Jared, but it was worth it for you to meet Wyatt."

"Yes, what a whirl wind and I guess it was fun whilst it lasted."

Alex stopped suddenly and looked at Connie, "what do you mean was it just a fling? I thought it was more than that?" she asked

"I would love it to be more than that, but he's been gone four days and I haven't heard anything from him."

"You know fellas, and he's probably travelling and gigging and on a totally different time zone, did you give him your phone number?"

"I'm not sure, everything just happened so fast, but surely he's got Rivolli's phone number?" Connie felt daft now not even exchanging phone numbers, not even a schoolgirl error because surely that's the first thing a schoolgirl on a romantic quest would do!!

"Don't worry Con, if it's to be it'll be, love will find a way" said Alex sounding much wiser than she felt after her recent romantic fiasco!

The girls arrived at Romero's just after eight, Alex dressed in a white slim fitting sleeveless dress teamed with gold stiletto sandals and matching bag she had curled her hair and applied lashings of mascara and lipstick, "I know it's supposed to be Summer, but I've been in trousers every day since I've been back home, it's nice to put a dress on for a change!"

Connie wore a new dress she had bought from Sorrento's weekly outdoor market, tangerine red floaty and strappy, teamed with white strappy sandals and matching bag, she put her hair up in a loose bun and fastened a delicate gold and crystal bracelet to her wrist,

"That's beautiful Con, is it the one Wyatt gave you before he left?"

Connie nodded remembering lying luxuriously in Wyatt's hotel bed as he took it out of the box on his bedside cabinet and fastened it onto her wrist.

"It's beautiful!" she had exclaimed at the time.

"Not as beautiful as you" he had replied kissing her.

He had bought it for her during the evening they had spent in Capri; he had secretly paid for it when she had been browsing, thinking he was just buying a present for his mum.

"And you don't think he feels the same way as you?" exclaimed Alex, "sounds to me as if he's smitten!"

They arrived to a wonderful welcome, from Ricardo, Gianni, Sofia and a few other acquaintances who were always ready for an impromptu get together and after all, it was the weekend.

Alex was smiling widely and hugging everyone and drinking at least 3 glasses to everyone else's one!

"Is she ok?" asked Sofia taking Connie to one side and nodding towards Alex who was laughing loudly with her arm wrapped around a guy from the local bank who they knew vaguely

"It seems she's out to prove to herself she's going to have a good time!"

Connie approached Alex and the 'guy'.

"Hey Al, fancy something to eat, you know to soak up some of the drink?" asked Connie.

"Oh no I'm fine!" slurred Alex, "Con, thith ish Ben, Beneeeto!"

"Beneeeeto!" she exaggerated his name, "isss Connie my besht friend in all the world!!!"

Benito smiled politely, "Hi nice to meet you" Benito looked around their age and was dressed in a cream shirt and jeans with dark curly hair and a goatee beard.

"Come on Alex, you haven't eaten anything let's go and grab a pizza or something" Connie tried to get Alex to go with her but then a song she liked came on and she dragged Benito off to dance

"I think I'll get some food anyway and see if I can get her to sit and eat something" Connie told Sofia, Sofia called the waiter over and the girls ordered a load of different dishes.

"I've never seen Alex like this before" said Sofia frowning and looking in the direction of Alex writhing around a slightly embarrassed looking Benito.

"She'll be ok, just needs to get 'home' out of her system I think", Connie emphasised the word home, but wondered if Alex would ever get Jared Jones out of her system.

Finally, they persuaded Alex to eat something, and Connie got her to drink water instead of any more alcohol.

"I think we'll call it a night" said Connie at eleven O'clock; Alex was almost sleeping at their table,

"We'll walk back with you" said Ricardo, "come on Sofia"

Gianni had vanished earlier with a glamorous blonde no one had ever set eyes on before, and Benito had made his excuses and left too.

Connie and Ricardo maneuvered a very drunk Alex between them out of the bar with Sofia following carrying various handbags belonging to the girls.

"She'll be ok after a good sleep, lucky there's no work in the morning," said Connie.

"I've hardly seen Alex touch a drop of alcohol before tonight I mean she never goes out, what do you think made her like this?" asked Ricardo.

"I think it's got something to do with an ex, it has to be, who's that one she was with forever, before she stayed in Italy?" said Sofia

"It's not really my place to say, but yes I think it's probably got something to do with him" answered Connie not wanting to betray her friend's confidence.

"I knew, she sounded so sad when I spoke to her when she said she was coming back, we didn't expect her back yet, I knew it had to have something to do with him," said Sofia.

The four were at the entrance to Alex's apartment now, Ricardo lifted her into his arms and carried her up the stairs and gently laid her on her bed.

"Thanks Ricardo don't think I could have managed her on my own" said Connie gratefully.

"That's what friends are for" he answered, "now you look after her and yourself, whilst I escort this other young lady home"

"Mm young lady I like the sound of that" laughed Sofia, linking his arm "come on- old man."

The two left then and Connie slumped down onto the bed next to Alex, who was sleeping soundly, Connie stroked Alex's head, "well Al, me and you never learn, broken hearts again at our age!!"

Connie woke first next morning stiff from falling asleep next to Alex, she got up and stretched, grimacing at her aching back.

"Morning Con" came a croaky voice from within the bed, "I feel awful."

"Don't worry I'll get you a nice strong black coffee and some paracetamol now,"

Connie busied herself in the kitchen making coffees and finding a hangover cure for Alex.

She returned carrying coffee and tablets,

"Thanks Con, did I make a fool of myself?" asked Alex who was trying to sit up, but her head was spinning too much

"You were fine, you had a drink well a few drinks, a dance and then a sleep, here take these" Connie gave her 2 paracetamol tablets to take.

"I don't know what happened, I was so determined to have a good time and forget Jared bloody Jones!"

"You had a good time, up to a certain point anyway, and you forgot about him for a while."

Alex shook her head "aww that hurt" she rubbed her eyes

"Here drink this" Connie propped her up and gave her the mug of black coffee.

"I'm a mess!" wailed Alex.

"Don't be silly, you had a few drinks too many, who hasn't, have a rest, then if you feel up to it later, we'll have a bit of sun on the balcony and a bite to eat and discuss what I'm going to do with my life next!" said Connie.

"Ok auntie Connie" teased Alex, but laughing made her head hurt, suddenly she remembered "that reminds me, in my suitcase there's a letter for you, your gran gave it to me just before I left, she said she thinks that it's from your aunt Constance's solicitor as they have finalised her estate, the letter came just yesterday morning so she popped it around as mam had told her that I was coming back and she thought it safer for me to bring it in case it got lost, go and see Con."

Connie was surprised and wondered what it could be about. Aunt Constance had passed away at Easter time; her body had been brought back to her native Wales for the funeral. Connie hadn't seen her since her own mother's funeral, Connie remembered some sort of argument that had occurred between her Great Aunt and her grandparents after Laura Devereux's funeral and as far as she remembered they hadn't spoken again.

Connie went over to where Alex's suitcase lay open against the wall, half unpacked, she picked up a few items of clothing and moved them to one side when she came across an important looking sealed brown envelope addressed to Miss C Devereux at her grandparent's address.

"Open it Con" said Alex eagerly, temporarily forgetting her `bed ridden' state.

Connie got a manicure scissors out of her makeup bag and slit open the top of the envelope and took out the folded letter and read the contents of it to herself.

"Alex I've been left Aunt Connie's entire estate, I know she had a house in London, we lived with her for a while, but I can't remember where it was or even what it looked like, do you think she's left me her house?" Connie looked up questionably from the letter.

Alex now was rapidly recovering from her hangover," What? Oh, Connie that's great, I mean it's sad she's gone but fantastic that she wanted you to inherit everything!"

Connie read through the letter again, "they want me to contact them as soon as possible so they can proceed."

"Ring them Con see what they have to say."

"I wonder why she's left everything to me, I feel awful I mean I hadn't seen her for ages, you know what my grandparents are like, if I'd been in touch with her, they wouldn't have liked it after their falling out, and I don't even know what they fell out about!"

"Well Con she obviously wanted you to have everything, after all you were named after her and as you said before, she and your mother were very close."

Connie nodded, "Yes mum thought the world of Aunt Con"

Even though it was a Saturday the girls weren't working as Ricardo thought it would be nice for them to spend the weekend together catching up before Alex came back to work on Monday.

Connie checked the time considering the hour time difference between Italy and the UK.

"Do you think they're open yet it's just past nine in the UK," said Connie.

"Try Con" urged Alex.

Connie keyed the phone number into her mobile phone that was printed on the top of the letter from 'Harding, George and Launchberry Solicitors', as it rang, she read the gold embossed address: - 10-12 CHARLES Road,

Camden Town

LONDON

NW1.

"Good morning, Harding, George and Launchberry's, how may I help you" the well cultured ladies voice answered on the other end of the line.

"Er Hello Good Morning, my name is Connie Devereux and I have received a letter from you regarding my great aunt's estate" answered Connie.

"Hello Miss Devereux, I shall just put you through to Mr George" answered cultured voice.

"Well???" mouthed Alex.

"I'm being put through to one of the solicitors" whispered back Connie.

"Hello Miss Devereux? This is Edward George; I have been dealing with your late Aunts estate, may I offer my condolences" came a husky posh voice.

"Hello er thank you" stuttered Connie.

"As you have read in the letter addressed to you, you have inherited the late Miss Devereux's entire estate.

"WHAT??" gasped Connie.

'Do you need me to repeat Miss Devereux?' came back the slightly amused sounding voice.

"No sorry it's just a surprise" answered Connie trying not to sound so incredulous.

Alex was now up and out of bed and sitting next to Connie who was sitting crouched on the bedroom floor with a look of pure amazement on her face.

"When are you able to come to the office to discuss your inheritance?" asked posh husky Mr George.

"Oh, er I hadn't thought, erm," Connie stammered," "I'm living in Sorrento now so I'm not sure when I'll be able to come but erm, shall I ring you back?" Connie was still in shock.

"Of course, Miss Devereux, you let me know when you can return to the UK and we'll set up a meeting, if you can bring in some ID too, I'll look forward to meeting you."

"Yes yes, thank you I'll ring you as soon as I have sorted myself out, thank you."

"It's been my pleasure Miss Devereux, looking forward to meeting you soon, goodbye or should I say Ciao!" husky voice laughed a sexy husky laugh.

"Er yes bye" Connie pressed the button to end the call

"Well?" asked Alex "what did he say?"

"Al, I've inherited all of my aunt's estate, whatever than consists of, I'm guessing her house!!!"

"WHAT!!!!" Alex was now as shocked as Connie, "London, my goodness houses there must be worth a small fortune did you have any idea???"

Connie shook her head, "No, I don't suppose I ever gave it much thought."

"Bloody hell Con, if I didn't feel so rough, I'd say let's celebrate!"

"I've got to go to London to sign some paperwork"

"When?" asked Alex.

"As soon as I can, I can't believe it!" said Connie "You're back here and it looks like I'm moving on, look like I'd better look for a flight to London Al!"

Chapter 14

"Hello, mam?" asked Alex as the telephone was answered in her mother's flat.

"Oh, Hello babe, how are you? How are things?" answered mam sounding pleased to hear Alex's voice.

"I'm okay thanks mam, enjoying the sun and being back in work, can't believe I've been back almost a week already, how are you, I hope my father is looking after you!"

"yes fair play he's been pulling his weight, making meals for me and endless cuppas, don't worry about me I'm fine, well as fine as I can be with this blooming plaster on my arm and leg" Carole laughed gently, she did sound alright Alex was relieved to hear , her voice sounded happy, she hoped her father wasn't giving Mam any romantic ideas, as if reading her mind Carole added, "and before you ask, yes he's in your room, no he hasn't tried his luck and I think you know by now that there will never be anything between us again, that boat sailed long ago."

"Good I'm glad to hear but does `he' know?" asked Alex.

"Oh, I think he knows, anyway never mind about us, how are you, Connie gone yet?" Carole was up to speed on Connie's latest 'wind fall', Connie had rung her grandparents to let them know and Mary had been around to fill Carole in with all the news.

"Flew to Heathrow last night, she messaged me this morning she has an appointment later on today with the solicitors, she's staying in London for a couple of days and then she's back home to Porthcawl, I expect Mary and Sid will be glad to see her."

"Oh yes, Mary is afraid that she will settle in London now she has inherited a house, but like I said she doesn't know anyone in London, so why would she, but there you go, who knows what she'll decide, I mean a month ago she was serving ice cream down the road, then she was off to Sorrento and now in London!"

Alex agreed, "Yes life has been a bit crazy for us all over the past few weeks."

"What about you love, have you thought anymore about Jared?" asked Carole gently.

In truth Alex hadn't thought about anything else these past few weeks, her comfortable single life had been turned upside down and thrown back down to earth with a bang since laying eyes on Jared Jones again and the revelation that he had someone special in his life.

"I'm trying not to mam, I'm getting back into my routine, back to normal, I'm ok."

Carole knew her daughter better than that, even though her words sounded positive the tone of her voice sounded said something different, Carole answered "You know where I am if you want to talk things over."

"I know mam, I'm fine don't worry, I'll ring you soon."

After saying their goodbyes, Alex went to her apartment balcony to sit down and relax, it had been a busy day at Rivolli's – no rock stars looking for villas this week, but a succession of people wanting to buy E500,000 houses on E150,000 budgets and hating everything Rivolli's had for sale in their price range! Alex slipped off her cream heeled shoes, her feet were aching, well here she was back home in Italy back to work and back to normal, but she didn't feel normal, since she had returned to Porthcawl and walked into Doctor Jared Jones office everything had changed, even being back here in Sorrento where she loved-she didn't feel herself, didn't feel settled, she just didn't know what to do about it – didn't know what to do at all!

Connie had felt like a jetsetter as she boarded the plane to return to the UK, she and Alex had had a lovely few days together even though Alex had been in work most of the days, every evening they had made an effort to go out for dinner- trying bars, cafes and restaurants that they had fancied but hadn't been to before, making a list of the best ones for when they were together again. Gianni had pulled the short straw again as he was nominated to take her to Naples airport, he said he hadn't minded as he had a "bit of business" in Naples, Connie guessed that it probably involved a 'bit of pleasure' too knowing Gianni! They had chatted politely on the journey and had parted quite amicable which Connie was relieved about.

Connie had booked to stay the night in a hotel close to Heathrow airport as she wasn't due to land until close on midnight, she didn't really fancy travelling across London in the middle of the night to a hotel close to the Solicitors and hoped after a good night's sleep she would be better off travelling in the morning and in the light. Her appointment was at 2pm so she had plenty of time to find the Solicitors and organise accommodation for a longer stay if needed in London itself.

Connie had lived in London until she was seven but could barely remember anything about her time there. She had lived with her mother and presumably her father for some of the time, with Aunt Con.

Aunt Constance had moved to London as a young girl and had been married twice to what appeared to be two quite well-off men, both having died before Connie had been born. She had never had any children of her own, and always regarded Laura and her daughter as her nearest and dearest.

Laura her mum, had said they had moved to London to keep Aunt Con company whilst Laura pursued her career as an artist. Her mum had never said much about her father Giacomo, or Giac (Jack) as he was known locally. She knew he was Italian, and they had met when he had come to Porthcawl looking for work, as a young man and fell in love. They moved to London, Connie was born, Giac left, they moved back to Porthcawl and that's as much as Connie knew. What had happened between her parents she didn't know, she felt so stupid here she was at the grand old age of 27 and she had no idea what had happened to make her father leave and never to be seen again. She had tried to broach the subject with her mum and her grandparents but was always palmed off or the subject changed, until she gave up asking or even wondering, that was until lately.

The next morning Connie caught the train into London and then the tube to Camden town where the solicitor's office was also based, being brought up in Porthcawl, where there was no train station, this had been quite an adventure for her, she was glad to exit the hot and full tube, she had stood all the way and had been pushed, squashed, and her feet trodden on! She checked the time and had an hour and half before her appointment. She checked out some B & B's, in case she extended her stay and then re checked her walking route to the Solicitors office on Google maps on her phone to make sure she was going in the right direction.

She arrived in plenty of time at the smart double fronted office of 'Harding, George and Launchberry' Solicitors, it looked as if it was straight out of a Victorian drama from off the TV, with high box sash windows and double shiny black doors adorned with brass numbers and knobs. She smoothed down her blouse and trousers, checking her reflection in the highly shiny brass name plate on the wall next to the door took a deep breath and pushed opened the door to enter.

"Good morning, how may I help you?" she was greeted by a black-haired girl around her own age, made up professionally with a large pair of black framed spectacles covering her startling blue eyes and amazingly long, probably false, eyelashes.

"Good afternoon, I have an appointment at two pm my name is Connie Devereux" answered Connie feeling a bit scruffy in comparison to the 'model' sitting in front of her, her hair had started to escape from its bun and her lipstick had worn off several tube stops earlier not to mention her smudged eyeliner, 'Model' must arrive by car, thought Connie to herself!

"Good afternoon, Miss Devereux, Mr George will see you shortly, would you like to take a seat" 'model' had elegantly risen from her desk now and was showing Connie to a waiting area, "could I get you a drink?"

"A water would be great thanks," answered Connie gratefully sitting down on one of the chairs in the waiting area, she picked up the top magazine from the small table next to where she was sitting to flick through whilst she waited,"

HAS THIS COWGIRL FOUND HER COWBOY?" the headlines of the magazine asked, the photo emblazoned across the front of the magazine was of Wyatt Morgan with his arm around the shoulders of a young blond girl wearing a cowboy hat- Connie stared at the photo and didn't notice the return of 'model' with her glass of water.

"Ohh Wyatt Morgan he's so gorgeous, "Connie jumped slightly as 'model' spoke looking over her shoulder," he's with Jayde Johnstone, the country and western singer, they're at some concert in Texas together, the papers are full of it" Model laughed a light airy laugh" Lucky girl, all the paper's recon there's a romance going on."

Connie felt as if a dagger had been thrust into her chest, no wonder he hadn't been in touch, with   America's latest bloody singing star to cuddle up to! She took the glass of water with shaking hands that 'model' had given her, taking an unsteady sip she could feel her throat burning with unshed tears, as she glared down at the magazine cover.

Wyatt and Jayde inseparable – is it love? She read underneath the photo.

"Miss Devereux" a husky voice cut into her thoughts, she looked up and there in front of her, arm extended was a man, aged in his early thirties, dressed in an expensive looking grey suit with a smart shirt and matching tie, smiling broadly on his suntanned face, "Welcome to 'Harding, George and Launchberry' I'm Edward George, one of the partners handling your late aunt's estate."

Connie shook his hand, he had a firm handshake, "please come into my office" he indicated to a slightly open door to the left, Edward George was very handsome, but as poor Connie was still in shock after just reading the magazine headline about Wyatt, she wouldn't have noticed if he had had two heads!

"Are you alright Miss Devereux?" he asked with concern as Connie just stared into space, "Miss Devereux?" he repeated her name now, concerned that she seemed quite distant.

Connie focused her eyes on him, "yes sorry erm" she stuttered, "long journey and I'm a bit hot!" she excused herself with this white lie, even though she had just returned from living in a country at least 10 degrees hotter than it was today, she hoped he wouldn't press her on this point.

"Have a sit down you do look rather flustered, here's your water" he handed her the water 'model' had brought.

Connie sipped it and tried to gain her composure.

"Thank you, I'm ok now!" she smiled despite feeling very 'un- OK!'

"Take your time Miss Devereux "Edward smiled at her again and took a seat at his desk, he smoothed his golden blonde hair back as he opened a file in front of him.

"Have you brought your ID? I'll call Cordelia to photocopy it"

Connie fished around in her bag for her passport as Edward summoned 'model' to copy it.

"Right, everything seems straight forward, a few documents and legal bobbins for you to sign and we can get the ball rolling "

Connie smiled at the term 'bobbins' as it sounded funny coming from a young, cultured gentleman, like Edward George, he caught her eye and gave a small laugh "I'm so sorry that didn't sound very professional did it."

"It sounded fine" answered Connie, relaxing slightly as his pleasant demeanor put her at ease.

He discussed Connie's inheritance which consisted of a house and a sum of money, Connie signed a few documents which took about three quarters of an hour.

"Miss Devereux, I think that's us done now," Edward looked up from the paperwork on his desk, I have a set of keys here for your aunt's property here in Camden Town" he opened a safe box in his desk and handed Connie a bunch of keys.

Connie looked at the bunch, one large silver coloured key that looked like it was for a gate or a shed type building, 2 smaller silver-coloured keys and a typical brass coloured front door key, on a bunch with a key ring, a rather worn leather with the initials C and D on, Constance Devereux.

 Connie stroked the letters with her thumb, her initials too, suddenly her eyes filled up with tears, and they just started to fall uncontrollably down her cheeks, Connie tried to wipe them away with the back of her hand before Edward could see, but they fell faster and heavier and she let out a big sob.

Edward rushed to her side bending down on one knee her gently handed her a handkerchief," Oh I'm so sorry Miss Devereux, this has been rather a lot to take in I could see that you were upset about your aunt as soon as you walked in."

Connie cried even harder, bloody Wyatt Morgan, breaking her bloody heart, and then seeing this old worn key ring feeling guilty about not seeing Aunt Con for years and then thinking about her mum, it had all been too much and the all the feelings had totally engulfed her leaving her a howling wreck in front of this poor bloody guy!

"I'm so sorry" sniffed Connie wiping her eyes, mascara all over the place, and blowing her nose noisily.

"Don't be silly, is there anything I can do?" asked Edward as a look of concern spread over his handsome face.

"I'm ok now, just been a hard day" Connie forced a smile, "Can I use the bathroom please I must look a dreadful sight."

"Of course, er, I mean the bathroom not that you look a sight" Edward blushed slightly.

Connie was shown the direction to the toilet, as she entered, she looked into the mirror in the elegantly decorated toilet area, yes, she definitely looked a wreck, she washed her face under the cool water, popping it dry with the paper hand towels provided, despite living in the sun for several weeks, a ghost like face stared back at her.

She applied some lippy and mascara and pinched her cheeks in order to give them a little bit of colour, then she brushed out her hair and left it in bouncy curls around her shoulders, "Come on Connie girl, pull yourself together, this poor Edward George will be thinking you're a basket case!" she chided herself, "and he's got a passing resemblance of Christian Grey too!!"

She reentered Edwards office, "I'm so sorry, I'll go now if we're done, I think a bit of fresh air might do me good."

"I hope you're feeling better now, you are certainly looking better" Edward smiled then blushed again, "not that you didn't look good before" he blushed deeper now.

"Thank you Mr George" Connie smiled, he was just so nice

"I'll see you to the door" said Edward regaining his composure, what was wrong with him, he was acting like a giddy schoolboy, but this Miss Devereux was very attractive even with red eyes and streaky makeup! Edward saw Connie to the door of the solicitor's office, "it's been a pleasure meeting you today, Miss Devereux, if there is anything you need or you can think of that we haven't discussed please ring me", Edward swallowed hard then added, "or if you would like to meet me for dinner or even a drink" there he'd said it now, he'd asked her out they weren't supposed to be dating clients but as their business had now concluded he felt that she was now no longer a client.

"Thank you" Connie shook hands with him and then she was gone Edward returned to the office, oh well he'd made the offer, she had his number, albeit his office number, the ball was in her court now, so to speak, but he did wish that she had said "yes that would be nice" instead of just "Thank you."

Chapter 15

Connie entered her aunt's house address into her phone, the map showed only a five-minute walk from the Solicitors office, so she decided to walk, in the hope that she would clear her head. What a day! As soon as she arrived at her aunts she would phone Alex, two of them now unlucky in love- two with broken hearts- bloody men- when would she ever learn! And now this Edward bloody George- handsome as he was- asking her out! A month ago, she would have bit his hand off but now- well now she decided all men were off limits!!

She had arrived! she stood outside a smart looking terraced house with a small forecourt in front, the gate was open, so she walked up the short path and felt around in her handbag for the bunch of keys, she was right the brass key opened the front door, she pushed it open picked up her case and entered the hallway pushing the door closed behind her.

 The decor was quite Victorian- esque- burgundy walls, mahogany woodwork and patterned carpet covering the hall and the stairs leading upwards, Connie went through the first doorway which led into a front room this had quite dark decor too with heavy mahogany furniture and a wall unit full of china tea sets and ornaments. The second doorway along the hall led into a lighter room with a pale blue theme, Connie at once recognized the adorned the one wall as those of her mothers, she had a distinct style of painting. One was of Porthcawl harbour, one of tower bridge in London and the other of a garden full of colourful flowers, Connie took a closer look, all were signed L Devereux, she smiled, feeling both proud and sad at the same time. Mum's paintings were beautiful, she could imagine her sitting at her easel, like she remembered her doing at home in Porthcawl, her hair piled up on top of her head, wearing a paint smudged old shirt, lost in a world of artistry.

Connie went upstairs and found fresh bed linen in the airing cupboard and dressed the double bed in the back bedroom, she thought that she may as well stay here than at a hotel or b & b. The house had two more bedrooms too and an upstairs bathroom, Connie also found clean towels in the airing cupboard which she put in the bathroom so she could have a bath later.

She remembered passing a small corner shop on her walk here, so she went back out to get some supplies as she had planned to stay here over night. Armed with bread, butter, milk, toilet roll, a bottle of wine and a microwave lasagna she arrived back at the house, putting the wine in the fridge she sat down on the sofa in the 'blue lounge' and pressed ALEX on her phone.

Alex answered straight away obviously waiting patiently for her call, Connie filled her in about the magazine featuring Wyatt, breaking down in Edward Georges office, the house, everything down to the name of the bottle of wine she'd just purchased in the corner shop,

"And now I'm absolutely wrung out between travelling and the news about Wyatt I think one glass of wine and I'll be fast asleep!" Alex had sympathised over Wyatt she knew exactly how it felt to be let down by a man!

"Are you going to stay for a couple of days in London?" she asked Connie.

"I don't know I might do Mario isn't expecting me back yet so I can take my time I suppose, there's loads of stuff in the house so I think I'll need a few days to sort it out, it's lovely and clean here , Mr George said that she had a cleaner and that she has been popping in just to keep the house clean, apparently a direct debit was set up to pay her and it hasn't been cancelled and fair play she's continued to come here and keep it nice, I'll get in touch with her tomorrow"

"Ok as long as you are alright now, I don't believe a word I read in these magazines they take a photo and read what they want to into it and persuade their readers to believe it too!!" said Alex indignantly.

"It's on the internet too apparently, I haven't looked Al, I can't I'm afraid what I'll see" Connie could feel herself filling up again

"It'll be the same crap Con, he was on the same bill as that Jayde in a couple of festivals someone photographed them sitting together and put two and two together and made five, typical tabloid rubbish!"

"Even if it is rubbish, why hasn't he rung me, or texted even? He's not interested in me I was a bloody fool to believe it, as if he would be, I was a bit of available fun, a holiday romance and now it's over, I've got to get over it, I really thought we had a connection, but obviously not, oh Al, me and men why does it always go wrong?"

"Huh, I'm a good one to ask, it took me five years to get over Jared Jones and now I'm back to square one, fine pair we are Con!"

The two consoled each other for a bit longer then promised to be in touch the next day just to check that each other was ok.

Connie was right one glass of wine, and she could hardly keep her eyes open, she went up to bed in her aunts, now 'her' house, and fell asleep hoping that things would feel better in the morning.

Connie awoke to a sound of knocking, she sat up suddenly wondering what on earth it was, and where was it coming from! The knocking came again, and this time she realised it was someone at the front door knocking the big brass knocker. She got out of bed and tied her dressing gown around her as she padded down the stairs and to the front door. Cautiously she opened it.

"Hello lovey, I'm Sarah Smith, you must be Constance's young niece Connie" a woman much shorter than Connie beamed up at her, and held out a plump little hand and shook Connie's hand in a firm but friendly manner, Connie smiled back, "Er, yes that's me," Connie's puzzled look prompted the woman, "oh I'm sorry lovey you must be wondering who I am," she went on "I'm your aunts cleaner, well friend too, me and Constance go back many years, she was a lovely woman."

"Oh right, sorry "Connie apologised, "come in."

Sarah followed Connie into the kitchen, "I'm sorry did I wake you lovey, I was just on my way home from cleaning in the solicitor's office in town, and I was chatting to that lovely Mr George from the solicitors, and he said you'd moved in, so I just wanted to come and say hello."

"That's nice, I'm so sorry I wasn't up, think all the travelling and one thing and another must have knocked me out!" apologised Connie again- why was she apologising – Connie didn't know- but just felt that she needed to.

"Oh lovey, come from Italy so I hear" Sarah was smiling again and looking like she was ready for a chat.

"Yes, been a busy few days, er, can I get you a cup of something?

"Offered Connie feeling that Sarah wasn't in any rush to go, and needing a cuppa herself too.

"If it isn't too much trouble, a cup of tea one sugar would be just nice."

Connie made the teas and sat next to Sarah who had made herself comfortable at the kitchen table. "Thank you for keeping Aunt Cons house so clean, I really didn't know what to expect when I arrived, with her having passed away a while ago."

"Oh, it's been my pleasure, I'm still being paid to clean even though it's only a bit of sprucing up here and there, what with no Constance here anymore, God rest her soul" Sarah crossed herself Connie smiled thankfully and nodded," It's a lovely house I can hardly remember it from before though, apparently I lived here when I was very young."

"Yes, you did, I remember you were always smiling and singing and your lovely mum Laura, a beautiful girl, her and your dad made a handsome couple."

"You remember me?" Connie looked up surprised.

"Yes, for sure I do, I've known Constance for a long time, I only live across the way, we were friends for over thirty years."

"You knew my mum and ....my dad?"

"Oh yes I remember you all living here with Con, but then your dad went to America and you, and your mum moved back to Wales"

"America! Did my dad go to America?" Connie put her mug down suddenly "yes, yes lovey, you didn't know?" Sarah looked concerned now, she touched Connie's arm gently.

"No, I guess no one really said anything and I was only little, I know it sounds stupid, but I didn't really know where he went, mum said he went away to work and being young I just kind of accepted it and then the years went by, and life moved on and mum died" Connie shrugged and looked sadly at Sarah.

"Yes, yes I understand, Con always said that your grandparents weren't keen on your father and Laura going away with her condition and everything" Sarah nodded sagely.

Connie looked at the little woman in front of her, obviously they had been acquainted when Connie was a child, but she didn't remember her, and here she was now telling Connie things about her family that she knew nothing about. She had guessed there was no love lost between her grandparents and her father, but she had never been told he had gone to America, and this little lady seemingly knowing all about her mum's illness, Connie felt that a virtual stranger knew more about her young life that she did.

Sarah went on, "He worked in the city you see, your dad, that's why they came up to London to live with Constance, Con loved having the three of you here, then his company were expanding in New York, and he was offered this great new job there. Con knew that your mum wouldn't follow him she said she would go and take you when he had found them somewhere to live, but time went on and then Laura was quite poorly, it was her heart condition, I remember Con saying they had wonderful surgeons and hospitals in the states, but your grandparents wouldn't hear of it. Then you and Laura went back to Wales and that was the last time I saw either of you"

"I didn't know any of this, so if mum was too ill to travel, why didn't my father come back? Why did he never contact me?" now Connie had been told this information about her life, she wanted to know more.

"I don't know it all my lovey but from what Con had told me, your grandparents made quite a few decisions and your parents appeared to go along with them."

"You mean they kept him away and made mum go home with them!" Connie searched Sarah's plump face for answers

"Connie lovey I don't think it was that cut and dried, remember Laura was poorly and they loved her and you dearly and thought they were doing the right thing, you'd have to speak to them about it,"

"But mum was always well when I was young it was only the last few years that she was frail."

"She had a relapse just before you went to Wales, do you remember she spent time in hospital here that's why your grandparents came."

Connie shook her head, "no, I don't really remember much from then," and then added sadly "I don't even remember my father"

"Oh, poor Constance was so sad when your father left and when you both returned to Wales and devastated when your mum passed away, she thought of them as her own children, she was never blessed with children of her own, and she adored you" Sarah smiled at Connie.

"I was gutted when my mum died and then not to see Aunt Con again was a double blow, but you know what it's like when you're a teenager I was full of sadness and angst, and I just sort of put her out of my mind thinking she knew where I was if she wanted to see me, I suppose I thought the same about my father too."

Sarah nodded in understanding, "you went through a horrible time, Con understood, but she never forgot you, she said she didn't want to interfere."

"I suppose I felt everyone I loved had left me, I went through a bit of a bad time then" Connie shuddered remembering the tears, tantrums the wishing she had never been born episodes, her only sanctuary being Carole's home with her best friend Alex, and all the time spent at Nice Ice.

Sarah touched her arm gently again, "you know Con, and your dad were in touch, I remember popping in one day just after the postman had been, Con had a letter from your dad, she was always pleased to hear from him."

"No, I didn't know, why didn't he ever get in touch with me?" Connie's interest began to grow.

"Oh, but he did lovey, he wrote to Con here regularly, he would send letters here for you and your mum"

Connie looked stunned," but why didn't I ever receive any of them?"

"Con sent them all onto you at your grandparents address, but I guess they didn't pass them on" said Sarah sadly

"No, they didn't" Connie shook her head "but why?"

"Well when Con came to your mother's funeral, she found this out and there were words, bad words between them all and well you know the rest."

Connie couldn't believe her grandparents could be so controlling, "I can't believe they did something like that."

"They told Con it was for the best that they wanted to keep you and your mum safe with them, they must have been so afraid that he'd take you away to America and that they wouldn't see you again, they must have been so worried about your mum's health, and then when she passed away, I suppose they wanted to keep you with them in case they lost you too" explained Sarah.

"I can understand that, but to deliberately keep us apart, I thought my father had no interest in me and I never gave him much though, but you have opened up a whole new world to me now, he feels real, I know that sounds daft,"

"Wait there, I have something for you" Sarah got up and padded across the room and out up the stairs, Connie took a sip from her mug which had now gone cold, she made a face and tipped the contents down the sink, swilling the mug she put the kettle back on to boil.

Sarah returned carrying an old shoe box, "Con had kept all these" she handed the box to Connie, who looked at it in wonder "letters from your dad!"

Chapter 16

Sarah left just then, saying she would leave Connie in peace to read the letters.

Connie had made a fresh mug of tea and settled down on the settee

She gently lifted the lid off the shoe box and looked inside

Inside the box tied with craft string she saw a bundle of envelopes

She took the top bundle out, they were addressed to Constance, she put the bundle to the side of her on the settee and lifted the bundle underneath, they were addressed to her mum Miss L Devereux, all the envelopes bared the same script, and Connie guessed that they were all written by her father's hand

Connie took a sip of fresh tea whilst wondering which letters to read first.

She noticed Aunt Cons letters were all in date order the first envelope baring the date stamp July 1999 and the last December 2017- whilst the ones to her mum were dated from April 1999 to May 2004 – the month she turned 12.

The letters addressed to her mum were all still sealed she noticed as she went through them one at a time turning them over and wondering why none of them had been opened

These must be the letters returned from Sea Breeze Cottage

Had her mum seen these letters and sent them to Aunt Con unopened-but why?

Or had her Grandparents sent them on not wanting her mum to read them? She was confused-where had they come from?

Had they always been at Aunt Cons or had they been kept at 'Sea Breeze' until her mum's death.

Maybe that's why there had been a falling out with Aunt Con and her grandparents.

Connie touched the outside of the top envelope; she felt like a snoop, should she open them? They had remained unopened for all these years, was it her place to open them now?

She took another sip of tea, her phone rang suddenly, making her jump as she was lost in thought over the unopened letters- it was Alex.

"Hi, I just wanted to check you were ok?"

"Yeah, Al I'm ok, I'm glad you rang, I'm in a bit of a quandary," Connie told Alex all about the visit from Sarah next door and whether or not she should open the letters.

"Well Con if they can help answer some unanswered questions you have about your father, then yes I think you should open them, after all they were obviously kept for some reason" answered Alex carefully.

"I guess so, it's just that I feel a bit strange I suppose reading personal stuff, I mean what they going to say?"

"Well, you'll know when you read them Con, what about everything else, you ok being back in London after all these years?"

"It's been a bit of a whirlwind Al, to be honest, a lot to get my head around these last few days."

"Of course, and Wyatt?" Alex ventured.

"Wyatt bloody Morgan! got more important things on my mind at the moment!"

"Yes, course you have, you take care and ring or message me if you need to talk, promise."

"Promise" agreed Connie.

She picked her cup up to finish the tea, but it had now gone quite cold, she put it back down, feeling it was just being a distraction from the task in hand- opening the letters!

She slit open the oldest dated envelope which contained the first letter to her mum and took a deep breath and began reading

My Bella Laura

I am missing you and Connie so much- New York is a big, exciting city but feels so empty without you! I have a nice apartment just a few blocks away from the subway that takes me minutes to get to the office- so that's a plus. The guys are all a good bunch at work. I hope you are resting and feeling better now that you are back home by the sea. I have a meeting arranged with a doctor Howard who's been recommended to me by a colleague (his sister has had heart surgery, and has recovered fully), so I am so optimistic that when you are feeling stronger and can travel that the medical

experts here will be able to help you my darling I pray this every night

Give Connie a hug and a kiss from me and tell her, I love and miss her and her Mama.

Ciao Cariad

Your ever-loving Giac.

Connie folded the letter back into its creases and replaced it back into the envelope,

What went wrong? Her dad seemed so desperate for her mum to go to America for treatment- and Connie remembered mum getting better for a good few years and surely, she would have been well enough to travel- why hadn't she gone? Why hadn't she opened the letters? So many unanswered questions!

There were another three letters dated the same year all in the same vein her dad had met with this Dr Howard who wanted Laura to go to see him in New York to be assessed for possible treatment- her dad's pleas were desperate.

Every year there was a Birthday card for Connie sent care of Laura and a birthday card for Laura- all remained unopened – until now. Reading all the Birthday cards from her dad brought tears to her eyes- all those years when she thought that her dad didn't care about her or where she was and all along it was he that was being ignored and probably thought she had forgotten him or didn't want to know him- Why? Why had this happened why had she been denied any relationship with her dad- was it just Laura and her grandparent's fault or was Connie to blame too? After all she wasn't always a little girl- she could have tried to find out about him herself why hadn't she asked more questions? Why hadn't she bothered? Connie sat back against the cushions behind her on the settee- all these daughter cards signed "Ciao Cariad your ever-loving Daddy xxx" and the birthday cards to her mum signed the same "Ciao Cariad your ever-loving Giac xxx" All those years he had continued to send cards but never heard anything back from them!

All Giac's letters were signed off with Ciao Cariad- his bit of Italian and Mums bit of Welsh.

The last letter from Giac, as over the years they became less and less to only one a year the year her mum had died- it was in an envelope with a birthday card- her 12th-

My dear Laura and Connie,

I hope my letter finds you both well, I understand from Aunt Con that you Laura have been ill again, and I pray that you will recover soon. I am sorry that I have not ever received any communication from either of you, but I understand, and that is why I have always kept my distance. I know that if you wanted or needed me you would let me know. I relocated to New York in 1999 and as you can see by my current address, I have now settled in Sydney Australia these past two years. I have been lucky to have such a fulfilling occupation as I have missed you both more than words can say over the years. Aunt Con has kindly sent me photographs of you Connie as you have grown which have meant the world to me. I hope you are both happy in life and want to let you know that after so many years of being alone I have finally filled the void in my life- I have met a lovely lady by the name of Diane who has agreed to be my wife. As I always say if you ever need me, I'm here for you both- I won't write again but know you are both always in my heart.

Ciao Cariads

Giac xxx

Connie re read the letter- her poor dad he obviously didn't think she wanted anything to do with him- if she had been given these letters at the time would things have been different? So, her dad had lived in America and Australia- was he still there? And he was married- did she have any brothers and sisters? This letter was 15 years old – she wondered what had happened since then? Aunt Con had letters too more recent letters maybe she would find more out about his life- the last letter Con received was less than two years ago- Connie braced herself to read Aunt Cons letters from her dad. The first few were full of questions about how Laura and Connie were, and why had he not heard from them- she could only guess her Aunt Cons response- she obviously kept Giac up to date with Laura's health and with bits of news and photos of Connie, but what did she say about why they never replied to his letters?

Connie read through the letters which were dated up to when he last wrote to Connie and her mum in 2004, he had only sent one a year at Christmas to Aunt Con from then on, Connie was finding that she couldn't read them quick enough- after all these years of barely thinking about her father she now felt that she desperately needed to know how he was, where he was and what he was up to. He appeared to be happy with Diane and up until Christmas 2017 there was no mention of any children being born to Giac and Diane, so it didn't look like Connie had any half siblings.

The letter received from him following Laura's death was hard for Connie to read she felt his anguish through the words on the paper and had begged Con to give Connie his address and telephone number to get in touch if she wanted to. Why hadn't Aunt Con given them to her? Was that what the falling out with her grandparents had been over? It must have been Connie summarised- what an awful mess- why hadn't anyone been honest with her- let her make her own mind up about things- and her dad- after all he was her dad and from what she had read today he obviously loved her- and her mum- even if mum didn't want to go to America she could have still kept in touch- and then on the other hand- Connie thought- if he had loved them so much why didn't he come back? So many questions?

The last letter he had wrote had been sent from Italy –his homeland-his dad had passed away and he had returned to Italy after 30 years travelling the world.

Connie couldn't believe it -back to Italy- where she had been herself up to a few days ago- what if she had passed him on the street- she probably wouldn't even know him- She knew Italy was a big country- but from not knowing where he was to finding out he went to America and then Australia- and then Italy- it felt that he was closer now than ever- he felt so real and close now that she had read all the letters- she re-read the letter again- was he still there, was he back in Italy now?

So much to take in- should she ring her grandparents? Or should she go back to Porthcawl to confront them face to face- she wasn't angry- she just wanted some things clarified- after all she'd had a good life growing up in Sea Breeze Cottage, but would her life had been any different if she'd grown up knowing she had a father who loved her? She didn't know.

She put all the letters away in the shoebox- a lot to think about! She went upstairs to have a shower and to clear her head- what a week!

She was brushing her hair when the doorbell rang- Connie ran downstairs thinking it was probably Sarah, she opened the door, but it wasn't Sarah standing there-it was Edward George from the Solicitors.

"Hello, I'm sorry to bother you, it's just that I was passing, and I just wanted to say hi and see if you were ok?" He smiled nervously colouring slightly.

"Oh, Hello I er thought you were someone... oh it doesn't matter, er yeah I'm ok I guess!" and with that Connie burst into tears

"I'm so sorry, I..." Edward stuttered awkwardly thinking he had brought on this upset.

"No, I'm sorry" sobbed Connie, "So sorry, please come in" she opened the door wider for him to enter but fell sobbing into his arms.

Edward held her and managed to maneuver her inside and onto the settee he quickly found some tissues and offered them to her

Connie blew her nose noisily, "oh Edward I'm so sorry I seem to be in a mess every time we meet" she apologised.

"No need for apologies I'm glad I'm on hand to assist" he answered gently,

"I've had some surprises today shall we say! And I'm all topsy-turvy with my emotions; I'm not normally like this it's just well..." Connie trailed off and shrugged her shoulders.

After one that led to two strong coffees that Ed made, Connie felt a lot better.

"What you need is a nice afternoon out; clear the cobwebs away and a bit of a laugh!"

"Sounds good to me I think I could do with an uncomplicated stress-free day!" agreed Connie.

"I do a bit of am dram you know amateur dramatics and I'm off there this afternoon it's only a local group we're doing a production of Warhorse, trying to get our horse to come together but well you know the mechanics are a bit last century" Ed laughed, and his laughter was infectious as Connie felt her mouth turning into a smile.

"It sounds lovely Ed I'd love to come along if that's ok"

Connie was already dressed in jeans and T shirt she tied her hair back, "I'm ready!"

"Is there anything I can do to help- I know I'm a solicitor but I'm also a good listener and I don't charge for friendly advice" Ed smiled

"Ah Ed I'm ok, think I just need a distraction so thanks for that"

They left the house together and walked the short distance through a leafy suburb to St Thomas's church hall where the Thomas players were gathering ready for their next rehearsal, Ed turned the large rusty handle on the rather weather-beaten main door it had been green once upon a time but was now badly needing a lick of paint, it creaked noisily as the two entered the hall.

"Ed, great to see you glad you could make it," Ed was hugged by a small lady in her 50s, who was carrying a length of gray material which she draped over Ed as the two embraced

"Aunt Jean "said Ed untangling himself from the material, "This is Connie, I've brought her along to..." Ed didn't finish.

"Ah Connie hello "Jean the little lady boomed loudly, a voice that Connie didn't feel sounded like it belonged to such a small lady, she embraced Connie too, festooning her with said material, "come along to help, great, great always need another pair of hands!"

Connie felt herself hugging Jean back, she smiled and nodded, as Jean ushered her towards a large table in the corner of the room covered in various materials and bits of metal and wire

"This" Jean waved her arm over the contents of the table is our Joey!"

Connie looked at Jean puzzled, "Our warhorse dear!" Jean replied with a loud laugh.

Ed ambled over to the table, "Oh Aunt Jean, still no further on with the mechanics then?

"Well Steve knows a man who knows a man" she winked.

Theatrically at Ed and Connie, "and apparently he's a dab hand at creating stuff so hopefully he is starting Joey next week!" she smiled widely.

"Connie dear would you like to start on the backdrop we need lots of green paint for the fields."

Another lady approached the trio carrying two pots of paint and some brushes "Ah Caroline wonderful!" Jean spoke to the other lady whilst taking the paint off her and handing them to Connie and Ed, "there my dears you can start over here" she indicated to some large boards of MDF which had been hinged together to form a screen "This will be our green field, so carry on painting dears!"

Jean busied herself amongst a group of individuals who were sat in the corner of the hall "Sorry Aunt Jean is a bit er, full on," said Ed "Don't apologise it sounds very therapeutic, just what I need," smiled Connie.

Caroline the paint carrying lady re approached them carrying 2 overalls, "so you don't get paint on your nice clothes" she said smiling as she handed the slightly paint stained overalls.

Connie and Ed slipped them on over their clothes and started about the screen.

"So how long have you been doing this?" asked Connie dipping her brush into the green paint.

"Oh like, forever!" answered Ed, "I used to come in as a child with my mum as her and Aunt Jean has always been a bit theatrical, and I've been singing in the ensemble, painting backdrops, sewing stuff and generally mucking in for over 20 years!"

"That's great, I bet you have so much fun, are you "staring in this production?"

"Yes, got a part as one of the owners of the horse, been learning my lines too" Ed laughed, "the show opens in a couple of months, so we hope to get Joey up and running soon!"

"Sounds good!" answered Connie.

The two spent the next two hours painting and chatting about past productions put on by the Thomas Players, the various mishaps and triumphs, whilst a small group of Thomas Players made up of Caroline, another lady slightly younger and taller by the name of Suzy and two guys around Connie's own age called Dan and Ben ran through their lines in the corner, being aided and sometimes being chastised by Jean in her booming voice.

"We've almost finished, are you ok, to carry on until the end or have you had enough" Ed said, then smiled "don't be polite if you've had enough!"

"I'm fine 'til we finish only got this corner to go-I've enjoyed it"
answered Connie pushing a bit of stray hair back off her forehead
and accidently dabbing her nose with the bright green paint
They both laughed, "see I said it'll be fun."
When they had totally covered the boards with green paint, they
stood back to admire their handy work, as Jean bustled over to
inspect their handy work "Marvelous job dears well done" she
announced admiring the boards, "mind you, you've more paint on
you Connie dear than the board!" They all laughed, Connie realised
that she hadn't thought about her dad or Wyatt all afternoon, Ed
was right this had been a nice distraction; and just what she
needed, even though it had only been just for a short time!

Chapter 17

Alex sat on her veranda deep in thought; she had spoken to Connie the previous night; Connie had told her all about the letters and had so many unanswered questions. Alex had listened while Connie had poured her heart out to her.

"Go back home to Porthcawl and speak to your grandparents" advised Alex, "you need to speak to them about this Con, you need to go home don't stay in London on your own, you can confide in my mother too, I think it's important for you to be with family and people you know,"

"Yes, I think I will, I know I need to, I'm just worried about what they'll say, they have always been so wonderful, what if I don't like what they've got to say?"

"You'll only know if you speak to them, and then you can make your own mind up."

"I know you're right I'll get online now and book the coach home tomorrow, thanks for listening Al,"

"Are you ok, you know about Wyatt Morgan?"

"I can't think about him now, my head is full of my dad."

"Let me know when you're back, take care Con."

Alex wished she could be there for Connie, this was huge, in all the years that they'd been friends Connie had hardly mentioned her dad, and now practically overnight he had become the main focus in her life- Alex worried about her too even though she had said

Wyatt wasn't on her agenda at the moment, she knew how upset Connie was over him, she just hoped that she would be okay.

Connie had messaged Alex late last night to say she had booked onto the 8.30am National Express home. Alex checked the time, Connie would probably be on her way home now, and she just hoped that she would be able to get some answers.

Alex had rung her mother to let her know Connie was due home "I just wanted to let you know in case she needs a friendly face, I really don't know how it'll go with her grandparents, I'm worried about her mam."

"Oh, love her, poor Con after all these years, mind you Al, it might be a good thing, get everything out in the open, and you never know, might lead to her meeting up with her father again"

Alex hadn't slept very well first worrying and thinking about Connie which eventually turned to thoughts of Jared, she'd given up on any notion of sleep then, and got up to make herself a strong cup of coffee.

She wondered which direction her life would take next, she had been totally contented working for Rivolli's building up her portfolio and learning more and more Italian until she had felt quite confident in basic conversation yes, she had been happy with her lot- until she had laid eyes on Jared Jones again and her head, heart and life had been thrown into total chaos! She had ignored his calls changed her number- what was she afraid of? She hadn't seen him for years, had basically dumped him, and now she had the nerve to be 'gutted'? Yes, she had to admit she was gutted that he had moved on and obviously had someone new, who knows he might be married, might have kids! She sighed, should she still care? Did she have any right to care? Whether she did or didn't unfortunately she did care- she cared very much and now her happy content life was not as appealing as it had been before she had returned to Porthcawl when Carol had had her accident!

Connie had popped in to see Sarah to tell her she was going back home as she had things to sort out and didn't know when she'd be back, "If you see Ed from the solicitors, please will you let him know, tell him I'll be in touch soon."

"Are you thinking of selling up then lovey?" enquired Sarah.

"I haven't really thought about that yet, everything is still very new, you know, me inheriting the house and all the stuff about my father, I'm going back home for a bit to think and to speak to my grandparents."

Sarah nodded sagely, "of course lovey lots to talk about, good luck and safe journey."

Now here she was travelling again in just a few days, Sorrento to Naples, Naples to London then across London and now on her way back home to Porthcawl.

Connie rested her head back on to the back of the coach seat she felt tired, and emotional she closed her eyes and tried to rest.

She woke with a sudden jolt, her back ached and her eyes felt sore, she looked out of the window, they had arrived in Cardiff already, she glanced at her phone, 10.20am she had been sleeping for almost two hours, not like her at all, mind you after the past few weeks and with one thing or another, it was no wonder she had slept so heavily. Almost home thought Connie, home, Porthcawl, this was the longest she had been away from there and her grandparents since she had arrived all those years before with her mum. It had been a mad few weeks, wonderful, exciting times in Sorrento, which felt like some kind of exotic dream now, sun, sea, million euro houses and a whirlwind romance with a bona fide rock star! Then off to London with a broken heart a grand house and untold revelations about her father. She rubbed her eyes, her life had been like some kind of crazy romantic novel lately, and now back home she was going to face yet more revelations, she hadn't told her grandparents she was coming home and on Alex's advice she decided to call on Carole first to get her head together before she went home.

Soon the coach pulled into its stop in Bridgend, Connie got off and collected her bags and got into a taxi at the nearby rank, she asked to be taken to Carole's address.

Connie rang Carole's number, "Hiya Carole its Connie, can I come to yours I'm just leaving Bridgend in a taxi, I hope that's ok?"

"Of course it is babe, are you ok?" asked Carole concerned for this young girl who she had known since she was seven years old, and felt as close as an auntie to her.

"I don't know" Connie burst into tears, she didn't know why or how

"Oh, my love, I'll get the kettle on, don't cry, you'll be home soon!" said Carole, suddenly feeling herself filling up with tears too

"I'm sorry; I don't know what's wrong with me!" cried Connie

"You've had a shock and a lot to contend with, take care babe and I'll see you very soon."

Connie wiped her eyes and blew her nose and apologised to the taxi driver.

"Don't you worry love, you have a good old cry, my missus says everyone feels better after a good old cry!" he answered sagely

Connie smiled despite herself.

Soon they arrived at Carole's, she was waiting at the door, looking very worried, and when Connie got out of the taxi, she threw her 'good' arm around her.

"Come in and have a relax after that long journey, kettles just boiled, and I've got some nice chocolate biccis"

"Lovely, thank you" Connie hugged her back; it was good to see Carole again.

After a visit to the loo, and a cold splash of water on her face,

Connie felt a bit better; Carole had made her a steaming mug of tea and an opened packet of half covered chocolate biscuits stood on the coffee table.

Connie sat down gratefully and sipped the tea,

"Oh, my love if I had been up to my well old self, I would have come straight to London to see you, Alex is beside herself, she was all for jumping on a plane home, but I said let's see how things go once you got back home" Carole sat down and gently stroked Connie's hand.

"I'm ok really, it's just been a crazy couple of weeks, here I was a month or so ago working in Mario's doing nothing spectacular, just plodding along day to day, and then POW!!!! Well, you know the rest!"

"Well, there's no rush for you to go home, you go when you are good and ready, but I know Mary and Sid will be so pleased to see you, I think they have missed you, a lot."

Connie nodded.

"And love don't be too hard on them, whatever they did or didn't do, they obviously thought it was for the best at the time"

Connie nodded again, "It's just that I don't know why they kept all the letters and stuff from me, I mean, I doubt I would have gone with my dad as I was happy here, with them and you and Alex, but it would have been nice to have kept in touch with him and have visited each other, after all he was my father!"

Carole nodded, "Relax for a here for a while and then when you are ready pop over there and see what they've got to say."

"How are you though Carole, here I am moaning on, and I haven't asked how you are?" apologised Connie.

"Well as you can see, I'm managing better, only another couple of weeks they said in the hospital and these" she indicated to her casts, "will be off for good, I can't wait Con, they haven't half slowed me down, can't wait to get behind the wheel again, I've been missing my car, Johns been good, but now he's moved on to his brothers, I don't like bothering him if I need to go anywhere, and Mario, bless him, he's been taking me shopping"

Connie smiled; she was glad Carole was getting better and almost back to her old self.

After another cuppa and a chat on the phone with Alex to let her know, she had got back ok, Connie felt ready to go home.

It was a nice bright warm day, Porthcawl was busy, full of day trippers and holiday makers as Connie walked to her grandparent's house.

She walked past Mario's and could see Nicola and Mario busily serving customers, she would call in later.

She arrived at her grandparent's front gate and hesitated before lifting the latch, no turning back now if she was to speak to them about Giac, her father.

She went around to the back door and was greeted by Sammy next doors cat that came and brushed against her leg and purred contently as she bent to tickle her ears, her granddad as usual was in the garden going a bit of weeding.

"Granddad!" she called, "I'm home!"

Sid got up stiffly from where he was tending his plants, and turned to the direction Connie's voice came from, when he caught sight of his beloved granddaughter, he beamed a huge smile from ear to ear, "Ah Connie, we didn't expect you," he brushed the soil from his hands down his gardening trousers, "have you seen your gran, does she know your home?"

"No not yet "Connie went to him and kissed his cheek,

"We missed you Connie, I'm so glad you're home, come on in, your gran will be so pleased to see you," he ushered Connie inside the house and into the kitchen, "Mary, Mary, look our girls come home!" he called excitedly, Connie's gran appeared from the other room, "You're back Connie, but why didn't you let us know you were coming, oh it's good to see you love!"

Connie's face must have given something away as much as she hoped the walk here in the sea air would have calmed her,

"Are you alright Connie, Connie, Connie!!!" The last thing she remembered was seeing her Gran's face change shape and colour and her voice becoming very echo-ey and far away, Connie had fainted!

She came too, with her grandparents knelt by her side on the kitchen floor, "She's coming around Sid get her a glass of water!" her Gran Said worriedly.

She sipped the water slowly.

"Oh, Con you frightened us, are you alright?" Asked Gran.

"I think so, I feel a bit woozy" Connie felt quite weak.

"Come on love, we'll get you onto the settee" her grandparents helped her up slowly and onto the settee in the other room, putting cushions behind her and propping her feet up.

"All that travelling from a hot country, it's no wonder!" said Gran sternly, "you rest there, no more gallivanting!"

For once Connie was glad to be told what to do, as she felt so awful, "Get her a sugary tea Sid!"

"I'm ok Gran I just had a few cups in Carole's."

"Carole's, why on earth would you go there before coming here?" asked Gran sharply.

Connie realised what she had said, and as much as she didn't feel like divulging all she had discovered about her father at this precise moment, she knew that she would have to tell them everything.

"Well, I haven't come home directly from Italy, I've been in London for the past week" confessed Connie to her surprised grandparents, "Aunt Con has left me her house in her will, and I had to go to London to a solicitors to sign some things and I decided to stay for a bit."

Sid and Mary stared at her then at each other in surprise, "Con left you, her house? Well, I suppose it isn't that surprising as apart from granddad you are her only relative" said Gran taking this new information in.

"Tell us more love," said Granddad.

"Well, there was all these letters there to mum and to me," her grandparents exchanged glances, as Connie continues, "from my father"

"They were unopened, and I opened them and read them all, and to be honest I didn't know what to think, about the letters and cards," Connie hesitated "or about you two!"

Mary looked at Sid uncomfortably and Sid started rubbing and pulling at her sweater the way he always did when he felt awkward or uncomfortable, Mary spoke first, "And what did these letters say then?"

"Well that he wanted us to go to America and that he loved and missed us, I really thought that he didn't want us, all these years I honestly thought he just up and left without a backward glance, but he didn't did he?" Connie was feeling a bit stronger now and was starting to feel a bit angry.

"It was a long time ago love," said granddad.

"All he wanted was to take our daughter and granddaughter half way around the world when he knew how ill our Laura was, that her life expectancy was short, but no he didn't care, he was chasing a high-flying life and job, and our Laura knew she was too ill to go, who would look after you if she got too ill, not him no, too busy with work, and she knew she would die, and then what would have happened to you!" Mary's voice cracked then with emotion and tears ran down her face.

"Now, Now, Mary love" Granddad went over to Mary and gently put his arms around her, her shoulders were shaking from sobbing, Connie hadn't wanted to upset her grandparents, and now she felt bad.

"I'm sorry gran, but I didn't understand why the letters and cards were unopened and why I had never got to see them, I didn't want to upset you."

"It's like your gran said, your mum knew she was ill and going to die and that it was no use going to America as then who would have looked after you, she thought it best and rightly or wrongly we decided not to respond to Giac's letters, just to make a clean break, with hindsight maybe it wasn't the right thing to do, but we were afraid we'd lose not just our beautiful Laura but you too, it may have been selfish but when you are losing the most precious thing in your life then you will do anything not to lose the second most precious" Sid spoke quietly but steadily.

"But what about my father, didn't he lose the two most precious things in his life too?" asked Connie.

"Maybe, but he was young and ambitious, we knew he'd be alright and make a new life, I'm sorry Connie but at the time we all thought, your mum included, that we were doing the right thing," continued Sid.

Connie nodded, "I understand, but I would have stayed with you and Gran always, you should have known that I wouldn't have wanted to leave here, my friends, school, I would have just liked to have had a chance to get to know my dad too,"

"I'm sorry love, what else can I say" Sid shrugged his shoulders sadly

"Is that why you and Aunt Con fell out?" Asked Connie.

"Yes, basically, she had different ideas from us and well, that was that I don't know what else to say but sorry, Giac was a nice fella, but we didn't think he would be able to cope with your mum's illness, you and a career the other side of the world" Mary had recovered enough to speak now,

"Ok" answered Connie, what else could she say? Whatever she said now wouldn't make any difference and there was no point in arguing with her grandparents now, it was done, it was in the past and it was as she had expected, a bit unfair that her dad hadn't been given much of a chance to prove he could have coped, but then again what if they had gone and mum had died in America, what might have happened to her then? She just wished that she had had a chance to get to know him even if it had only been through letters and telephone calls and the occasional visit.

"Are you alright now, love?" Mary asked.

"I still feel a bit rough I think I'll go for a lie down if that's ok" Connie got up off the settee slowly as her head was still pounding and slowly went up to her room to lie down and think about her dad and what could have been and maybe what could still be! Connie awoke to the buzzing of her phone as it vibrated on her bedside cabinet; the noise indicated she had a message. It was dark in her room and the phone lit up making Connie blink, how long had she been asleep? She stretched out her arm to lift the phone to see what time it was, seven fifteen pm, she'd been asleep for hours, the journey and all the revelations had taken it out of her, she felt wrecked, her mouth was dry, and her head ached. Three messages showed on her phone.

The first was from Ed, "Hi Connie, I heard you had returned home I hope everything is alright, you know where I am if you ever need me, Ed ☺" Connie smiled, "aww lovely Ed."

The second was from Alex, "Con, mam said you were home, hope you are ok ring me when you get a chance xx" and so was the third, "Con, hope you're ok, haven't heard from you xx"- Bless Alex she had messaged her two hours ago and then again just now, she was such a good friend.

"I'm ok thanks, I'll ring you later xx" She replied to Alex's text, now she was awake she felt quite hungry and decided to ring Alex when she had had a bite to eat and then hopefully would feel more human. She stretched and rubbed her eyes as she willed herself up and out of bed.

She suddenly felt cold so found her old dressing gown hanging behind the bedroom door and put it on loving the feeling of soft fluffy pink faux fur against her, she felt comforted and safe wrapped up in it, she sighed deeply and walked downstairs and out to the kitchen where her gran was peeling potatoes at the sink.

"Hello love are you feeling any better after a sleep, I checked on you about an hour ago, but you were flat out," said gran

"I still feel shattered, but I'm starving!"

"Just getting these spuds on, chicken is just finishing up (gran gestured to the oven, boasting a golden-brown chicken) and some of your granddad's beans from the garden, look like you need feeding up after all that gallivanting!" Gran eyed Connie up and down, "hmm you are looking very peaky Connie!"

Connie sat down, she probably felt 'peaky' too whatever that meant, but she did feel washed out, maybe gran was right, and she needed a nice home cooked hot meal.

"Are you home for good now Connie?" gran questioned casually.

"I think so gran, well for a bit anyway, not sure what I'm going to do about Aunt Con's house yet, I don't think I want to live in it, I mean my job is here and much as I loved going to Italy and then to London, I can't really see me moving from Porthcawl" after the heartache and stresses of the past few weeks Connie was glad to be home, safe and cwtched up in her own bed.

Mary's hunched shoulders dropped the tension eased from them hearing these words, she had missed Connie, not that she would admit it, not to mention Sid, who had been quiet and withdrawn since she'd been away - their Connie was back and hopefully, for good!

Chapter 18

Alex was glad when Connie eventually phoned her, she was sat on her little veranda working on some marketing for Ricardo, not that he would ever suggest her take work home, but she just wanted something to get her teeth into and to give herself something to do

Connie had told Alex everything that had happened so far

"What are you going to do Con, will you try to find him?" Asked Alex when Connie had told her that her father could quite possibly be in Italy.

"I think I would probably like to, I know it's been a long time and there's been a lot of water under the bridge, so to speak, but yes Al, I think I would really like to meet him, especially now that I realise he did care and probably did love me" answered Connie truthfully

"You'll have to ring that 'Long lost Families' with Davina McColl, Con."

They both laughed,

"Yeah, I hope he won't be that hard to find, I thought of looking on Facebook or just googling his name, to be honest I haven't looked yet, all I seem to want to do is sleep, Gran made me a lovely chicken dinner, I was so hungry but then I struggled to eat it, I don't know what's wrong with me!"

"It's no wonder all you've been through lately, travelling and then all that shock, first the house then all that with your dad, you've had a crazy couple of weeks not to mention Wyatt bloody Morgan, have you heard from him?" (Wyatt had appeared to have gained a middle name of 'bloody' now, every time the girls discussed him!)

"No, I really thought we had something Al, but who the hell was I kidding a world-famous rock star and an ice-cream girl from Porthcawl"! aww God I sound like some cheesy lyrics from one of his bloody songs!" Connie laughed despite feeling helpless about the whole 'Wyatt' situation.

"You're too good for him anyway Con, his loss!"

"Yeah" answered Connie not feeling or believing this

"Well if you need me to nose around about your dad just let me know, I can see if I can find something out, what with me being here and all that" said Alex meaning she was in Italy

"You are welcome to find out whatever you can, I'm going to forget about Wyatt now and concentrate on finding my dad- think I'll forget about guys permanently!"

"Hey what about lovely 'Ed'?" Alex emphasised his name

"Oh no, no Alex, he's just a very nice guy, and I'm determined to keep him as my lovely guy friend and nothing else!" answered Connie.

"If he's that nice you should snap him up!"

"No not this time, Ed is definitely friend zone and that's all!"

The girls finished up their conversation and Connie decided to have a little browse online just to see if there was anything on Giac.

She keyed his name into the Facebook search when various suggested **Giacomo Santini** popped up, she scrolls down, and there was a young man around her age from Sienna, she looked at his photo, he had a definite resemblance to photos she had seen of her father, but he was too young, about thirty years too young, but there was definitely something about him. Tentatively, Connie clicked on this Giacomo Santini photo, his profile wasn't completely private, so she was able to scroll down to look at his photos.

This Giacomo's smile beamed back at her from various snaps surrounded by family and friends, some on a beach, some in a garden, some in a bar, all happy smiling people. Connie kept scrolling until she suddenly stopped on a photo of several people with the caption 'Celebrating Uncle Giac's Birthday'.

She clicked to enlarge the photo and scrolled across at the smiling faces, the first face she recognised as the young man Giacomo, the second an older man with greying hair and glasses who had his arm around another man who looked younger than the second man, thick black hair with a sprinkling of grey and deep brown eyes shining with happiness, Connie would know those eyes anywhere, she zoomed in on the face, yes this was definitely the face of her father staring back at her! She studied his face, older, yes definitely older of course, but this was him, she zoomed back out and looked at the last person in the photo, a woman who looked aged around her mid-50s with short blond hair, also smiling happily, Connie guessed this could possibly be her father's wife Diane. The date of the post was May of this year, so her father was in Italy this year, in Sienna, only a couple of hundred miles from where she had been in Sorrento, had he been there the same time? Had she been in Italy the same time as her dad? Was he still there? After reading all his letters and seeing her birthday cards she knew now that he had cared and loved her, and her mum too, even when questioned, her grandparents hadn't really hated him, probably hadn't even disliked him, after all he hadn't really done anything wrong, Connie zoomed in on him again, her dad, she found herself smiling back at his image, here he was surrounded by family, she guessed the other older man was his brother, and young Giacomo's father. She scrolled down and saw other photos obviously taken the same day on her dad's birthday surrounded by his family on his special day, but not his daughter, his child, maybe his only child. Connie clicked off Giacomo's profile and into messages and sent to Alex: -

"I've found my dad!"

Obviously, Alex rang her immediately; Connie told her friend how she had found him,

"He's in Italy; at least he was in May."

"That was quick work, what next?" asked Alex processing this information.

"I think I'll sleep on it and maybe send this Giacomo, who is my cousin, a message, I haven't got a clue what I'm going to say yet"

"How about, hello I'm your cousin" laughed Alex, "wow Con this is great news, the power of social media eh?"

"I didn't expect to find him this quick, I mean he might not still be in Sienna, but surely his family will know where he is if he isn't there," a thought suddenly occurred to Connie "but what if he doesn't want to see me?"

"I can't see that Con, but if you are sure you want to meet him then there's only one way to find out!"

Connie tossed and turned all night in bed, a mixture of sleeping all afternoon and wondering what she would say to young Giacomo in her message, kept her awake.

She eventually decided to get up at 7am, got showered and dressed and decided to go for a walk on the beach to clear her muzzy head It was a cool morning with a keen breeze in the air, so she put up her anorak hood and headed down to the sand, she passed a few dog walkers making the most of the quiet morning before the tourists and day-trippers descended onto Porthcawl.

This was her favourite time of day, she remembered early morning walks just after her mum had died, sometimes she just walked and walked, going nowhere in particular, lost in her thoughts, she always felt better with a clearer mind after an early morning walk, and hoped this would be true of her walk today.

She took the beach road and walked towards town and arrived outside Nice Ice twenty minutes later.

She tapped on the side door as the business was not yet open

"Connie my sweetheart, I didn't know you were back?" exclaimed Mario embracing her fondly.

"Hello Mario, I got back yesterday, this has been the first chance I've had to come and see you."

"Oh, I have missed you; the customers have missed you, and it's not the same without you behind the counter!" Mario waved his arms around expansively.

"I've missed all this too" and Connie realised how much she had, as soon as she had entered the ice-cream parlour.

"Sit down and I'll get you something warm to drink, it might be summer but there's a definite bite in the air!" Said Mario. exaggerating a shiver, "can never get used to this cold weather!"

"How was the old country, did you like it" said Mario as he busied behind the counter getting out 2 mugs for them.

"It was wonderful Mario, the food, the language, the people "

"In your blood too, oh how I miss home" Mario looked into the distance wistfully, even though he had lived in Wales longer than he had lived in Italy he always referred to Italy as home, it was still where his heart lied.

He filled the mugs with steaming coffee and sat opposite Connie

"I've found my father Mario!"

"Giac?" exclaimed Mario looking at Connie in surprise

"Yes" said Connie looking into Mario's flushed face

"Where, how, when?" He blustered.

"Well, I think I have, at least I've found his nephew, who is also called Giacomo Santini."

"But not Giac?" Mario stirred his hot drink slowly.

"No not yet, but I'm hoping to."

Mario kept stirring his drink, looking intently at Connie

 "So do you know where Giac is, my child?" asked Mario.

"No but I think he is in Italy, I haven't met or spoken to him, but I know he was in Siena in May, I want to make contact, but I don't know what to say, or even if he will want to be contacted by me"

Mario nodded slowly, "It's been a long time Connie, and do you think it wise to open up old wounds?"

"Oh" said Connie concerned, "I thought you'd be pleased Mario, I mean you two were old friends, weren't you?"

Mario stirred his drink again before answering.

"That was a long time ago my child, yes, a long, long time ago" Mario's eyes clouded over.

Connie was puzzled she had thought that Mario would be pleased that she had found her father, maybe she had been wrong, maybe they hadn't been such good friends, maybe he thought her father hadn't acted in her and her mum's best interest.

"Are you alright Mario?" she asked.

Mario nodded, "yes child, I just don't want you to get hurt, you have always been happy, happy here in Porthcawl with your grandparents, but I do wish you the best of luck" Mario touched her hand gently, "if that is what you want to do"

Connie nodded, "Thank you, Mario."

Connie left after finishing her drink, the visit to Mario hadn't helped at all, should she contact young Giac or not, she supposed Mario was just being a bit over-protective, afraid she would get hurt or rejected, and yes, he was right, she had been happy here with her grandparents, but now she had read the letters and had almost found him, she couldn't let it go- not now- she had to meet him or at least try!

 Connie walked on for a bit and then decided to sit in one of the shelters on the promenade; she took out her phone.

"Hello, you don't know me"- Connie typed but then deleted, that sounded a bit stalker-ish,

"Hi, I'm Connie Devereux your uncle Giac's daughter" yes that was better, **"I'd like to get in touch with him, if he would like to get in touch with me, please can you send me a message, thank you, your cousin Connie x"** Connie re read it to check what she had typed.

She decided it was now or never.

Connie clicked 'send'.

"Well, I've done it!" said Connie to herself.

Connie found herself glancing at her phone all day, she had made her way back to the cottage, where her grandparents were in the kitchen sharing a pot of tea,

"Connie there's early you are up and about love" said gran as she came through the back door.

"Been to see Mario, I'm starting back to work tomorrow."

"Oh Good, I bet he's missed you; it'll be nice to get back to normal" said Gran, Granddad nodded in agreement

"Yes, I think it will" answered Connie.

The next few days went by quickly, Nice Ice was very busy as it always was during the Summer months, and Connie didn't discuss her father again with Mario, deciding to see if young Giac would reply to her first, if the weather was hot everyone wanted ice cream, and if the weather was cold everyone wanted a hot drink and a cake, so it was always busy, which was good as it stopped Connie looking at her phone wondering if young Giacomo had replied to her message.

Early afternoon three days after Connie had sent the message she took her afternoon break, she collected her bag from a locker in the kitchen area and headed for the beach, it had been nonstop since her lunch break, and she was glad to get out and have some fresh air.

She found a patch of sand and sat down her back was aching and she realised how hungry she was, she dug around in her bag for a snack bar and her hand felt her phone vibrate. She took her phone out of her bag and saw that she had a message; she clicked on it and saw it was from young Giacomo!

'Hi Connie great to hear from you, I have only just got hold of Uncle Giac-he was very surprised when I told him that you had been in touch, he said that he would love to see you but he's in Australia at the moment, he is coming back to Italy next month and said that he will contact you when he is back, I hope this is ok-Gio x'

Connie read and re read Giacomo's message, her father was in Australia, but had probably been in Italy when she was there, he would be back in Italy next month and wanted to see her, she couldn't believe it, after all these years, she would finally see her dad, would she remember him? Would he recognise her? Would she remind him of her mother as everyone said she was so much like Laura; would he like her? Would she like him? So many things were running around her head, she jumped at the sound of her phone ringing, it was Alex.

"Hi con, how are you, I had to ring, have you messaged that cousin of yours, have you had an answer" Alex sounded excited

"Yes, and yes Al, he just messaged me, my dad is in Australia! but guess what, he was actually in Italy the same time as I was there, just a few hundred miles away, how mad is that Al!" answered Connie just as excitedly.

"Aw Con, that's great, when is he coming back? Is he coming back?"

"Yes soon, my cousin Gio said he will contact me when he gets back to Italy, hark at me, my cousin Gio, I didn't even know he existed a couple of days ago" Connie giggled.

"How do you feel about it all Con?"

"I don't know, it's mad, it's all happening so fast, I mean what if he doesn't like me Al, we hardly know each other, and I haven't seen him in decades!"

"He'll love you Con; you are his daughter after all, and now you are older you will be able to talk things over, you know, say stuff that couldn't or didn't get said before."

"Oh, Alex Stevens you are always so wise, always know the right things to say."

"I wish" said Alex, "If only that applied to me and my life!" an image of Jared popped into her head, tall, handsome, Dr Jared Jones!

"You'll work it all out too Al, maybe you should give Jared a call, I know he is constantly in your thoughts, isn't he."

"No, I can't do that Con, Jared is the past, and I need to move on!"

"But are you Al, are you really?" asked Connie gently.

"You know me Con, happy on my own," Alex gave a small laugh, which she knew was false and which Connie knew was false too, as she knew Jared Jones would never be in Alex's past!

"Anyway, keep me posted Con, and take care."

"You too Al."

Connie put her phone into her back pocket and walked back along the beach, she never grew tired of the feeling of warm crunching sand under her feet and between her toes, she loved the seaside, she breathed in the sea air deeply, yes Porthcawl was home, she could never see herself living in the city, and definitely not in London, she would miss the sounds, the smells, the sights, the whole being beside the sea, it always made her feel better, she couldn't imagine leaving like her mum and dad did to live in London, she felt that the sea was part of her, her mind wandered to splashing in the sea in Amalfi with Sophia, and him... Wyatt, gorgeous, sexy, warm, kind Wyatt, what happened? He was so lovely they had, had a magical time in Italy albeit a short time, every minute spent with him had been wonderful, not just the high end dates of sailing in private yachts to Capri and room service in 5*opulent hotels, but the fun they had had, just doing everyday things, browsing shops, paddling in the sea, and the deep and meaningful talks into the early hours, they had been on the same wavelength and definitely shared a special bond, talking about their families and the loss of her beloved mother and his beloved father, no she hadn't imagined it, they had truly felt like soul mates in that short time they had spent together, she couldn't believe that none of it had meant anything to Wyatt, it had all been so real, so genuine, he must have been a good actor, she thought bitterly, just a holiday romance , she read about these things in the magazines

Mario supplied for the customers at Nice Ice- always some poor girl who had met the most wonderful, sexy, caring man on holidays and who had swept them off their feet, who then a) never heard from him again, b) found out he had a girlfriend or married or c) realised she was pregnant and he didn't want to know, she remembered thinking, "how can anyone be such a fool!" and yet here she was back home with no word from Wyatt Morgan and him being splashed all over magazines and the internet with another woman! Now who was the fool!

Chapter 19

The next few weeks went slowly by as Connie waited for Giac to contact her. She resumed her shifts at 'Nice Ice' getting back into the old familiar routine, the weather was warmer and everyday Nice Ice was packed out with holiday makers and day trippers clamouring to the seaside to enjoy some summer sun. Connie was glad her shifts were busy as it gave her less time to dwell on Wyatt Morgan and her father. She and Alex would contact each other every day either by a quick exchange of messages or when they were feeling the need for a good chat, a proper old fashioned telephone call was the order of the day. Her grandparents had given her a bit of space and hadn't been badgering her about everything, which she was grateful for as she didn't really know how she felt about everything herself, life had been so straight forward just a few months ago, and now Connie felt that her world had been not quite turned upside down, but definitely been shook about a bit!

Connie looked up from the counter in Nice Ice where she had been serving, finally there was a lull, as she looked up she caught Mario staring at her intently,

"Connie my lovely, you are very quiet today, and not just today, are you alright?" Asked Mario sounding concerned.

"I'm ok Mario, a bit tired, you know, been a busy shift."

"Yes, you are looking tired, you know you can talk to me if anything is bothering you, don't you" dear Mario, he was always looking out for Connie, always had as far back, as she could remember

"I know I can Mario, thank you."

Her phone vibrated in her back pocket of her jeans, she took it out and saw it was an unknown number, "can I get this Mario, and it's nearly my break."

Mario nodded as she swiped to answer.

"Hello, is that Connie Devereux?" asked a man's voice on the other end, he spoke with a slight accent.

"Yes" breathed Connie, knowing before he had introduced himself to her, who he was.

"Ah Hello this is Giac Santini, I understand you have been trying to contact me" his voice was warm, smooth, and even though you could hear a touch of accent, but as he has lived in Britain, America and Australia, you would not immediately recognise as Italian

"Yes, yes" Connie suddenly felt a bit shy, after all these years she actually had her father on the telephone, and he was speaking to her!

"Well, it was such a surprise when my nephew Giac contacted me, a very nice surprise, how are you Connie?" Giac asked

"I'm ok thanks, I I er, I hope you didn't mind me trying to contact you" Connie stuttered.

"No, no of course not, as I say it was a nice surprise after all these years, yes a very nice surprise!" He sounded so warm, and Connie relaxed a bit.

"My aunt Con has passed away and I read all the letters and stuff from you, that I hadn't seen or known about before, and I just really wanted to get in touch with you to say hello and that I am so sorry" There, Connie had said everything she had wanted to say to Giac since reading his letters,

"I'm so sorry to hear about Constance, such a wonderful woman, but you my dear have nothing to be sorry about, but it is good now that you want to say hello" Connie smiled despite feeling shaky, she smiled across at Mario who was looking anxiously in her direction She mouthed the words, "My Father" to Mario, and Mario nodded slowly, and Connie may have been mistaken but something in Mario's expression changed, from anxious to somewhat sad, old memories, she guessed.

"I am coming to the UK in two weeks' time, I have some business in London, if you would like to meet up," her attention was taken back to Giac, "I would love to see you Connie, but only if you would like to."

"Oh yes, that would be lovely, I have some business in London too that needs attention" Connie thought of Aunt Cons house, she really needed to get it sorted ready for selling as she knew she would never want to live in London.

"Then it's a date" said Giac jubilantly, "now I have your telephone number I will contact you when I arrive and then we can arrange to meet, I am so looking forward to seeing you Connie after all these years."

"Yes, me too, I will wait to hear from you."

"Ciao dear Connie, it has been wonderful to talk to you, and thank you" said Giac gently.

"Thank you for ringing me, bye."

Connie couldn't believe she had just spoken to her father after all these years, she couldn't even remember him, no one ever spoke about him, and she had only seen a handful of photos of him

"What did Giac have to say?" asked Mario approaching the counter, looking intently at Connie.

"He's coming to London in two weeks and I'm going to meet him"

"He's coming here too?" Mario was frowning.

"No, I need to go to London to sort out Aunt Con's house, so it's an excuse now to get on with it and meet my father the same time" answered Connie.

"After all this time" Mario said it out loud, but it was so softly as if he was thinking out loud

"Yes, Mario I know it's been a long, long time."

Connie decided to contact Ed George, lovely Ed who'd been her knight in shining armor when she'd first arrived, an emotional wreck, in London. Ed would be an ideal boyfriend/husband, reliable, steady, and handsome, with a good job, but he was not for Connie, she needed a good friend in London and Ed was it.

Ed was pleased to hear from her, she told him she had decided to put Aunt Cons house up for sale but would first need to get it ready and would be coming to London in two weeks to get the ball rolling. She arranged to take some time off from Nice Ice, as she was due to leave at the end of her shift, Mario called her to one side.

"I have been thinking about selling up" he announced suddenly

"Selling up!" answered Connie in surprise, "But Mario this is your life, you are 'Nice Ice'."

"I'm getting older Connie and well I've been thinking about having more time to maybe go back home and spend some time there"

"Back to Italy Mario, but you can still do that and keep Nice Ice going."

"I thought of that Connie, but I was thinking of maybe buying a little place back in Italy and spending half the year here and half in Italy, or maybe even longer and I will need capital to do that, and to be honest I think now my children are grown up and doing their own thing I can relax and do my own thing."

"Was it me reminding you of Italy talking to my father?" asked Connie hoping she hadn't done anything inadvertently to make Mario want to leave.

"No, my child, Italy, home, is always on my mind, I would have returned years ago if, if, things had been different" he looked at

Connie intently, eyes suddenly shining with emotion.

"Are you ok Mario?" asked Connie suddenly concerned at Mario's show of emotion.

"I'm alright my lovely, don't you worry about me, I just think that now the time is right" Mario nodded to himself, "yes now the time is right!"

Connie left then, walking home to her grandparent's cottage along the seashore, what a day, her dad contacting her, her decision to sort out Aunt Con's house and then Mario's revelation to sell up! She had to tell her grandparents now that she was going to London, should she say she was meeting Giac? She'd think about that again- didn't want to stir anything up now when everything was going along peacefully- maybe when she had sold the house- she could get her own place, after all she was approaching 30 and still living at home, maybe she could make Mario an offer for Nice Ice- all these thoughts, Connie's head hurt and her back ached it had been a long and busy day!

"Hello love, busy day, you look tired," her gran greeted her at the cottage door.

"Yes, as usual, don't know how I feel so tired though, must be the heat", suddenly Connie felt quite dizzy,

"You ok love" said gran stepping towards her, "SID!!!" Mary shouted into the house.

Gran caught Connie's arm, "Come on love come and have a sit down" Sid appeared in the hallway looking worried.

"What's happened?" he asked looking from Mary to Connie

"Our Connie has come over a bit funny; help me get her to the settee."

Between them they helped Connie in and onto the settee, she lay back into one of Mary's soft velvety cushions, "Get her a glass of water Sid" instructed Gran.

"Are you ok now love?" asked Mary as Connie sipped gratefully from the glass of chilled water her Granddad had brought her

"Better thanks, I don't know what came over me, I was feeling fine walking home and then it just came over me, I felt so dizzy and a bit sick, sorry to frighten you both, I'm fine now, said Connie.

"that's the second time love that I know of, that you have come over funny like this, perhaps it might be a good idea to pop in the Doctors, and have a check-up, you might have low iron, got to be careful our Con" said Gran seriously.

"Yes, perhaps I will, but I expect it's just the heat and rushing around, plus I am feeling a bit hungry, it was so busy in Nice Ice today that I only had a bag of crisps for my lunch" said Connie a bit sheepishly.

"Well then, no wonder you are feeling faint!" chastised Mary, "silly girl I've got tea on now, but I'll bring you a sweet tea and some biscuits to raise your sugar levels."

Mary bustled out to the kitchen as Sid looked at Connie, "you sure you're ok our Con," he asked, his face full of concern.

"Yes, I'm sure thanks Granddad, don't worry I'll be fine after a bit of food" Connie reassured him smiling weakly, but wondering if she should actually make an appointment at the GPs as it wasn't like her to be like this, mind you after the whirlwind of her life these past few months, it was no wonder she was feeling lightheaded! The next two weeks dragged by Connie went from one emotion to another, she was excited to meet her father one day to the next she felt sick with anxiety- she was finally glad to board the National Express coach in Bridgend bound for London Victoria. She sighed deeply as she sunk into a window seat six rows from the front- she hadn't bothered to make an appointment at the GPs after all- between being busy in Nice Ice and making plans for her trip to London she had felt better but still really tired, but she put that down to being busy in work and tossing and turning in bed most nights with broken sleep with dreams/nightmares about Giac her father, Wyatt Morgan, Aunt Cons house, and giant ice lollies chasing her- she confided in Alex regularly which always helped at the time, but then the dreams would start again as soon as she fell asleep at night, with hindsight now she wondered if she should have gone to the GPs , but hoped that once she met her father and made definite plans for Aunt Cons house, that her head might start to clear a bit.

Somewhere just past Bristol Connie must have fallen asleep as she suddenly woke with a jolt as the coach came to a stop at London Victoria coach station. Connie stretched, well moved around in her seat as stretching wasn't really an option in the cramped seat, the sleep hadn't helped and she felt the beginnings of a headache appearing, she took a swig from her water bottle, which had turned lukewarm in her bag, getting off the coach she hoped the fresh air would clear her head and wake her up a bit. The air outside the coach was humid in the late August afternoon, Connie took another sip of the tepid water pulled a face and made her way towards the closest tube station to get to Aunt Cons house as quickly as possible. Her suitcase felt heavy as she hauled it along the pavement as she alighted from the tube, she fumbled in her bag for the key for the house as she approached the outside of the house. Connie put the key into the front door lock, turned it and pushed the door open. Closing the door behind her she was so glad to have arrived, it was Friday 3.25pm, she had had a telephone call from her father, last Monday to say he would be in London from tomorrow until Tuesday and would Sunday morning be suitable to meet, that gave her all day tomorrow to start sorting Aunt Cons house out, all her personal papers and items, and then all the bigger items. During a recent conversation with Alex, Connie remembered, she let slip that Mario was thinking of selling Nice Ice and Alex had suggested that she might think about buying it once Aunt Cons house had been sold.

Connie had thought about it regularly since that conversation, could she buy it? Should she buy it? Was Mario serious? Nice Ice without Mario would be like, Connie thought of something that would be strange, Take That without Robbie? NO that was a poor comparison as 'Take That' was still massively popular with or without Robbie Williams! Maybe Coronation Street without Ken Barlow, that was it- Mario was like Ken Barlow, she couldn't imagine either of them leaving!

She looked around Aunt Cons lounge full of all her treasured possessions, it would be a massive task sorting out all this, Maybe Sarah next door would like something to keep, she'd call in on her later and see if she wanted anything and if she had any suggestions for charity shops or local charities who could take the furniture. Connie felt quite sad that all her aunt's possessions would have to be given away, but she couldn't keep them, and she didn't want to live here, in London, she would obviously keep a few bits to remember her aunt by but hoped that by giving her possessions to charity her Aunt Con would be pleased that she was helping those less fortunate.

Chapter 20

Connie woke early Saturday morning; she had a quick cup of coffee and after a shower and getting dressed she decided to make a start on the downstairs. Sarah next door had been pleased to see her again last night and after a good hour or so of Sarah talking nonstop, how was Connie, was she selling the house, how was home, how was Giac, (Connie began to wish she hadn't mentioned getting in touch with her father) Connie managed to mention Aunt Cons possessions and Sarah promised she'd be around in the morning (today) to have that "nice mosaic lamp and those lovely matching porcelain ladies" and "if you don't want the floral tea set on the dresser I wouldn't mind having that either Connie" Connie assured Sarah she could have whatever she wanted and Sarah said she would ring her sister "who knew the woman who was in charge of the place that gave furniture and other bits to poor souls who need them" Connie thanked her whilst politely backing out through the front door, carrying the empty cardboard boxes Sarah had produced for packing Aunt Cons possessions in and before Sarah had chance to move onto another topic of conversation Connie was ready for an early night feeling tired after the day of travelling. Connie began packing utensils and crockery into the first of the cardboard boxes, when the doorbell went, guessing it was probably Sarah, she went to answer the door.

A disembodied voice came from behind a pile of cardboard boxes that they were carrying "Good Morning lovey, got some more boxes for you" Sarah poked her head around the boxes.

"Let me take them" said Connie stepping forward

"I'm ok lovey, balanced just right,"

"Come in and thanks" Connie opened the front door wide and stood to one side as Sarah entered.

"My sister has rung that woman, Linda, her name is, she was most grateful for the offer, got two young families in need, so she'll be around later with a van" Sarah puffed a bit as she deposited the boxes onto the lounge floor.

"That's great, thank you, best I get packing!" answered Connie

Between the two of them they packed up all ten boxes full of Aunt Con's kitchen cupboard contents and all the tea sets and ornaments that neither Sarah nor Connie had wanted to keep.

Connie obviously wanted to keep the beautiful paintings by her mother that Aunt Con had treasured all of these years and all the photographs and private letters, which she put safely to one side, Sarah bustled around taking the items she wanted to keep, back to her house and returned ten minutes later with freshly buttered toast and jam for her and Connie.

"Thanks, I'm starving" announced Connie biting into the toast,

"There's more where that came from, here's some bread, butter, milk and tea bags oh and a packet of biscuits, keep you going if you're here for a few days" said Sarah putting down a carrier bag full of goodies.

"Thank you so much!" said Connie through a mouthful of toast, "Let me get you some money."

"I won't hear of it, if Con thought you were here without me looking after you, she would be cross and even more cross if you were to give me any money! No!" Sarah was adamant.

"You have been so kind thank you for everything Sarah, I don't know what I would have done without all your help, I didn't really have a plan about how I was going to sort Aunt Cons stuff and you have sorted everything for me."

Connie suddenly felt quite emotional, and could feel tears welling up in her eyes, "I'm sorry, I don't know what's come over me" she apologised.

"Don't be silly lovey, I feel a bit tearful too, sorting all Cons stuff like this, only natural" Sarah gripped Connie's hand, "and you meeting up with your dad again tomorrow, after all these years"

Connie nodded," yes I suppose so" she smiled at Sarah, she was what her gran would call a 'busy body', but had a heart of gold, and was glad she had her there with her.

Connie rang Ed when the woman, Linda, who had been accompanied by a young chap Steve, also from the local charity, "Caring for Families" had left, Ed said he'd pop around that evening with someone called Cathy Henry, from a local estate agent that he dealt with frequently through work, for a chat and to put the wheels in motion for selling the house.

Linda and Steve had been so pleased with all Aunt Cons furniture and agreed to take it all (except one bed, as Connie needed somewhere to sleep until she returned home on Monday), they loaded their van up three times with all Cons furniture and the full cardboard boxes. Connie wondered what the young families would make of Aunt Cons ornaments, but Linda had said that the charity had a small shop where they sold bric-a-brac, books, clothes and other donated items to help them raise funds.

By the time Ed and his colleague Cathy arrived at 6pm Connie and Sarah were ready for a sit down and a cuppa, Sarah had had to lent Connie some kitchen basics as the charity had taken everything and she needed a few bits until she left on Monday.

"Just in time for a cuppa" Connie greeted the visitors warmly

"Great, I'm always in the market for a nice cup of tea" he answered just as warmly, "Hi Mrs Smith good to see you again, Ed called into the kitchen, "wow, have you been robbed?" he looked around the empty rooms.

"Oh, hello lovey, been doing our bit for charity haven't we Connie," Sarah popped her head around the kitchen door to greet Ed, "Everyone, this is Cathy Henry from Metropolitan properties, known to all as "MetProp," Ed introduced a tall slim woman in her early thirties with a shiny red bob cut, dressed in a smart green trouser suit and carrying a, Connie guessed, designer briefcase, she smiled brightly at everyone.

"Hi, pleased to meet you" she stepped forward and shook Connie's hand lightly, Connie felt so scruffy next to sleek Cathy, as she brushed down her dusty t shirt and pushed the strands of hair from her face that had escaped from her untidy bun.

"Thought, I'd better empty the house before I try to sell it" said Connie replying to Ed's early quip about the empty house

"Is it alright if I look around and take some photos?" asked Cathy

"Yes of course, if you need any help give me a shout" answered Connie.

Sarah made them a cup of tea each then made her excuses, before returning to her own house.

"Sorry I can't offer you a seat, the charity took everything"

Ed laughed, as he got down on his haunches in the 'blue lounge'

"I'm ok here thanks, will you manage ok though?"

"Yes, I'm returning home on Monday, I'm hoping that everything that is needed to put the house on the market can be done before then, so I don't mind too much, I was just glad that they could take everything, I've still got a bed, and Sarah has lent me some crockery."

"Oh right! I suppose you won't need to stay" Ed's face fell slightly, at the thought of Connie returning home so quickly.

"I might be thinking of buying a business back home in Porthcawl when I can sell this house," Connie had only told Alex about the possibility of Mario selling Nice Ice and it had been Alex's suggestion that Connie might buy it, she had surprised herself by saying it out loud, let alone out loud to Ed-a solicitor!

"Oh really," Ed sounded interested, "what type of business?"

"An ice-cream parlour!" announced Connie," its where I've worked since I was a teenager and I suppose it's the one thing that's been a constant in my life since I first went to live in Porthcawl when I was a child" saying it now out loud made Connie realise that it was true, Nice Ice and Mario had always been there, always in her life, through her school years, her mother's illness and her subsequent death, the ups and downs of her love life, yes, Nice Ice and Mario were part of her.

The more she thought about it, the more she knew that if Mario sold Nice Ice, then she had to have it, she couldn't risk losing it, it would be bad enough losing Mario, if he did as planned-move to Italy, she knew that she couldn't lose Nice Ice too!

Cathy returned to the blue lounge where Connie and Ed were crouched on the floor drinking tea,

"Very cozy" she quipped,

"I'm sorry I can't offer you a seat" apologised Connie.

"Oh, don't worry about me, this is a palace compared to some places I've been to, to sell" Cathy knelt down too, "I've taken photos and had a good look around, so when I'm back in the office on Monday I'll upload everything and then we'll be ready for viewings."

"Here take the spare set of keys" said Connie as she unhooked them from the "CD" key ring she kept in her handbag.

Cathy took the keys and then they agreed on an asking price for the house, which was way beyond Connie's expectations, she knew prices on properties were high in and around Porthcawl let alone in cities, but this price was amazing, and Connie hoped it would sell quickly, so she would be in a good position to make Mario an offer for Nice Ice if he definitely decided to sell.

"We're off to Baristas Bistro for a couple of drinks if you fancy joining us?" said Ed as they got up ready to leave.

"I'm ready for an early night to be honest, been a busy day" said Connie suddenly feeling very tired after a busy day sorting Aunt Cons house.

"I'll pop in Monday morning before I go into the office, with all the paperwork for you to sign," Said Cathy "around eight thirty, is that ok."

"Yes, that's great, see you then, thanks Cathy, and thanks Ed" Connie accompanied them both to the front door, and bid them goodbye. She returned to the lounge looking around at the empty room where only a few hours ago Aunt Cons furniture, pictures and possessions were, she suddenly felt sad and very lonely.

"End of an era" she thought sadly, it had been her aunt's whole life in here and it had taken her only a matter of hours to dispose of it and to put the house up for sale, had she been too hasty?

No, she knew that she didn't want to live here, and leaving it empty for any longer than necessary would be pointless as well as risking the possibility of the house getting broken into or getting into a poor state of repair. Would Aunt Con have wanted her to live here? Connie didn't know, she wished that she had kept in touch with her and she would have known what her wishes would have been- too late now, Connie knew deep down that it was the right thing to do, even though she felt sad about the house, but after all, that's all it was, 'a house' not a person, it was too late to make amends with her Aunt, but hopefully not too late to make amends with her father, and tomorrow was her chance to make amends with him!

Connie slept well that night, it must have been all the hard work that went into emptying the house that had made her fall into a deep sleep the minute her head hit the pillow, she hadn't gone to bed straight away, she had phoned Alex first, to give her an update. "Really that much?" shrieked Alex, when Connie had told her the price the house was going on the market for.

"You'll be able to buy a villa here in Sorrento and still have change!" laughed Alex, "Well I have been thinking more and more about Nice Ice after what you said" admitted Connie.

"Really?" said Alex.

"Yes, I've been giving it quite a bit of thought to be honest, I'm going to have a chat with Mario when I get back home," said Connie

"Great, it's a good business opportunity, "answered Alex, forever the estate agent.

"How are you feeling about tomorrow and your father?" asked Alex

"Ok I think, it's something that I need to do, it's so long overdue, so yes, I think I'm looking forward to meeting him now."

"Good, and what about the eligible Ed?" laughed Alex, enquiring about Ed George.

"Still eligible, but not for me, I think there might be something in the making for him and Cathy the estate agent!" Connie was sure she saw Cathy's eyes light up when she declined to join them for drinks, she was glad for them, she knew that she wasn't interested in Ed, and after Wyatt she hoped that she would never be interested romantically in another man again!

Connie got out of bed and stretched, it was the best night sleep she'd had in a while, after showering and blow-drying her hair, she carefully applied her makeup. She wanted to look her best to meet her father. She decided to wear a red and white floral dress she had bought in Sorrento, as she slipped it on, she remembered the last time she had worn it, on a day out with Wyatt, where they had strolled hand in hand along the streets of Sorrento, window shopping and popping into a gorgeous little bar overlooking the Bay of Naples for drinks and a sharing dish of mixed cheeses and hams, they were so happy as they gazed into one another's eyes and chatted about anything and everything, it just felt so right with Wyatt, so real, she felt a real pain in her chest when she thought about him, it was like real heart ache. She finished putting on her dress teaming it with white sandals and a white bag. She stood in front of the mirror, which was attached to the bedroom door, she looked better than she felt, she felt a bit sick, was it lack of food, or was it just nerves?

She had arranged to meet her father in 'Joe's Cafe' which was only a short walk from Aunt Cons house, he had suggested it, as apparently it had been a favourite when they had all lived in London all those years ago when she was a little girl, and her father was thrilled to discover that the cafe was still operating and still called Joes. She remembered seeing Joe's Cafe the last time she had been here, when she had accompanied Ed to the church hall for his 'am dram' group. She had asked him last night how their proposed show of 'War Horse' was coming on, as she had enjoyed the time spent in the hall painting scenery with him. Ed had laughed and said it was still a work in progress!

Finally ready and trying to ignore the butterflies in her stomach, Connie grabbed a white cardigan from the bottom newel post on the stairs, in case she needed it, as she hadn't checked the days temperature, together with her handbag, closed the front door behind her and made her way in the direction of Joes Cafe- and her father!

Chapter 21

Alex sat at her desk in Rivolli's absently checking emails whilst glancing at her blank phone screen, waiting and wondering how Connie was getting on. It was a big day for her best friend, meeting her father at last. As long as they had been friends Alex had never known anything about Connie's dad except that when Connie and her mother had returned to live in Porthcawl all those years before, he hadn't joined them and as far as Alex knew, he had never been back since.

Sofia appeared at Alex's desk placing a file on the edge of it,

"Can this one can be filed now Alex?" she asked tilting the buff-coloured file upwards, showing the name MORGAN W

"Yes, please Sofia, that's all been finalised" answered Alex,

"Did you read about him" Sofia nodded her head theatrically towards the file,

"What, about him and that American Country singer?" Alex answered contemptibly.

"Yes, and I thought he and our lovely Connie had something special," Sofia imitated the action of spitting on the floor, "Men! All the same!"

"I hope that doesn't include me Sofia!" Ricardo's voice came from the other side of the office.

"I hope not too Ricardo" Sofia replied tartly, but then giving him a big smile.

Alex watched the two of them, was there something going on?, Ricardo didn't usually join them for after works drinks, but since that first night she had returned from Porthcawl when she had got really drunk and had to be put to bed,(she still scurried past the bank where Benito worked burning with shame about that night), yes, Ricardo seemed to join the after works contingency to Romero's regularly now, even Alex had tagged along sometimes, but thinking back, there was always lots of giggling from Sofia when Ricardo was regaling them with various tales of real estate and even he seemed very gregarious, more like his brother Gianni than the usual taciturn Ricardo. Alex would more often than not leave early, but Sofia and Ricardo would always remain chatting and laughing over something that had happened in the office earlier, barely even noticing her leave.

Alex's phone beeped and flashed, momentary taking her attention away from Sofia and Ricardo, she glanced at the screen, it was Connie thanking her for her earlier message where she had wished her good luck in her meeting with her father. Too early yet for any news on the meeting, Alex thought.

Connie arrived at Joes Cafe five minutes before the time agreed with her father; she smoothed down her dress and patted her hair back into shape in case it had got untidy during the short walk to the rendezvous. She took a deep breath and put her hand on the cafe door and pushed it open.

The smells of fried bacon mingled with fresh coffee invaded her nostrils, she felt nauseous between the smells, and the anticipated meeting, and the cafe was looking quite busy, with several tables taken up by customers.

"Can I help you?" a friendly voice came from behind the long counter to her right, startled from her being in a little world of her own, Connie stuttered," I'm meeting someone, my my er"

"Connie!" another voice this time coming from further inside the cafe, a man rose from a chair, two tables in front of where she was standing, she looked at where the voice had come from, and there he was, her father! She knew him instantly, recognising him from the photos she had seen on his nephew Gio's face book page

"Connie, bella cariad!" he called, then her father walked towards her, catching her right hand in both of his hands and bringing it to his face kissing her hand and then smiling broadly, "come and sit down."

She followed him to the table he had vacated and sat down opposite him with her back to the cafe door, "I haven't ordered yet, what can I order for you?" asked Giac still smiling at her.

"Just an orange juice please" Connie answered, she looked at Giac as he bid the waitress to their table, he ordered a Late and a cake for himself along with Connie's juice. He was wearing a light blue open necked shirt, with the sleeves neatly folded back to the elbow, he had a leather strapped watch on his right wrist, his hair was still wavy but was now the peppered with grey, his dark eyes crinkled as he smiled a white straight toothed smile from a craggy but still handsome face.

"I'm so glad you contacted me Connie, it's been a long time, but I would know you anywhere, so like your dear mama" Giac clasped Connie's hands across the table, his voice was still tilted with a slight Italian accent, even though he had lived all around the world

"Thank you for meeting me" answered Connie, she couldn't believe after all the years here she was sitting across a table from her father

"How are you my cariad?" he asked,

Connie smiled 'Cariad' was always the name he had for her and her mother, it was the only Welsh he had known and would end his letters and cards 'Ciao Cariad' a little bit of Italian and a little bit of Welsh, like her, she thought, a little bit of both.

"I'm ok thanks" Connie answered, after all these years and she didn't really know what to say and her mouth suddenly felt very dry,

"Tell me about yourself, are you working have you got a young man, where are you living?" Giac looked at her eagerly,

Connie swallowed, "Well" she began nervously "I'm still living in Porthcawl, with my grandparents," she glanced down, she felt a bit uncomfortable mentioning her grandparents, after the chat with Sarah and the letters and cards scenario "I haven't got a young man, and I'm working in an Ice Cream parlour."

Saying all this out loud made Connie feel like she hadn't done much with her life, here she was 27, still living at home, no man and her career was no more than a teenager's weekend job!

"Not much to say really," she apologised, "But I'm in London sorting out some stuff and I'm hoping to buy my own business and my own place when I get back to Porthcawl" she added in a bid to make herself seem a bit more mature.

"That's good, but I can't believe a beautiful woman like you has no man in her life!" Giac looked serious.

"Well, I haven't had much luck in the love department" answered Connie truthfully, hoping Giac wouldn't press her on this subject

"Well all the young men in Porthcawl must either be mad or blind!" announced Giac.

The waitress brought their order to the table and Giac let go of Connie's hands which she was glad of, as she felt a bit uncomfortable sitting with a man albeit her father, that she barely knew, holding hands!

They sipped their drinks, and Giac offered her some of his cake which she declined, they chatted some more about her recent visit to Sorrento and how much she loved it there and about her Aunt Cons house, and Giac told her briefly about the different places he had lived and his return to Italy.

"I can't believe you were in Italy the same time as I was there" said Connie, "but I didn't know all about you then."

"All about me?" frowned Giac.

"Yes er, when I was sorting Aunt Cons things I came across letters from you, I didn't realise, I always thought you had abandoned me, I, I "Connie was stuttering again, she stared down at her empty glass wishing she still had juice left so she could distract from this conversation she had stared.

"Abandoned? No never" at this Giac clasped her hands again, "is that what you thought?"

"Yes, I suppose I did, I mean I never saw you and I don't really remember you, so yes, I'm so sorry" Connie's eyes met his

"You've got nothing to be sorry for, I am sorry that you thought that, Connie."

Connie nodded, "I've read all the letters now and the cards, I just wish that I had had chance to see them before."

It was Giac's turn to nod now, "I'm sorry, I should have come back to see you, talk to you, I was the adult, will you forgive me?" Giac squeezed Connie's hands tighter, his face a mixture of seriousness, caring and sadness!

"Of course I forgive you; I've had a great life in Porthcawl, I miss my mum of course I do, and I would have loved to have had you in my life, but ..." Connie hesitated.

"I wish I'd tried harder, come to Porthcawl, I didn't know if I was wanted, it's no excuse cariad, I should have made more effort" apologised Giac.

"Well, we are here now, together" Connie smiled at Giac in a bid to make him feel better, sorry that she had upset him, "but I just wondered, why didn't you take me with you, to America, I mean?" Giac looked seriously into her eyes, and answered "but cariad, you were never mine to take!"

Alex's phone rang it was almost her break time, she picked up her mobile and indicated to Ricardo that she was going on her break five minutes earlier, it was Carole her mother.

"Hiya mam, everything ok?"

"Yes, fine babe, went to the hospital yesterday for my checkup" answered Carole breezily.

"Oh, mam I'm so sorry I didn't realise it was yesterday, I thought it was next week!" Alex exclaimed.

"Don't worry Babe, nearly forgot myself, luckily Mario remembered, he had kindly offered to take me," Carole explained.

"Are you ok? "Asked Alex feeling awful that she had forgotten.

"Yes, everything is how it should be; I'll be back on those skates before you can say..."

"Over my dead body!" shouted Alex.

Carole laughed, "Only joking, but at least I'm allowed to drive again now."

"Don't try to do too much too soon now mam!" warned Alex

"I won't, anyway," went on Carole," I went for my appointment and Jared Jones wasn't there, apparently he's gone abroad to work"

Alex was taken aback by the mention of Jared, just the mention of his name made her heart miss a beat and for a lightheaded feeling to come over her,

"The girl there couldn't say anymore, you know, not supposed to tell the patients the doctor's business, but, well what do you think of that?" said Carole sounding quite animated.

"Oh right," what else could Alex say, she had blocked him, tried to cut him out of her life and her thoughts, the latter not so well

"Yes, I wonder where he's gone?" said Carole.

"No idea mam, but it doesn't matter to me if he's in Porthcawl or outer Mongolia!" answered Alex shortly.

"I just thought I'd tell you" Mam sounded a bit hurt.

"Sorry mam, it's just that, I don't care or want to know where Jared is" even saying this out loud to her mother Alex felt like the biggest fraud, who was she kidding, of course she wanted to know where he had gone, and why had he gone, and who was he with? The questions were endless.

"Sorry love I know things are difficult between you two"

"I'm sorry I was nasty mam, I'm glad you're ok and feeling better, look I've got to go there's someone waiting to see me" Alex lied, wanting to end this conversation, any conversation about Jared Jones, why did he still upset and unsettle her so much?

Connie looked puzzled at Giac, "what do you mean, not yours, but you are my father, aren't you?"

"I thought you knew; I thought Laura would have told you?" Giac looked anguished.

"Told me what, she never spoke about you?" Connie was puzzled

"Cariad, when I first met Laura, she was already pregnant with you!"

Connie was stunned with this new revelation, already pregnant??

"What?" she couldn't comprehend what Giac was saying

"I'm not your biological father, I couldn't have loved you anymore than if you were mine, but that is why I couldn't take you with me" Giac explained,

Connie couldn't believe what she was hearing, all these years not really thinking about him, then the letters, stirring up all kinds of emotions within her and now meeting him to find out that he was not her father after all!

"I had no rights to you Connie, I wanted to take both you and your mama to America, but your grandparents wouldn't allow it, I was young I made a fuss, I thought your mama would get better in America, but she wanted to stay, I never adopted you, you weren't mine, so I went, and you both stayed."

Connie's head couldn't take anymore, this new revelation was unbelievable, "Excuse me!" she cried as she pushed her chair back and ran to the cafe toilet, suddenly she felt very, very sick!

Connie pushed open the door labelled LADIES, rushed to the first cubicle and vomited down the toilet- her body shook all over, her head felt like it was on fire, when she finished being sick, she flushed the toilet and went to the wash basin to wash her face under the cold flow of water and leaned back against the washroom wall. When she had stopped shaking, she wiped her face and hands and adjusted her smudged makeup in the mirror- this was getting a habit- making herself look and try to feel better in strange toilets in London! She had to go back into the cafe and face Giac- her father- no not her father- then who the hell was????

Connie returned to the cafe- luckily as it was full of chatter and busy people, no one except Giac had seen her rush to the toilet, she walked a little unsteady back to their table, as she was still feeling a bit queasy.

"I'm so sorry I don't know what came over me, it must have been shocked" apologised Connie, as she took the chair and sat back

Down.

"Oh, my goodness Connie I am so sorry, I should never have sprung that on you, I just thought that surely after all these years you would have been told" Giac looked concerned, "are you alright my cariad?"

"I'm ok, it's not your fault, even though I'm in shock, I've not been feeling very well for a couple of months, I've fainted a few times and been sick and I'm always so tired" as Connie said these words, she began to wonder, when Giac's kind voice broke into her thoughts.

"I remember your mama feeling the same," he said softly, "that was when she was pregnant with you!!"

Connie felt a massive feeling of panic come over her; she stared at Giac incomprehensibly,

"I need some air" Connie scrambled back out of her seat and ran blindly through the cafe door, pushing past a middle-aged couple who looked at her in annoyance, she could hear Giac's voice calling her, but she kept running, then another voice, "Connie?"

She looked up through tearful eyes and there in front of her was Ed!

"Connie what's happened?" his voice sounded full of concern

She ran straight into his open arms and cried big sobbing tears onto his chest.

Ed held her and guided her to a bench just off the street on a grassy area.

"Hey hey it's ok, tell me what's wrong?" he asked gently.

"Everything" sobbed Connie, hardly believing that she was crying all over poor Ed yet again.

"Connie!" Giac had caught up with them after hurriedly paying the bill in the cafe and rushed up the street hoping he had chosen the right direction to find her.

Giac and Ed looked at each other, and back to Connie.

"She just ran off; I was so worried" explained Giac.

"I'm sorry" sobbed Connie, "I felt that I just had to get outside, and then it all became too much"

"I'm Ed, Connie's friend, you must be her dad?" Ed freed his left hand from comforting Connie.

Giac took it and shook it, "hello Ed, yes I am Giac"

"But not my dad" sobbed Connie.

Ed looked puzzled" sorry I ..."

"It's a long story Ed, but yes and no" Answered Giac as he gently touched Connie on the shoulder, "I'm so sorry I have upset you, Connie."

"I'm sorry too, and I'm so sorry Ed that I'm crying all over you again" Connie mopped her face with the tissue Giac offered her.

"That's what friends are for" answered Ed as he smoothed down his tear splattered shirt.

"I've had a bit of a shock that's all, sorry."

"No need, are you alright now?" asked Giac concerned.

"I don't know and that's the honest truth, if you are not my father then who is?" Connie looked searchingly at Giac.

"I honestly don't know, it was your mama's business, I loved her and respected her decision when she didn't tell me, maybe that was the wrong thing to do" Giac shrugged.

Ed squeezed her hand gently in support.

"And then the other thing" she glanced at Ed under her eyelashes and looked back at Giac, Giac took this as a signal not to impart his earlier observation.

"that's really thrown me, I think I need to get back to Aunt Con's and start packing its time I went back home."

Connie rose to her feet a little unsteadily.

"Can I accompany you back?" asked Giac.

"No, I'm fine now thank you, I'll walk with Ed, if that's ok Ed?"

Ed nodded.

"Thank you for meeting me, I've got a lot to think about now and to find out too" Connie held out her hand to shake Giac's, he took her hand and kissed the back of it.

"It's been my pleasure, I'm just so sorry that I upset you my cariad"

"No, thank you for telling me the truth, at least now I can move forward, and perhaps find out who my father actually is"

Giac hugged her and kissed both her cheeks, "whoever he is, he is a very lucky man to have you as his daughter, please keep in touch cariad, and take care,"

"Thank you I will."

Ed and Connie walked off in the direction of Aunt Con's house

"Are you alright now?" asked Ed as they approached the house

"Yes, I think so, thank you for walking with me Ed, I hope I didn't hold you up to wherever you were going."

"No, it's fine, I was meeting Cathy for lunch, but no worries, there's a gang of us going so she won't be on her own."

"I'm sorry, you must go, oh no your shirt!" Connie exclaimed looking at Ed's creased and stained shirt after her tearful episode

"I'll pop home and change; this is becoming a habit" Ed smiled

"I know, oh Ed what must you think of me?"

"That you are a very lovely lady, that in another time and another life I would have hoped to have got to know much better, but being your, what did you call me, your knight in shining armor, will do" Ed smiled.

"Thank you Ed, you have been more than a knight in shining armor, you have been a wonderful friend to me, and Cathy is a very lucky girl!" Answered Connie. The two embraced as she watched Ed walk off towards his home, yes in another lifetime Ed could have been the one, handsome, kind, funny, with a good job and future, but that was Connie all over, unlucky in love, and now it was looking very likely that there might be a pregnancy to deal with too! She closed the front door behind her - she was done with London now, tomorrow she would leave for good.

Chapter 22

"So, after telling you that he wasn't your father, he dropped the bombshell that he thought you were pregnant too, oh Con, what are you going to do? Have you had a test yet?" Alex was beside herself, there she was stuck thousands of miles away when Connie needed her most.

"No, not yet, I'm going home in the morning when I've signed the paperwork for the house, I'll pop in a chemist on my way to the bus station, I can't believe this, but Al, I don't think I need a test to tell me, I think I've known for a while, I've been faint and now sick and have ignored it being so wrapped up in everything else, I've been so bloody stupid, getting pregnant, I should have known better."

"Oh love, millions of women have said that before you, and millions will after you."

Connie couldn't believe it herself, what a bloody fool she'd been, caught up in the sun, sea and romance of it all, she must have left her common sense back home in Porthcawl as she hadn't packed it and taken it to Italy with her, and if she had she must have forgotten to take it on those dates with Wyatt Morgan!!

Giac had been worried about her and had rung her that evening to see if she was alright, she had assured him that she was fine, and they agreed to stay in touch when she returned home to Porthcawl.

Connie closed the front door on Aunt Cons house for the last time the next morning, Cathy from Metprop had been true to her word

and had come around to the house at 8.30am on the dot for Connie
to sign all the paperwork to do with the sale of the house,
everything was now done, Sarah met her on the doorstep of her
own house.

"Goodbye Connie love, I'll be sorry not to see you coming and going
into next door anymore, but I wish you the very best for your
future" Sarah embraced her.

"Thank you Sarah for all your help, you have been marvelous"

"My pleasure lovey" Connie returned her embrace; she took a last
look of the house, oh what a house it had been! There she had
found out more about her father who turned out not to be her
father, and then the revelation that she was probably going to have
a baby, talk about history repeating itself! And if Giac wasn't her
biological father, then who was??

Connie found herself a seat on the coach, which was leaving
Victoria bus station for Bridgend, and sat down to contemplate her
morning.

After she had concluded the 'house' business with Cathy and bid
Sarah goodbye, she had popped into the chemist on her way to
Victoria coach station.

A visit to the public toilets in Victoria told her what she had already
guessed – the pregnancy test was positive!

She closed her eyes as the coach started to move off- what now?
She tried to push the thought of who her father might be out of her

head as she had more urgent things to think about, in the shape of a baby!! A baby- she didn't know how she felt about it- yes, she would have money to look after herself and a baby once the sale of the house went through- maybe buy Nice Ice and a little flat or even a small house, but could she do it on her own? Then she thought of her grandparents- what would they say? She wasn't a girl, she was a woman of 27, but she still felt a bit like child, still living with them, did they expect more from her than to get pregnant with no sign of the father, just like her own mother! But they had loved and cared for her and her mum, she just hoped that they would understand.

She arrived back to Bridgend late afternoon, as she stepped down from the coach she wondered if there were any taxis free, as she turned the corner from the bus station wild waving caught her eye, "Connie over here!" called the familiar voice.

"Alex?" Connie looked at the figure waving; yes, it was Alex, but how, here in Bridgend.

"Come on I've got mam's car to take you home."

Connie picked up her bag and ran to where Alex was standing ready with the car door open, the two hugged tightly, "but how are you here?" asked Connie bemused.

"I was due some time off and after our conversation yesterday, I wanted to be here for you so I asked Ricardo if I could take leave from today and booked myself onto the next plane home and well, here I am!"

"Oh, Alex you will never believe how good it is to see you" Connie hugged her friend again.

"Come on get in, let's get you home."

They got into Carole's car, and Alex indicated and pulled away

"I can't believe you are here!" exclaimed Connie tears welling up in her eyes.

"I had to come home; I knew you needed me even though you would never say."

"I do."

"And the test?" asked Alex giving Connie a sideways glance

"Was positive, I'm going to have a baby Al!"

Alex swerved slightly at the news "How do you feel about it or is it too soon?"

"I'm not sure, but I want it Al, I've messed about with life for too long, I'm going to make a good life for me and the baby."

"I know you will Con" Alex briefly took her hand off the steering wheel and squeezed Connie's hand "Bloody Hell Al, keep your eyes on the road!" exclaimed Connie.

"Don't worry Con, I'm used to drivers in Italy!"

"That's what I'm worried about!" Connie laughed then, it was good to see Alex, even if she was doing a good job of trying to kill them both!!

"Where to first?" Alex asked.

"How about an ice cream with Mario, I've got a proposal to make him" announced Connie.

"Righto, let's go!"

"Ah my two favourite girls!" Mario boomed as the girls walked into Nice Ice.

"And our favourite ice cream seller" answered Connie smiling, it was good to be back home.

"Sit down and I will bring you over your heart's desire!" said Mario smiling widely.

"Lovely, have you got time to join us too?" asked Connie

The cafe was reasonably quiet even though a queue had formed outside for takeaways, but Nicola was more than capable with dealing with it.

"I always have time for my favourite girls" answered Mario

He bustled about behind the counter bringing them both over two Nice Ice specials, sitting down opposite them

"How did London go?" he asked Connie apprehensively

"It's a long story Mario, but I'm back for good now, and I was just wondering?" Connie hesitated, scooping up a small spoonful of ice-cream that was threatening to escape from the over full bowl in front of her, "you know that you mentioned about possibly selling Nice Ice?"

Mario nodded seriously, "yes, I have been giving it a lot of thought, but don't worry about your job Connie, I will tell whoever buys it that they must keep on the best waitress in Porthcawl!"

Connie smiled, "It wasn't that Mario, I wondered if you would consider selling Nice Ice to me?"

"You?" Mario looked astonished.

"Yes, I am selling my Aunties house in London, and I really want to buy a business to set myself up for the future, and Nice Ice would be my first choice, you know how special it is to me" Connie looked at him eagerly.

"Well, then, there is no one I would rather sell Nice Ice to than you my bella Connie, I am meeting with my solicitor later in the week and I will definitely give you first refusal, nothing is decided yet, but I will keep you informed don't worry" Mario smiled gently, "yes, no one more than you Connie."

Connie smiled widely "that's wonderful Mario, of course I have to sell my aunt's house first, but Cathy the girl I have been dealing with thinks it will go as soon as it hits the housing market as it is in a sought-after area, so fingers crossed!" She jumped up out of her seat and hugged him.

Mario mopped his eyes, "it is good to have you back Connie, you too Alex."

The girls finished their Ice Creams, "That sounded positive" said Alex, referring to the possible sale of Nice Ice.

"Fingers crossed Al, I hope it all comes together now, the sale of the house and this place and hopefully somewhere I can buy to live in too, I need to turn everything into a positive and once I've got my head around this one" she stroked her stomach, "maybe I can find out who my real father is!"

Connie called into the local GPs who spoke to the anti-natal unit and arranged for her to have an appointment the following week "I think I'm going to wait until after my hospital appointment before I tell my grandparents" She confided in Alex.

"Good idea you can give them a date then to get ready for their great grandchild!" Alex smiled mischievously.

"I don't think I need a due date I know exactly when this one was conceived," answered Connie remembering that blissful night and morning she had spent in Wyatt's 5* suite, "I wonder how they'll take the news, how do you think your mother would if it was you?

"If I know mam shed be planning and plotting to keep me here and hoping that I wouldn't go back to Italy or else she'd probably sell up and come back with me!" Alex laughed, "You know mam!"

Connie smiled at the thought of Carole's possible reaction to becoming a grandparent and suddenly realised her baby wouldn't have a grandparent, her mum being dead and her dad not being her dad after all, "I hope my grandparents will be ok, they'll be this baby only relatives, apart from me"

"Oh Con, don't forget their auntie Alex and great auntie Carole" said Alex catching under Connie's arm as the two walked towards

Carole's flat.

"Thanks Al, you've been wonderful, thank you so much for being here for me today"

They entered the main entrance to the block of flats where Carole lived and Alex tapped on Carole's door before opening it with her key, "Mam, we're home" She called out.

Carole appeared at the kitchen doorway looking much more mobile than the last time Connie had seen her.

"Connie love, how are you?" she asked full of concern, not knowing the facts of the visit to London or the impending baby news, but knowing something was up due to Alex coming back home so quickly.

"Hiya Carole, I'm ok, how are you, you're looking better than the last time I saw you, are you getting about ok?"

"I'm getting there thank you babe, the plasters off and I'm driving again, thank god, I hated having to rely on others," the two hugged, "cup of tea?" Carole offered the two girls.

"I'm ok mam, just had a special in Mario's"

"Oh lovely, what about you Connie?"

"No, I'm fine too thanks Carole."

"It's lovely to have you back Alex and having you two around here is just like old times, have you been home yet Connie?" asked Carole

"Not yet, I wanted to see you first" answered Connie.

"Oh right" Carole sat herself down on the easy chair, sensing Connie was about to ask her something important.

"You know that I've been to London"

Carole nodded.

"I went to sort out the sale of my aunt's house and to meet my father" continued Connie.

"But, well, to cut a long story short, I met him, and he told me that he isn't my real father!" Finished Connie.

"Well, I never..." Carole was lost for words.

"So basically, I was wondering if you might know who my father is" Connie looked at Carole hopefully.

"Oh love," Carole took hold of Connie's hand," I don't I'm sorry, I didn't really know your mother before she went to live in London, what with her being a few years younger than me, and I never got to know your father, sorry, Giac, what did he say Con, "

"Well, he was very nice and everything" Connie glanced at Alex, "but he said that he wasn't my biological father and that he didn't know who was."

"Have you spoken to your grandparents, would they know, or what about Mario, I think he knew your mother and Giac?" suggested Carole.

"Yes, I need to speak to my grandparents, about a few things" she glanced at Alex again, "and maybe Mario too, thanks Carole."

"I'm only sorry I can't help; it must have been a shock for you," said Carole.

"It was yes, I'd only just started thinking about him again after all these years and then to discover he is not my dad was a bit of a shock!" Agreed Connie.

"I'm glad you're back home though Connie and getting this lovely surprise visit from you too Alex, nice for you girls to have a catch up, and for me too" Carole smiled from one to the other of the girls, wondering if there was more to Alex returning home but deciding to wait until she was ready to confide in her.

"Speaking of absent fathers' Alex gave Carole a sideways look, "where has mine gone again?"

"He's still with his brother, your uncle, mind you Al, he was a God send running errands for me, I know what you're going to say' warned Carole, "but no he hasn't asked to move in, and you know that I'd say no, but credit where credits due, he has been marvelous!"

Alex snorted; she didn't trust him, he never did anything for nothing, "I'm just borrowing the car again mam to pop Connie home, is that ok?"

"Of course, it is, ta-ta Con see you soon babe," said Carole

Connie hugged Carole goodbye as the girls left for Alex to take her home.

"How do you feel being home again?" asked Connie.

"Cold!" laughed Alex, "but it was good to see mam and to help her out for a couple of days, and what about you? Are you glad to be back?"

"Yes, I think I am, you know me Al, a Porthcawl girl at heart" answered Connie.

"Your grandparents will be glad to see you"

"Yes, until I tell them about this one" said Connie tapping her still flat abdomen.

"I think once they know you're back for good that is if you definitely buy Nice Ice, they'll be pleased no matter what"

"I hope so Al, I've had enough drama lately, with all that business with my father and now this, I just want a quiet life"

"Not so quiet with a new business and a new baby!"

"I know it's enormous, isn't it? I just hope I'm doing the right thing, who would have thought a month ago, me being a business owner and a mother?" Connie looked at Alex widening her eyes to add drama.

"You'll be great Con, and you can bring the baby to visit Auntie Alex in Italy to sample new flavours of Ice Cream."

Connie nodded, she hoped, no prayed everything would turn out ok, it had to, simply had to!

Chapter 23

As Alex had predicted Connie's grandparents were so happy to have her home, she had spoken to them about her plan to hopefully purchase Nice Ice when the sale of Aunt Con's house came through along with a place of her own. They told her that there was no need to move out but realised that she may want to now she had an inheritance, but of course there would always be a home for her in Sea Breeze.

"When I was in London, I met Giac Santini!" There, she had told them, she looked at her grandparents and waited for their reactions

"What? But how?" blustered her Gran.

Her Granddads mouth opened as if to say something, but no sound came out.

"I contacted his nephew and Giac rang me and as he was going to be in London the same time as me, we arranged to meet" answered Connie.

"After all these years, but why Con? Was it those letters, I knew they would cause trouble!" said her Granddad at last.

"Don't you think I had the right to meet him?' asked Connie

Her grandparents exchanged meaningful looks.

"You knew, didn't you" she added, and it was then that Connie knew that they had known all along that Giac was not her dad!

"Knew what?" asked her gran her face colouring.

That he isn't my biological father!" Answered Connie, almost shouting.

"Now look here Con..." Granddad started.

"You knew didn't you, and you never told me!" Connie was trying to keep her voice steady and staring at them both in turn, waiting for their response.

Mary and Sid looked aghast as they exchanged glances- It all fitted into place now, how they had the upper hand when it had come down to keeping her mother and herself here and not supporting the move to America.

Her Gran was first to speak, "I'm sorry Connie, but it wasn't our place to tell you, your mother, our Laura, had never thought you needed to know and with Giac long gone, we thought that it was best left unsaid" she went on "when she had found out that she was pregnant she told us that 'the baby was hers and that's all that mattered' and it was left at that, shortly after she met Giac and they moved to London so everyone else just assumed the baby, you, was his."

"It was Laura's decision, and we agreed, we never asked who your father was, and she never told us, Constance tried to interfere, and Giac Santini thought he knew best, but when all was said and done, they both knew you were best here with us, and your real father was never mentioned!" Granddad spoke now with a passion in his voice Connie hadn't heard before. If she hadn't found the letters and other things and hadn't contacted and met Giac she would still be in the dark- she felt hurt by this, that no one had thought she needed to know, why? Was her real father a bad person, a one-night stand, married?? The possibilities were endless.

"But I always thought I was half Italian; everyone says I look like I am from Italy or Spain? I don't understand?" Connie had voiced her thoughts.

"Well Granddad is half French, maybe that's why, I don't Know Connie, maybe your real father was from Europe, I'm so sorry my love, but we were never told who he was, and we respected your mother's decision" her gran had tried to explain.

"I wondered why I was Devereux and not Santini and why the father part on my birth certificate was blank, but mum had said that it was because she wasn't married and registered me when my dad had been working away and I just believed it all" Connie looked from her gran to her grandfather and felt tears prick in her eyes.

"Oh, Connie love" Granddad held open his arms to give her a hug, "we are so sorry, we thought we were doing the right thing, even fell out with our Con about it all" Connie had become to realise what the falling out had been about, "what can we do to put it right?" Connie didn't know, she had no idea where to find out about her father now, now that her grandparents had no idea either and everyone else had thought she was Giac's child, was it worth asking Mario, she thought probably not, she would never now find out who her real father is!

Alex stayed long enough to accompany Connie to her first anti natal visit, Connie had told the midwife that she was probably ten weeks pregnant, and a scan was arranged for a fortnight later. "Oh, I wish you could be here with me for my scan, but it's been great having you here now," Connie said to Alex as they left the appointment, "I wish I was too, if you want company mam will go with you, you know that don't you," said Alex.

"I know, thanks Al, I might take her up on that, suddenly I'm starting to feel quite alone."

"Don't say that Con, I'm sure once your grandparents know they will be there for you."

"I hope so; we fell out a bit over them not telling me Giac wasn't my father, so I don't know whether to wait until I've had the scan and then maybe by showing them a photo the news might be received a bit better."

Alex nodded, "and what about Wyatt Morgan, will you tell him?"

"Chance would be a fine thing, I have no idea how to contact him and to be honest I don't think he'd want to know, and anyway, like my mum said about me, this is my baby and that's all that matters!"

"It's his baby too Con, I think you should think about telling him, Sofia said he only had eyes for you and that he was definitely well into you."

"Oh yeah, so well into me he forgot about me the minute he left Sorrento!" Connie raised her voice angrily.

"I'm sorry Con, you are right it's none of my business, but you don't want the baby to end up like you have, wondering about its father! Come on let's not quarrel on my last day here, let's go and treat ourselves in Nice Ice, "said Alex sorry that she'd mentioned him

"Yes, I'm sorry too Al, anyway I had some good news today, I've had an offer on Aunt Con's house, so I can get things moving with Mario soon."

"That's great news, come on let's go, 'Mammy!'" Alex smiled as she emphasised the last word.

"I like that it sounds lovely, now come on Auntie Alex, let's go" Connie smiled back at her.

The girls linked arms and walked back to Carole's car that Alex had borrowed again, best of friends and always there for each other!

Mario was as pleased as always to see the girls, "Connie you can't keep away, not that I am complaining" Mario referred to the fact that Connie had returned back to work at Nice Ice a few days previously.

"Can't get enough of your Ice Cream, I don't know what I'll do tomorrow when I'm back in Sorrento!" teased Alex.

"You tinker!" laughed Mario, "Ahh I wish I was coming back with you."

"You might be soon Mario, I've had good news on my aunt's house today, hopefully things will move quickly and then I can buy Nice Ice and you will be as free as a bird to fly off to Italy!" said Connie.

"Fantastic news, keep me up to date Connie, well what can I get you two bella signoras?"

The girls ordered and sat down at their favourite table with a view overlooking the beach.

"You've been wonderful Al, thank you so much for being here this last week, it's been great having my 'bestie' here", Connie squeezed Alex's hand in a friendly gesture, "I'll miss you when you go back, mind you I only think you came because you knew there would be no chance of you bumping into Doctor Jones."

Alex looked away, Jared Jones was never far from her thoughts and Connie knew this.

"It's my turn to stick my nose in now" said Connie cautiously, "why don't you ring him or message him even if it's just to get closure"

Alex shook her head, "No, I'll forget about him when I'm back in Italy."

They both knew this wasn't true-maybe they were both destined to be losers in love.

"What time are you leaving tomorrow?" asked Connie changing the subject.

"Er, not until lunch time, I've got an evening flight from Bristol" answered Alex absently stirring her coffee.

Connie didn't want thoughts of Jared Jones spoiling her and Alex" last day together, so she suggested a meal out together for that evening, "That would be great, chance to dress up a bit and a couple of glasses of fizz" Alex smiled, "thanks Con, that would be great."

The girls finished their coffees and bid Mario goodbye.

The girls parted company as Connie declined Alex's offer of a lift as she thought a walk back home across the beach would do her good, she slipped off her sandals to feel the sand between her toes and the gentle crunch beneath the soles of her feet, she loved the beach, and remembered back to when she and her mum first moved to Porthcawl, the excitement of actually being able to visit the beach every single day. Her grandparents had told her that she would probably tire of it now that she was living here, but she had never tired of it. It was her go to place, her happy place, if she was sad, it made her feel better, if she was angry, it calmed her down, if she was happy, it kept her mood high, she was definitely a beach baby at heart. It was always a good place to go to, to think, and she was thinking now of being on the beach in Amalfi, splashing and laughing in the sea with Sofia and Wyatt, had she really got it so wrong? She was so sure that they had had a connection, it had felt so right, so easy, they had talked and shared about their families it had felt as if they had known each other for ever, she had been so certain that he was 'the one', why hadn't she heard from him? What was going on between him and this country star?

Was it just spin or was he in love with her? Connie had been a fool to think a world-famous star would be in love with her, an ice cream waitress, when he could have any woman he wanted, she had been swept off her feet like a gullible fool and now here she was pregnant and alone. She breathed in the smells of the seaside, on the beach outside Nice Ice the smell was always from the donkeys who were a familiar sight on the beach, and from the fish and chip bars, as she walked along the beach the smell changed to a fresher sea smell, the smell of home.

The girls had a lovely last evening together at the local Italian restaurant, Connie was sad to see Connie off the following day as she waved her goodbye. The following few days passed with Connie being busy in Nice Ice and Alex being back in work at Rivolli's, when Connie's phone rang on her way to work.

"Hi Connie, its Cathy, I've got some good news" it was Cathy from MetProp the estate agents dealing with the sale of Aunt Cons house "I've received an offer today on the house, the full asking price, the buyer is a first-time buyer so no chain and are looking to get the go ahead asap!" announced Cathy excitedly.

"That's wonderful news!" answered Connie almost shouting as she was so pleased.

"Are you happy to go ahead with the sale?" asked Cathy, knowing what the answer would be.

"Oh yes, definitely, yes!" answered Connie excitedly

"That's great I'll get the ball rolling and will be back in touch soon" answered Cathy, "bye."

Connie arrived at work; Mario was already there.

"Good news, I've had an offer on the house so hopefully we can start talking about me buying Nice Ice," announced Connie as she waltzed through the shop door.

"Ah good news Connie, I've been looking at some places to buy in Italy, online" he added frowning.

"What's wrong with that?" asked Connie.

"Not the same as seeing them with your eyes, taking in the place the sounds the smells" Mario shook his head.

"But at least it will give you an idea" answered Connie encouragingly.

"I think I must go to Italy soon and look for myself"

"That will be a lovely thing for you to do Mario"

"Yes, I thought maybe my son Marco, or my daughter Gabriella might want to accompany me, and see where my family and their mama's family came from, but..." Mario shrugged his shoulders, "they were not interested."

"Aww Mario perhaps they are busy, I expect they will all love to visit you if you do decide to move to Italy" said Connie sensing Mario's disappointment in his children's lack of interest. Mario nodded sadly, "yes maybe, I thought they would have jumped at the chance, with it being in their blood, you loved Italy though didn't you Connie, see it's in your blood."

Connie hadn't mentioned to Mario about Giac not being her dad, "No it isn't Mario, when I met Giac in London, he told me that he wasn't my real father."

"What?" Mario looked visibly shocked" "what do you mean Connie?"

"Well when I told you everything went ok with London, oh Mario it didn't, it couldn't have been further from the truth" answered Connie sitting down at the table closest to the counter

Mario, his face full of concern stood at the counter and beckoned her to carry on.

"Well, I met Giac as planned and we chatted and then he told me that my mum was already pregnant when they met!"

Mario could feel the ground coming up to meet him as the shop swirled around him, "Mario!" he heard Connie's voice call out in anguish, but he was falling, falling and then nothing!

Chapter 24

The ambulance arrived outside Nice Ice just after the paramedics had arrived, Mario was checked over and taken to the local hospital strapped to a stretcher, it was believed that he had suffered a slight stoke.

Connie had telephoned 999 when Mario had slumped to the floor, quickly followed by calls to his children and then to Nicola, to ask her to come into work to cover.

Gabriella his daughter lived only a few miles away, so she arrived shortly after the medics and accompanied him to hospital in the ambulance.

The morning in 'Nice Ice' flew by with a steady flow of customers, Gabriella telephoned late morning to let Connie know that Mario was comfortable in hospital and would be there for a few days following what the doctor had described as a 'mild stroke' she said that she would pop into 'Nice Ice' on her way home.

Nicola had come straight into work and Connie was so grateful as it was her day off. There was a quiet lull late afternoon, so they took a break.

"Poor Mario I wonder what had brought on the stroke?" wondered Nicola.

"I don't know, we were chatting and then he just keeled over, it was so frightening, I didn't know what to do, so I just got him comfortable and rang 999, I'm so glad he's going to be ok, and thank you so much for coming in, Mario would never have forgiven me if I'd closed, you know how he is" Connie smiled thinking of Mario who would have the parlour open no matter what.

"Yes, only closes Christmas Day and New Year's Day" added Nicola, "it was no problem coming in, Mario has been good to me, and I was only going to clean the house, so I've been saved from that!" she laughed.

The door opened and Gabriella, Mario's daughter entered Nice Ice, she didn't come there very often, and Connie didn't think she had seen her for about two years. She had her dark hair pulled back into a ponytail and had a multi coloured scarf-come wrap, around her shoulders, her eyes were so like Mario's, big and brown and friendly, but with a worried look today, she threw her arms around in wild gestures in a manner so like Mario's.

"Connie" she went to Connie and threw her arms around her in a big hug, Connie hugged her back, "I'm so glad you were here with papa the doctor said that your quick action phoning for an ambulance may have saved his life, as he needed immediate medical attention, thank you."

"I'm so glad he's ok, but I didn't really do anything" answered Connie.

"The sooner he sells you this place the better, he needs to rest, and you know that he wouldn't if he didn't sell, he's in here every day as it is, he just cannot stay away!"

Gabriella shook her head in a gesture so much like her father.

"I know we were just saying how he would have been cross if I hadn't opened today," replied Connie indicating to Nicola.

"Oh, I'm so sorry, you must think me so rude" said Gabriella "you must be Nicola" she extended her hand to Nicola,

Nicola returned her handshake, "Yes hello."

"Dad keeps me up to date with the business even though I haven't been here for ages, Connie I'm so pleased he is selling to you, he knows you will look after it, you are part of Nice Ice as much as the ice cream" Gabriella smiled fondly, "me and Marco never showed any interest in the business as papa was always fond of berating us over it, but you Connie, well you were his protégé."

Connie smiled feeling a bit embarrassed, all this protégé talk, she was glad that Nicola knew about the possibilities of her buying Nice Ice, even though it wasn't public knowledge, as Gabriella was talking quite openly about it.

"I'm hoping that the sale of the house will go through as soon as possible as there is no chain and the buyers are very keen, so fingers crossed" Connie smiled from Gabriella to Nicola.

"Yes, the sooner the better, papa can rest then, hopefully" she emphasised the word hopefully "before he starts gallivanting around Italy!" she shrugged her shoulders and sighed, so much like Mario in her gestures.

Gabriella adjusted her shawl and added, "are you ladies ok to run this place until papa is recovered, or you buy it, whichever comes first, you've got my number if you need anything, I'd better go the children will be home from school soon" she air kissed twice and then she was gone with a "ciao."

"So that was the famous Gabriella!" laughed Nicola, "I've heard plenty about her from Mario, but this is the first time I've actually seen her."

"Yes that force of nature was the one and only Gabriella" agreed Connie, I haven't seen her for ages, when we were younger she worked here one summer for extra pocket money, but all she did was moan and complain until Mario sent her home as he had had enough of her" Connie laughed remembering the teenage Gabriella too grand to get her hands dirty in the ice cream parlour, she had been a couple of years older than Connie and Alex and always so glamorous even when they were in school.

"I can imagine"' laughed Nicola, "what about the son, Marco is it?"

"Yes Marco, he's a year older than Gabriella, he lives in Cardiff, I remember when he was younger all the girls used to fancy him, me included," laughed Connie, remembering when she and Alex would moon over him whenever he was in Nice Ice, tall, dark and very handsome and no time for silly giggling schoolgirls!

"Mario must have lost his wife a long time ago," said Nicola.

"I never remember her, I think I remember Mario saying that she had died when the children were small, before I was even born, so sad he never re married, been on his own a long time" answered Connie.

"Yes, mind you I think that Mario was married to this place I don't know what he'll do when he retires, if he doesn't go back to Italy to live, he'll be in here every day looking to help out!" smiled Nicola

"Yes, probably if I know him, maybe he'll meet a nice lady when he goes over there, you never know' said Connie, mind you I will miss him, think I've seen him almost every day I've lived here, he's like family" mused Connie.

"I know what you mean, he is such a lovely man, I'll miss him too" agreed Nicola.

"Look at us talking like he's gone already, I'm just glad he's ok, Hey Nic, when I take over, fingers crossed' she added crossing her fingers, "you will still work here for me, won't you?"

"If you want me, then 100% yes!" answered Nicola.

"Thank you, I'm so glad, and I'll need you, my manageress' more than ever now that I am pregnant!" there Connie had told someone else now too.

"Pregnant, oh congratulations Connie, when are you due?"

"Not until next March, but with me taking this place on and being on my own I need know I have staff I can rely on, and I'd like you to be manageress, with a pay increase of course" added Connie.

"I don't know what to say" said Nicola smiling, "except thank you very much, I accept."

"I haven't told anyone yet about the baby, not even my grandparents, so if you can keep it to yourself, I'd be really grateful" said Connie quickly.

"Of course, but if you ever need to talk or need anything, please let me know, I know how hard and lonely it can be bringing a baby up on you own" said Nicola kindly, "but wonderful too" she added

Connie felt that it was the right thing to do, to confide in Nicola, she knew that she was more than capable of managing the parlour and that she was always keen to do extra hours, the next job would be to interview some new staff as Connie knew she would need lots of help over the next few months, but first things first would be to exchange contacts so that Nice Ice would be hers.

Cathy had rung her back to say that the offer had been agreed and as the couple were cash buyers hopefully the sale of the house would be completed by the end of the month and that Ed would be in touch in due course.

Everything was finally coming together and over the next week Mario became stronger and Gabriella had been back to Nice Ice to let them know that he was coming home to stay with her in her home in the nearby village of North Cornelly, until he was strong enough to return to his own home, and that his solicitor had been in touch and everything was in place for Connie to take over as the new owner of Nice Ice as soon as the funds were transferred from the house sale.

"Is he up to visitors?" asked Connie, "I've missed him."

"Why don't you come to mine when he's home, he'll be glad to see you, he's been asking about you."

"And Nice Ice too no doubt," laughed Connie.

"Oh yes, but I've told him it will no longer be his concern after this month" announced Gabriella.

"How is he feeling about that?" asked Connie.

"Oh, you know papa, fussing about how you're coping, will you cope etc., I said papa you will make yourself ill again! Connie is more than capable of running Nice Ice with her eyes shut and her hands tied behind her back!" said Gabriella in an exaggerated way Connie laughed, "I don't know about that, but yes we are coping fine, it's quieter this time of year we are almost over the summer rush!"

When Gabriella had gone Connie realised she hadn't told Mario about the baby, she had been about to when she had been telling him about London and Giac not being her dad, but then he had collapsed and well, the rest was history, she would tell him when she visited him in Gabriella's next week.

The following week Connie had her appointment for her 12-week scan, as Alex had suggested she asked Carole to accompany her. If Carole was shocked by the news of her being pregnant, she did a good job of hiding it and Connie felt much braver entering the scan room now she had Carole's support.

Connie was told to lie down on the examination table whilst the midwife, who was probably younger than Connie, and introduced herself as Georgia, applied a gel to her lower abdomen. Connie winced slightly at the touch of the cold slimy gel as the midwife rolled the electronic wand or transducer over her gelled area.

As the midwife moved the transducer around, sounds came through the machine accompanied by a picture on the screen that reminded Connie of the TVs weather forecast pictures for cloudy weather. The midwife made measurements and moved the transducer around on Connie's stomach which made her want to have a wee with having drank a pint of water earlier as requested. The midwife turned the screen towards Connie and Carole and pointed out the shapes on the screen as babies head, arms, legs, internal organs, as she checked that everything was growing and as it should be.

"Oh, Con isn't it amazing!" Said Carole, her voice full of emotion, "your baby!"

Connie stared at the screen, it sure was amazing, and this little mass of dots and blobs was her baby!

"And this is babies' heartbeat," said Georgia the midwife, "Good, strong heartbeat" she added, as a sound similar to a galloping horse or a train running along a track filled the room.

Connie listened in awe, her baby, she couldn't believe it, seeing him or her on screen and listening to the heartbeat made it all so real now.

"Everything looks fine, you are 12 weeks and one day pregnant" announced Georgia, just as Connie had predicted, she then finished all the checks and measurements of the baby and printed off the scan photos for Connie to purchase and take home, the estimated due date was calculated and Connie had already guessed that it would be just before Easter time, the following year.

Carole was overcome by emotion and blew her nose and wiped her tears away with a tissue as the two left the hospital.

"Thank you for coming with me today, I'm going to tell my grandparents tonight, now I know everything is ok" said Connie clutching the scan photos to her.

"It was my pleasure Con, it was absolutely marvelous, I'm sure Mary and Sid will be thrilled, surprised at first but thrilled!"

"I hope so!" answered Connie sounding more confident than she felt, "I'm going to phone Alex to let her know everything went well"

"I'll just go and get the car, send her my love babe and tell her Ill ring her later," said Carole.

As Alex was at work Connie made a quick call to her and Alex was happy that everything had gone well at the scan.

Connie had arranged to call to see Mario, on her way back from her scan, Carole who had taken Connie by car to her appointment dropped her off at Gabriella's house on their way back.

That morning when she had been picking up a cake from the local deli to take to him, she had had a telephone call from Ed, lovely Ed, to say things were moving well and the sale should be completed by the beginning of the following week. Ed was also acting on her behalf on the purchase of Nice Ice and everything was ready to be finalised as soon as the house sale was completed so in effect Nice Ice could be hers as early as next week! Everything was good, Mario was recovering well, she would soon be a business owner and she had also thought about putting in an offer for an apartment in Carole's block so she might even be a homeowner too soon. Why couldn't her private life be so successful? Ed had told her that he had proposed marriage to Cathy, and she had accepted, Connie knew that they made a lovely couple, then why did she feel a jealous pang when he told her? She had been in constant touch with Alex, who was living the life of a hermit again; would either of them ever be lucky in love?

She arrived at Gabriella's smart semi having caught a local bus into the town and making the short walk to her home, 'I must learn to drive, having a baby and owning a business I definitely need to drive' Connie told herself, there were bikes, balls and other games strewn on the front lawn belonging to Gabriella's two young sons, Connie smiled, that would be her in a few years' time, side stepping toys and bikes.

She was greeted by Gabriella after ringing the doorbell, "come in, papa is in the conservatory."

Connie walked into the house behind Gabriella, she followed her up the hallway and off to the right into a room full of the boy's toys, "Excuse the mess, this is the boy's playroom" apologised Gabriella, the boys were nowhere in sight. Just off the playroom was the conservatory where Mario was sat in a big comfy chair covered with an oatmeal faux fur throw, he was watching a gardening programme on the small TV in the corner. He looked up when he saw them arrive in the doorway.

"Connie how lovely to see you, come and sit down!" he looked smaller than she remembered, older, but his voice was still powerful.

Connie gave Gabriella the cake that she had brought, "a little treat for you, for later" she said.

"Later nothing,' said Mario, "Gabriella cut us a slice each and make us a nice coffee to go with it!"

"Yes sir!" Gabriella made a mock salute, "as you can see Connie still as bossy as ever!" she marched off towards the kitchen.

"I was so worried Mario, how are you?"

"Better now child, how are you, how is Nice Ice, not mine for much longer though so I hear from my solicitor, Congratulations Connie!" Mario smiled and touched her hand gently.

"It's such good news I'm really looking forward to it, I have some news to tell you too, I was going to tell you the other day, but then you collapsed and well you know the rest" Connie paused, "I'm pregnant Mario!" she'd finally told him.

She waited for it to sink in and added, "It doesn't make any difference to me taking over Nice Ice though, so don't worry, Nicola is going to be my full-time manageress and I have been interviewing new staff too."

"Connie, are you happy? If you are happy then I am happy, and I know you will make Nice Ice a success," said Mario.

"Yes, Mario I think I am happy; it was a shock of course and not the greatest timing but I'm more determined than ever now to make a success of everything for myself and for my baby," said Connie

"You will be a wonderful mother, just like your own dear mother, bella Laura" Mario's eyes misted over when he mentioned Laura, Connie's mother.

"I was telling you about Giac remember, when you collapsed, about him not being my father," said Connie.

Mario nodded slowly, "yes child I remember, I have been thinking about it a lot."

"I know you knew Giac and my mother, but Mario did you know he wasn't my father?" asked Connie.

"No, no I assumed that he was," answered Mario.

Gabriella returned then with cups of coffee and the cake cut into slices, she handed them around, "I'll leave you two to it, you've probably got lots to talk about not having seen each other for a couple of weeks" she excused herself sensing that they wanted to talk privately.

"So, you have no idea who my father could be?" said Connie despondently.

Mario took a sip of his coffee and then placed it onto the side table next to him; he rubbed his chin thoughtfully and replied slowly.

"I might have an idea my bella Connie."

Connie looked at him intently, "Really, who?"

"Well, my lovely, before Giac came to Porthcawl, I had just lost my dear wife to cancer, it had been a hard time, she was only 32 and we had two small children, I think Marco was 4 and Gabriella just 3, I was running 'Nice Ice' back then I had bought it the year me and Maria had got married. So, you can imagine a young widower working all the hours God sent to keep a roof over my baby's heads, I was nothing more than a bereaved workaholic husk of a man when the most beautiful woman I had ever seen walked into the parlour one summers day, she wanted to paint Nice Ice and asked if I minded, she explained that she was an art student. I obviously didn't mind or quite frankly care, my head just being in my work, but bit by bit day by day having her pop in and out of the parlour always with a kind word and with that sunny personality I began to realise that there was more to life than burying myself in work, work, work" Mario stopped and took another sip of his coffee

Connie interrupted, "it was my mother wasn't it, it's the painting you have on the back wall in Nice Ice the one she painted."

Mario nodded, and continued, "Laura your mother was a breath of fresh air in my stale life."

Connie listened intently imagining her younger mother, with her artist equipment sitting, painting, young and beautiful, she remembered how lovely she had been, and could see how she had turned Mario's head, as the saying goes Laura was beautiful inside and out.

"We fell in love Connie, I didn't expect it to happen after losing Maria so tragically, I never thought I would smile again, let alone love again, but that day your mother walked into Nice Ice changed everything."

"You and my mother were in love?" Connie was incredulous, "I had no idea."

"Yes, very much in love, but she wanted to travel and have a career in Art, and I had my babies, they needed stability and I could never ask her to give up her dreams for a life of being a stepmother to two young children."

"So, you parted?" asked Connie.

"Yes, it was for the best, my heart was broken all over again, then Giac came to Porthcawl, and they fell in love and moved to London," Mario took a tissue from the box on the coffee table and mopped his eyes.

"So, what are you saying Mario, are you my father?" asked Connie, she couldn't believe what she had just heard.

"I don't know Connie, I honestly thought Giac was your father, but when you told me that he wasn't on that day in the parlour, it was such a shock."

"I'm sorry Mario, it was my fault you had a stroke" Connie was anguished.

"No don't be silly," he squeezed Connie's hand gently, "but I have been lying in that hospital bed rolling it over and over in my head and I do think that I could possibly be your real papa Connie" announced Mario.

Chapter25

Alex had called into Luca's on the way home from work at Rivolli's that evening, she would usually call in, in the morning before work for a coffee and a 'social media' catch up on her laptop, in between catching up on various emails, but lately she had begun calling in after work too. Luca would make comments about her 'working too hard and not having any fun', Alex would just laugh it off and say that she was fine and that he wasn't to concern himself about her, but she was finding the evenings after work long and boring, she had lost her 'mo-jo'. Every day she got up showered, dressed and called in to Lucas for her daily coffee, went to work, usually working on as she didn't really have anything to do or want to do once she had left for the day, she declined Sofia and Ricardo's invitations to Romero's feeling like a gooseberry as their friendship had developed into romance, even when Gianni had tagged along, she hadn't really felt in a socialising mood and his constant flirting had irritated her. She had started calling into Lucas for her tea most evenings, so that the rest of the evening spent at home wouldn't feel so long. Why did she feel like this? She used to love sitting on her veranda taking in the sights and sounds of the city, but now nothing seemed to interest her. She stirred the ice around her glass, she was deep in thought, she had enjoyed going back home to Porthcawl, being there for Connie, now Connie was doing really well with a new business and new baby to look forward to, it was nice seeing her mam too, she had felt wanted, needed, but here she had begun to feel like a spare wheel in the office with the 'love-birds', not that she begrudged them, she was pleased for them really, but here she felt that she lacked purpose. Yes, she had enjoyed going back home and Connie had been right that she was safe in the knowledge that she wouldn't bump into Jared Jones, but was that what she secretly wanted, to bump into him again? What would she say? Would she play it cool, or would she bawl "who is this special person? She doesn't love you like I do?" there she had it, she loved Jared, and nothing would change that, no matter what she did or what she told herself or others- she needed to speak to him, for closure if nothing else and then maybe, hopefully, finally she could move on.

She flicked through media news on her laptop, when something caught her eye, the headlines read: -

Wyatt Morgan parts company with manager amid allegations of bullying, controlling behaviour.

She attached her headphones to the laptop and put them in her ears as she clicked on the video below the headlines.

It was from a news report in America where a news reporter was stood outside a hotel, the reporter said.

"News coming in, that British music star Wyatt Morgan has parted company from his manager Pete Dolan, sources close to Morgan have said that Dolan who has been Morgan's manager for ten years has become increasingly controlling, to the point that he would not allow Morgan a cell phone. Lawyers are involved on both sides, but Morgan has hit back by releasing a song independently of Dolan and his record company. 'My Celtic Girl' is racing up the download chart both sides of the Atlantic- but who is this Celtic girl, not Jayde Johnstone who is definitely an all-American girl-watch this space-this is Jo Brown reporting for Network Z in San Francisco."

Alex scrolled down for more information, but it was basically more of the same, she hadn't met Dolan but from what Ricardo had said about him was that the man was an obnoxious character, she even felt a bit sorry for Wyatt Morgan, maybe that is why Connie hadn't heard from him, if it was true that Dolan was so controlling and had taken his phone from him. Maybe there was nothing in this media reported romance with country star Jayde Johnstone, and what about this new song?

Alex searched for the song and sat back sipping her cold drink as the music started.

The words of the song were basically about a beautiful dark-haired girl, who he had met by the sea in a romantic trip to a hot country, they had fallen in love, but he had left, and his heart was broken. Alex couldn't believe it, surely this song was about Connie! Either he had just used the experience of meeting Connie and turned it into a lovely catchy ballad, or he did really love her!

Alex sent the song attachment to Connie with the message, 'Listen to this Connie, if it's not written for you, about you, then I'll eat my hat (even my Valentino one LOL!!) xxx'

Connie was sat next to Mario holding his hand; he had become so emotional after telling her about her mother and himself.

"Connie if you are mine, why oh why didn't she tell me? She knew I loved her, why didn't she tell me when she came back from London, she and Giac were over then, I don't understand" he looked at Connie desperately.

"I think we need to get a DNA test before you get any more upset" said Connie trying to take in everything that he had told her and worried for his health.

"Yes, yes how do we do that?" asked Mario.

"Don't worry Mario I'll look into it, but please don't upset yourself anymore, Gabriella will be banning me from visiting you" Connie tried to make light of the situation.

"Never, she wouldn't dare!" said Mario raising his voice in anger.

"Mario!" warned Connie, "you must rest."

"I'm sorry" said Mario in a more subdued manner, he squeezed Connie's hand, "my lovely Connie, nothing would make me happier than to be your papa, but if I had known all those years ago, all those lost years."

"I've spent most of my life in Nice Ice Mario, I don't think you would have seen any more of me if we had tried" Connie smiled.

"You are right Connie, Ice Cream was in your blood, you always showed far more interest in the parlour than my two" Mario smiled back at her.

"Come on let's eat up this cake or Gabriella will be wondering what's wrong," said Connie.

Her mind was racing but outwardly she wanted to keep as calm as possible not to get Mario worked up again and risking another stroke, she left not long after, telling Mario to rest and that she would return in a few days with a DNA test, she waited in the bus stop, and noticed she had a message from Alex on her phone;

"Listen to this Connie; if it's not written for you, about you, then I'll eat my hat (even my Valentino one LOL!!) xxx"

She clicked play put her phone to her ear and listened to the song When it had finished, she messaged Alex.

"Nice song who is it??"

Her phone rang, it was Alex,

"Wyatt Morgan, it's obviously about you Con!" said Alex excitedly down the phone.

"Oh right," she answered.

"Con is that all you have to say?" Alex was amazed by Connie's lack of interest.

"Sorry Al, I've just had a bit of a shock, that's all, Mario and my mum used to be a thing and he thinks that he might be my real father" answered Connie.

Alex inhaled sharply "What!!!! oh my goodness Con," she was incredulous.

"Sorry Al I'll have to ring you later my bus is here" answered Connie as her bus approached, indicated and slowed down towards the bus stop.

Alex put her phone in her bag as Connie had hung up, well what next she wondered, as she tucked into her tuna salad, at least Connie's life had taken her attention away from Jared Jones, however briefly!

The bus dropped Connie a short walk from Sea Breeze cottage, she walked up the path and pushed open the back door to the kitchen, her grandparents were both inside, Mary her gran had just poured the tea, "oh hello Connie, tea?" she greeted Connie.

"No, I'm fine thanks Gran, er, can I have a word with you and Granddad?" answered Connie apprehensively.

"Yes love, go on into the lounge, granddads in there, is everything alright?" Gran regarded Connie, she had been looking a bit peaky lately, and she hoped that everything was alright.

Connie smiled and went ahead of Mary into the lounge where Sid was sat reading the local newspaper, he looked up as Connie entered, "Ah hello con love, you alright?"

Connie sat down on the settee, as Mary took the opposite easy chair to Sid's, and looked at Connie, waiting for her to impart whatever it was she needed to tell them.

Connie took a deep breath, "I'm pregnant!" there she'd said it

Mary put her cup and saucer down on the coffee table, and Sid looked up again from his newspaper.

"How? No not how obviously" corrected Mary "but when did you find out, oh Con" she shook her head and tutted.

"I found out when I was in London, but I wanted to make sure everything was alright, I had my twelve-week scan today, "Connie fished around in her bag and brought out the precious scan photos, "look Gran, your great grandchild."

Mary looked at the scan pictures, "How are you feeling love, no wonder you were fainting."

"Better, and better now that I have told you and Granddad" Connie looked towards her grandfather who had been silent throughout

"Well, your mum did a good job with you Connie, so I've no doubt you'll make a fine mother, and you know that we are always here for you both," said granddad.

"Thank you granddad that means a lot."

"Is there a father on the scene?" asked Mary cautiously.

"No this is my baby Gran" said Connie forcefully.

Mary nodded, "well you've got Cons house and ideas of running the Ice cream shop, you've got money behind you, and we'll help where we can, as long as it's what you want."

"Yes, yes Gran it is" answered Connie, there, she had told them at last but now there was another pressing matter, was Mario really her father?

Connie had ordered a paternity DNA kit for Mario and herself to do and the results came back the same day as she became the official owner of Nice Ice, Mario was now back in his own home, and Alex had been filled in with as much of the details of Mario and Laura's affair as Connie had been told. Alex had more news too, that Ricardo had asked Sofia to become his wife and the two had set the date for the end of September, just weeks away.

"Why wait" they had said, "we have known each other for five years, we spend every day together."

Sofia had already moved into Ricardo's apartment, and they were now looking for their forever home together, everyone was moving on with their lives, except for Alex.

"Tell Connie there will be an invite for her too and one for your Mama" said Sofia excitedly as she flashed her exquisite sapphire and diamond cluster on a gold band engagement ring for Alex to admire.

"It's beautiful Sofia, congratulations" Alex hugged and kissed them both warmly, "I'm so pleased for you both."

"We are getting married in Amalfi Cathedral on the 28th and then a wonderful party for all our family and friends at my Aunt Francesca's restaurant, we will party all night!" announced Sofia excitedly waltzing around the office.

Ricardo shook his head fondly as he looked at her with adoring eyes, Alex looked away quickly, feeling like an interloper in this romantic setting, when did someone last look at her like that so lovingly so adoringly?

Connie knocked on Mario's front door, the results of the DNA test still sealed in the envelope that it was delivered in that morning and zipped inside her handbag, Mario answered, he was looking better than the last time she had seen him, when he had been tucked up under a blanket in Gabriella's Conservatory, he smiled widely when he saw that it was Connie by the door.

"Come in, how are you my lovely, what is it like being the owner of Nice Ice?" he said jovially.

Connie kissed him on the cheek as she entered the house, "it's good thanks Mario how are you?"

"Glad to be back home, nice and quiet, can do what I want, no Gabriella fussing about me" Mario tutted, then added, "come into the front room it's nice and light in here."

Connie had never been to Mario's house before as he practically lived in Nice Ice, it was very old fashioned and reminded her of the decor in her Aunt Cons house, she followed him into a small room at the front of the house.

"This is where I spend my time, Connie; it's more pleasant in here as the sun rises early on the front, please sit down" he indicated to one of the two large easy chairs either side of the fireplace.

Connie sat down, "I've got the results" she said unzipping her bag

"Have you looked at them yet?" Asked Mario apprehensively

Connie shook her head, "I wanted us to know together."

Mario sat down in the other chair; Connie tore open the envelope

and took out the results, there was list of letters and numbers on

the DNA report, as Connie scanned it over, and there at the bottom

was what she was looking for, 'The alleged father is not excluded as

the biological father of the tested child', she read on and looked up

at Mario,

 "It says here that 'the probability of paternity is 99.9998% certain'

oh Mario I am your daughter, and you are my father" she said as

she passed the report to him to read.

Mario read the results, "Connie, my daughter" tears rolled down his

cheeks, Connie went to him, and they hugged, her tears fell then

too, they sobbed together which felt like an eternity before Connie

broke away from their embrace.

"I can't believe it, all this time, all these years and we knew

nothing" she said wiping her tears away.

"My bella, bella girl, I am so proud to be your papa, I can't love you

anymore than I already do and now you are going to make me a

grandpapa again too," Mario was quite overcome by emotion

"I couldn't have wished for a better father Mario" agreed Connie.

"We will have to think about this 'Mario' too, is it too soon for you to call me papa, I would be honoured if you did, my darling precious daughter," said Mario.

"Papa, I like it, it might take some getting used to," she smiled fondly at him, but then added "what about Gabriella and Marco?" Connie realised then, that if Mario wanted to be known as her papa, people would have to be told the truth.

"I will speak to them tonight and tell them that they have a sister" said Mario proudly.

Connie suddenly realised that her grandparents must be told too!

"I have been thinking about moving to Italy," said Mario, "I am going to sell this house, far too big, I should have sold it years ago, buy myself a little flat closer to the sea front here, and then a little house in Italy, I can spend a few months there and then a few months here, I don't want to be away from you and this little one for long" he smiled, "I wish I had known about you, why didn't Laura tell me?"

"maybe she thought it for the best, you had already gone through the heartache of losing your wife and knowing how ill mum was she probably didn't want to put you through that again, we will never know what she was thinking, but it seems as if she pushed Giac away when she knew how ill she was and maybe that's why she didn't tell you about me in case you wanted to be with her again and she didn't want to hurt you" Connie tried to reason

"At least we know now, whatever her reason" agreed Mario.

"I'm going back to Italy too at the end of the month for a wedding, myself and Carole, Alex's mum are flying to Naples on the 26th we are staying with Alex for a few days and then attending the wedding of the couple I worked with in Italy, Alex's colleagues, in Amalfi in that wonderful church with all the steps" said Connie.

"That sounds wonderful, I remember going to the Amalfi coast when I was a young man, before I was married, maybe I could fly out with you both and I could hire a car and see the old country and check out some possible homes" said Mario excitedly.

"Yes, that would be great, and you know Alex works for Rivolli's estate agents she'll be able to help you look for a house over there, do you think you're up to travelling?" asked Connie

"Definitely! The doctor has given me the all clear so I'm raring to go!" laughed Mario.

They chatted some more about Nice Ice and the new staff Connie had taken on, Tom a mature University student and Chloe a sixth form student, so far they had both been reliable and efficient and the customers seemed to like them, Nicola was thriving in her new post as Manageress and Connie had no worries about leaving Nice Ice in her capable hands when she went to Italy at the end of the month. Mario who was now allowed to drive again gave Connie a lift back to 'Sea Breeze' her grandparents cottage to tell them the latest news. Mario had wanted to tell them too, so Connie relented, and he parked his car outside the gates of the cottage and walked up the path together and Connie let them both in with her key.

"Hello, I'm home" Called Connie, as she walked into the house "I've brought Mario back, we've got some news."

"In here love" answered Mary her voice coming from the lounge Connie pushed open the lounge door, Mary and Sid were watching the television, Mary turned down the volume when she saw them "Mario how are you, Connie told us that you have been ill," said Mary.

"Better now thank you, how are you both, Mr, Mrs Devereux" he acknowledged Mary and Sid.

"Gran, Granddad, Mario and I found something out today and we have come to tell you both," said Connie.

Her grandparents waited for the news in anticipation,

"That I am Connie's real father," said Mario.

Mary and Sid looked at each other in surprise, as Mario went on to tell them the same story that he had told Connie about how he had met and eventually fallen in love with Laura, but it wasn't to be, and she met Giac and moved to London with him assuming like everyone else that Connie was Giac's daughter.

"Well, this has come as a big surprise, we never had any idea that there was anything going on between you and Laura, did we Sid?" said Mary.

Sid shook his head, "no idea" he agreed.

Connie told them about the DNA test and that she and Mario were more than happy to know that they were father and daughter, and that Mario would be telling his children tonight.

Her grandparents were shocked and somewhat subdued by the news, but both agreed that it was a good thing for them all to know the truth at last.

"Does Mario know he is going to be a grandfather?' asked Mary once Mario had left the cottage to first speak to Gabriella at her house and then his son Marco over the telephone to let them know that Connie was his daughter.

Connie nodded.

"And have you told him anything about the baby's father?" asked Mary.

Connie shook her head.

"Now Connie you don't want history repeating itself, you know how you have been over Giac and then finding out about Mario, you don't want to do the same to this baby and its father" Mary continued.

"It's Connie's business, Mary" said Sid in Connie's defense, "but your gran is right, it is something you should give a lot of thought too, as you know what a shock it's been for us all finding out about Mario after all these years!"

Chapter 26

Connie was glad to climb into her bed that night, what a day it had been!

Seeing and hearing her baby for the first time, that had been amazing and then finding out that Mario was definitely her father- that was equally as mind blowing, not to mention that she was now finally the owner of her own business 'Nice Ice'. And what about this song that Alex was all excited about 'Celtic Girl' Connie had listened and re-listened to it, and unless Wyatt had been meeting and dating lots of girls in a hot climate then it certainly did sound as if the song was about her and their brief romance, did he mean what he said in the words of the song?

'My Celtic Girl, will you ever forgive me?'

'My Celtic Girl I wish that I had never left you'

'My Celtic Girl you mean the world to me'

Connie tossed and turned despite her tired state, her mind would not settle and when she finally dropped off to sleep her dreams were filled with a mixture of scan pictures which had photos of Wyatt on them, and the sound of the babies' heartbeat intermingled with his song 'My Celtic Girl!'

The next two weeks passed without any more days being quite as eventful. Mario had spoken to his children Marco and Gabriella who had been quite understandably shocked at first to hear that they had a half-sister, angry that they hadn't known, and then slightly more understanding when Mario had explained how he and Connie had only found out themselves.

"Connie was always your golden girl" sulked Gabriella, "are you sure that you didn't already know, or had guessed?"

"I assure you my love, I had no idea until Connie spoke to me about Giac not being her real father!" answered Mario, "If I had known then of course I would have taken my responsibilities very seriously!"

Marco had been more concerned that Connie had paid a fair price for Nice Ice and that it would affect his inheritance now that Connie would have to be taken into consideration too.

"Money! Is that all you can think of, Connie and I concluded business before we even had known that she was my daughter!" Mario had answered back quite angrily, "and for you information she paid a fair price and yes it will affect your inheritance now, as Connie is as much my daughter as you are my son!"

After a few days they had both thawed a bit and Mario was glad, as he had managed to book a plane ticket to Italy on the same flight as Connie and Carole and didn't want to leave on bad terms with his children, no matter how they had angered and disappointed him over the Connie revelation. Connie had sorted out the rota for Nice Ice and Nicola assured her that she could deal with suppliers' customers' staff and anything else that came her way.

"Everything is fine here, don't worry, just go and pack and look forward to having a lovely couple of days away, you deserve a nice break" she had told an anxious Connie.

"Are you sure, you've got my number if there's a problem and Mario said if you need help to ring Gabriella" Connie wasn't so sure about Mario's suggestion of Gabriella, but Connie conceded that she had been around the business since she was born so maybe she would be able to help if it was an absolute emergency

"Connie please don't worry everything will be alright" Nicola smiled confidently, and Connie knew that Nicola was more than capable of dealing with any problems that would arise, it was just that now Nice Ice was hers she felt rather protective of it, maybe it was her mothering instinct kicking in, she thought stroking her abdomen gently.

Connie had spent the last few days putting items of clothing into her suitcase, ready for Italy, Alex had informed her that the weather was still warm during the days but cooler into the evenings. When she had been in Sorrento during the summer Connie remembered that every day and night was very hot and that she hadn't needed a jacket or even a cardigan all the time she was there. This time she decided to pack some light jackets and a pashmina to wear over her dress that she had picked out to wear to the wedding. She couldn't believe it when Alex had rung with news of the wedding and then the sub sequential invite- Sofia the eternal party girl and Ricardo the confirmed bachelor- who'd have thought it! Now if Alex had said Sofia and Gianni had got together then yes, she could see that, not that it would last as they were so similar, but not Ricardo, then again who was she to summarise with her track record of romance! Maybe opposites did attract- her and Wyatt had opposite lives definitely, him living the rock star life of nonstop travelling, buying hilltop villas and being hounded by the press and she lives a very modest life, with her only adventure of travel being in the last few months, but on a personal level she had thought that they were very similar and had connected from day one- exactly- what did she know! She was so happy for Ricardo and Sofia though, as she had liked them both so much and they had made her feel so welcome when she was in Sorrento, maybe Sofia felt it was time to settle down and leave her party girl life behind her. Connie had decided on her pink bardot dress that she had worn to her cousins wedding and then on that amazing date with Wyatt, it was made of a slightly stretchy material which was comfortable and fitted over her expanding waistline, teamed with a pale gold pashmina shawl and matching sling back sandals would be ideal for the wedding. Connie folded the dress carefully the touch of the material took her back to 'that date' with Wyatt, being collected in the limousine and then chauffer driven to his luxurious hotel, seeing the suite he was staying in and marveling at all the splendour, and Wyatt in his grey suit looking handsome and very sexy, and that wonderful evening, night and morning that they had spent together. Connie sat down on the edge of her bed remembering it all, and after a wonderful, whirlwind affair, nothing! He hadn't contacted her since he had left Italy, she was sure that he had forgotten about her, but all the media coverage of the split between him and his manager Mike Dolan and all the allegations and now this song, 'My Celtic Girl' Connie just didn't know what to think. Her time and thoughts had been taken up with finding her father, becoming a businesswoman and most importantly coming to terms with her soon to be a mother status! She opened the top drawer of her bedside cabinet and took out a small leather-bound box, which she opened, inside there was the pretty gold bracelet that Wyatt had bought for her on their trip to Capri, she hadn't worn it since she left Italy, she fingered the crystals on it, then closed the box suddenly and put it in her case, no use looking back when there was a lot to look forward to, she told herself.

Connie, Carole and Mario were flying out to Naples a couple of days before the wedding, Mario had booked a taxi to Bristol airport as he didn't know how long he would be staying in Italy so it was easier than taking the car and then having to decide how long to park it for, he had told them the day before they were due to fly, Carole agreed as she was hoping to stay on too and help him with the house hunting, it looked as if Connie would be returning to Porthcawl on her own.

"When you are ready to go home Connie, I will sort out a taxi to collect you and take you home from the airport, so don't worry" Mario had told her.

Connie had reassured him that she would be fine, but he insisted, so she just nodded in agreement, Mario was enjoying his newfound 'papa' status.

Carole had fancied a break in Italy as she hadn't been for almost a year and after being confined to a wheelchair and to her apartment was desperate for a holiday, so it was agreed that she would accompany Mario on his house finding venture.

After a discussion, Connie and Mario had decided it was the right thing to do, to tell Giac that Mario was Connie's real father. Connie had volunteered to telephone Giac as she was the one who had recently met him and had instigated the discovery of her father. Giac was pleased to hear from her.

"Connie, how lovely, how are you?" He asked, his voice sounding as warm and friendly as she had remembered it in London.

"I'm fine thank you, I've got some news" answered Connie suddenly feeling anxious at the news she had to impart to him.

"Baby news?" he asked hesitantly.

Connie had forgotten that it was Giac who had alerted her to her current state of impending motherhood.

"Yes, you were right, and I knew myself too deep down, I am due next March, I'm feeling much better now no more sickness or

Fainting."

"Wonderful news I am pleased that you are well."

"I have other news too, about my father" she said.

"Oh right, so you have found out who he is?" Giac sounded anxious now.

"Yes, it is Mario, you remember Mario from Nice Ice?"

"Mario? Of course, I remember him, but I had no idea, had he always known?" Giac sounded surprised.

"No, but when I told him about you, he put two and two together, so to speak, and we had a DNA test and it confirmed that he is my father."

"All these years and only just finding out," said Giac sympathetically.

"Yes, and thanks to you, and of course Aunt Con keeping all those letters that led me to you, we have finally found out the truth" answered Connie.

"How does Mario feel about finding out after all these years?" asked Giac.

"He's here with me if you would like to speak to him" Connie turned to Mario who was sitting tentatively to the side of her.

"Thank you Connie, I would like to" answered Giac.

Connie nodded to Mario and handed him the telephone.

The two men started talking and went on in Italian, both shedding tears of past memories and regrets and happiness that the truth had now been discovered, when they had finished their emotional conversation, Mario hung up and wiped his wet cheeks with a tissue "We have agreed to meet when we go to Italy, it's been a long time, but it's something we would both like to do," said Mario.

"That's good" Connie smiled, the two had precious memories to share.

Mario nodded, "Yes, I think it will be good for both of us."

The day came when the three would fly out to Italy, Mario lamenting about his early life there, Carole looking forward to a holiday and Connie looking forward to seeing Alex again and the lovely friends she had made in Sorrento, it had been arranged for Gianni to collect them all from Naples airport. When they came through departures and out into the warm Italian afternoon sun, and saw Gianni slinked over the bonnet of his Lamborghini waving nonchalantly to them, wearing his signature sunglasses, white jeans and pale blue open necked shirt, Connie suddenly felt very emotional. It had only been a few months before she had walked these same steps being met by Gianni, who would have thought so much would have happened in such a short space in time.

"You ok babe?" asked Carole suddenly aware of Connie brushing away her tears.

"I'm fine thanks Carole it's just being back here, you know" Carole knew and understood, she had been filled in about Wyatt and the whirl wind romance that had left Connie heartbroken and pregnant, she squeezed Connie's hand tightly.

"You'll be ok babe, you got me and your papa and our Alex, we'll always all here for you, not to mention Sid and Mary" said Carole protectively.

Connie nodded then braced herself for Gianni's embrace and kisses, she smiled despite herself, "Gianni, he never changes!"

The view on the journey from the airport was as breathtaking as the first time she had arrived in Naples, Mario 'ooed and ahhed' remembering the last time he had seen the bay of Naples, wiping his eyes as he became emotional. They got caught up in heavy traffic halfway into their journey as they all summarised it was probably the busiest time of day for road travel, as they watched numerous vespers weaving in and out of the slow traffic. Finally, after almost two hours of travelling in Gianni's car, they were on the main road in Sorrento, Connie looked at her watch, it showed quarter past six, her stomach was rumbling as she hadn't had anything to eat apart from a toasted sandwich and a tea on the plane and that was hours ago.

"Alex has booked a table for this evening in Romero's" announced Carole reading a message coming through from Alex as her phone was in her hand, she was just about to phone to let Alex know that they were nearly there.

"Good I'm starving!" announced Connie.

Connie was to stay with Alex in her apartment and Carole and Mario had booked a two-bed roomed apartment further down towards the port, Alex had raised her eyebrows and hinted about a holiday romance when Carole had phoned her the previous week to tell her this, but Carole had answered, "Oh for God Sake babe we're grown adults sharing an apartment, in separate rooms!" Alex had laughed and said that Mario was a good-looking single man, and Carole had tutted and said that they were, "Just good friends!" Alex was outside waiting for their arrival, Gianni slowed down and stopped outside her apartment, whilst he got Connie's suitcase from the boot, Alex hugged and kissed her mother and Mario and gave them instructions as to how to get to Romero's for 8pm, Gianni drove them on to their apartment as Connie followed Alex up to her apartment.

"I'm so glad you're here Con, I've really missed you and mam since I've been back here" Alex hugged her tightly, "how are you feeling, I was worried about you travelling,"

"I'm fine, tired and hungry but nothing a shower and a bit of food won't fix" smiled Connie, "I've missed you too, it's been a mad couple of weeks!"

"I bet, "Alex laughed, "You don't do anything by half do you Connie Devereux!"

"No, do I ever!" answered Connie, "Not every day you get pregnant by a rock star, find your father after twenty years only to discover

301

he's not your father but the fella you work for is!"

"And becoming a business owner to boot!" added Alex.

"Sounds crazy saying it out loud!" agreed Connie "Am I ok to grab a shower?"

"Of course, I'll fix you a sandwich too, you know Romero's, table booked for 8, but by the time everyone orders, and it gets served it'll be 9!"

Connie showered and dressed in a beige shirt dress with matching cardigan and sandals she ate the sandwich Alex had made whilst she dried her hair, Alex had dressed in a powder blue body con dress with navy heels, the girls liked to dress up a bit for Romero's as it was one of the nicest restaurants in town.

"It was a hell of a surprise about Sofia and Ricardo!" said Connie

"I know I couldn't believe it myself; I had guessed that there was something going on before they had come out as a couple, but then the engagement and the wedding, it was all so fast!" agreed Alex

"It's lovely news though and getting married in that beautiful cathedral in Amalfi too!" a shadow cast over Connie's face

"You feeling ok Con?" asked Alex suddenly worried.

"I was just remembering when I first saw the cathedral, I was with Sofia and Wyatt, we were eating ice cream and laughing and chatting, it was a lovey day" answered Connie.

"Will you be ok going there; I did worry when Sofia invited you,"

"I'll be fine, I'll be happy to see two lovely people get married, and I'll be there with my Bestie, what more can I ask for" Connie reassured Alex with a smile, determined not to let anything upset her.

Chapter 27

Connie woke early the next morning, the sun was peeking through the shutters on Alex's spare room where she had slept, it had been a lovely evening at Romero's, Carole and Mario had been the life and soul of the restaurant. Mario was in his element being back 'home' as he called it, being back in Italy, and now Carole was fully recovered following her accident she was determined to have a good time! The girls had left at ten thirty as Connie was tired, so they had left Mario and Carole to enjoy the night chatting and dancing with the locals in Romero's.

Alex was already up and had made them a fresh coffee each, welcoming Connie as she entered the lounge area of the apartment "How did you sleep?" asked Alex handing Connie her coffee

"I think I fell asleep as soon as my head hit the pillow, it's been a busy couple of weeks, it was a nice evening though, I think your mother and my father were a hit in Romero's."

Alex laughed, remembering their parents dancing to the live band the previous night, who had played after dinner, "yes definitely, they seem to have become quite close, we might end up as sisters soon!"

"Yes, they do appear to have got quite friendly over the past few months, Mario, or papa" Connie smiled as she emphasised the word 'papa' "was taking your mum to her appointments and out shopping, after your dad moved out, and since she's been back on her feet, they've been out walking and beach cleaning, which has been good for papa following his stroke."

"Well, they are both free agents, I think it's great for them both," said Alex.

"Me too, they've both been on their own for a long time, so you never know, hope they are luckier in love than us!" said Connie.

Alex agreed, "Sofia asked if we'd like to join her tonight in Romero's, again, she's having a little get together, a hen night, bit mad the night before the wedding, but she said she would only be having one or two drinks as she is spending the night at her parents, being all traditional before the big day and wanted to be, what did she say, grown up and sensible!"

"I never thought I'd hear Sofia say those words, Ricardo has certainly made an impression on her!" laughed Connie.

"Must be love!" Alex said, "As it is their last day in work today before the wedding and honeymoon, Ricardo said we will close half day, and then next week I'm in on my own, they are off on their honeymoon to Rome for a week, so if you fancy a change from ice cream selling you can always stay on and give me a hand."

"The last time I did that I ended up getting pregnant!" answered Connie.

"True, but at least you won't get pregnant again!" Alex laughed as Connie launched a cushion off the sofa at her.

"I should be home by lunch time so if you fancy a bite to eat, we could go to Luca's he'll be pleased to see you back" suggested Alex

"Sounds great, this morning I said I'd meet your mum and Mario, sorry, papa, "Connie corrected herself, "It's strange calling Mario papa after all these years, nice, but strange."

"I'll bet, how is it going 'the papa daughter situation'?" asked Alex as she busied herself getting ready for work.

"Good, and as I have Nice Ice now the times when we see each other is leisure time not busy work time which is good, mind you he still likes to know what's happening in the parlour, it was his entire life for so long" answered Connie.

"I'll bet he doesn't know what to do with himself" joked Alex

"I think getting his house sorted for selling and his plans for Italy have been keeping him busy."

"Yes, he's already mentioned to me about helping him find somewhere over here, that's our plan for next week and apparently he's put in an offer for an apartment in mam's black of flats too!" said Alex brushing her hair back into a mid-ponytail and fastening it in place with a scrunchie.

"Yes, it's a nice apartment, I had thought about maybe putting in an offer, but it's on the top floor and I didn't think it would be a good idea once the baby is born, what with a pram and everything, so I mentioned it to Mario and he loved it, and it's close to your mum!" Connie smiled and raised her eyebrows.

"They've got it all worked out by the look of it Con" Alex laughed,

"Have you seen anything suitable for you and my little niece or nephew?" she asked.

Connie shook her head, "No nothing at the moment, I haven't found anywhere that has everything I think I want, I'd like a garden and somewhere not too far from Nice Ice, Mario suggested his house, but it's just so big and needs so much work on it, don't think it's been modernised since he moved in, plus he drove to work as it's a bit far out, and that's something else I need to do when the baby is born. Learn to drive!"

"Sounds like you've got a busy couple of months ahead of you, new home, new baby and possibly new car, on top of a new business, I'm so proud of you Con, you are making such a good life for yourself and the baby" Alex put down her hairbrush and picked up her handbag.

"I hope that I will, I've still got a long way to go, but it's definitely all coming together."

"You know that if you change your mind, I can always help you find an apartment here in Sorrento to buy and then Nicola can run Nice Ice and I can help you look after the baby over here" Alex winked, Connie wasn't sure if she was joking or not, although the idea was mad it did sound quite tempting too!

Alex left for work then and Connie decided to get ready to meet Mario and Carole. She had bought some comfy palazzo pants with elasticated waists; she had felt, especially over the past two weeks that she had put on weight around her abdomen as the baby was growing bigger. The trouser pants together with a loose skimming top would be both comfortable and smart for the coming months, she dressed in a navy and white striped pair with a matching white top and white slip-on loafers, and she tied her hair up in a bun and surveyed herself in the mirror. Yes, she had definitely put on weight she turned from side to side. She was hoping to pick up a few bits for the baby here in Sorrento, as she had remembered spotting a baby boutique back in the summer that had exquisite clothes and accessories for little ones. Who'd have thought that she would be back here almost four months later with the view to purchase baby things!

Connie spent a lovely morning strolling around Sorrento with Carole and Mario, it was warm but not too hot, Mario wanting to buy the baby boutique out, exclaiming excitedly to anyone who would listen, that he couldn't wait to become a 'grandpapa' again!

They all met at Lucas for lunch, Luca remembering Carole from past visits to Sorrento and being pleased to make the acquaintance of Mario, the two talked away excitedly in their native tongue, "Luca said he knew you had to be Italian, the first time he set eyes on you!" announced Mario excitedly, he beamed at Connie, tears sparkling in his eyes" My beautiful daughter!"

Connie smiled back, dear Mario; he was so happy that he had finally found out that Connie was his daughter.

"Mario, Ricardo has asked if you would like to join himself and Gianni and a few others tonight for a couple of drinks as we are meeting up with Sofia," said Alex.

"I would love to, it's so good being home, and new friends now too" Mario mopped his eyes as he became emotional for the third time that day, the first being in the baby boutique, the second when he spoke of Connie to Luca and now here, he was again wiping his eyes.

The 'Boys' were off to a little bar down by the port, not far from where Carole and Mario were staying and had arranged to meet at 7, whilst the 'girls' had arranged to meet at Romero's at the same time. Sofia arrived wearing a beautiful green lace dress, following the tradition of brides wearing green for luck the night before their wedding day. She threw her arms around Connie as she entered the venue, kissing her on both cheeks, "Connie how are you; you look so well!" she stood back and eyed Connie up and down her eyed stopping on her middle, she looked at Connie curiously, "Connie?"

"Yes, I'm pregnant!" said Connie in answer to her curious look

Sofia hugged her again, "and is it Wyatt Morgan's baby?" she asked, never being one to hold back.

Connie nodded, "Yes, and I haven't seen or heard from him, but this is my baby and were going to be just fine!"

Sofia smiled and answered, "Yes! I think you will Connie Devereux"

The girls were shown to their table, Connie, Alex and Carole together with Sofia, her sisters Lucia and Isabella took their seats and were quickly joined by Gabriella, Maria and Emilia, Sofia's friends.

When they had finished their meals, Connie got up to go to the toilet and was joined by Sofia, "I couldn't believe it when Alex told me about you and Ricardo, talk about whirlwind!" said Connie.

"I know, all that time he had been 'under my nose', all those wasted years with silly boys and my knight in shining armor, my prince, had been there all along!" Sofia laughed dreamily.

"I'm so happy for you both; you make a beautiful couple." said Connie.

"Seeing you today has made me very broody, so I hope we will have beautiful babies too very soon," laughed Sofia.

As the girls entered separate cubicles Connie felt a pang of jealousy, Sofia was so lucky, Ricardo would make a wonderful dad, whilst her baby probably would never get to know his or her dad.

Sofia ordered prosecco all around and made a toast, Connie stuck to fizzy water,

"Thank you for all coming tonight, my last night as a single girl!" The others whooped.

"This is my last glass tonight as I want a clear head to marry my prince tomorrow!" the others joked and whooped again.

"Drink up girls and I'll see you tomorrow, I'll be the one in the white dress!" Sofia laughed as she raised her glass in a toast.

Everyone raised their glasses to a hubbub of 'good lucks' and 'all the bests', Connie and Alex exchanged meaningful glances, Alex wishing it was her wearing the white dress tomorrow and seeing Jared Jones standing at the altar with his green eyes looking on at her adoringly, and Connie wishing it was her with Wyatt Morgan looking handsome and smiling at her as she walked down the aisle to him.

Connie and Alex walked Carole back to her apartment when they left shortly after Sofia.

"She's a lucky girl, landing herself a fella like Ricardo Rivolli" Said Carole as they walked through the streets, quieter than during the day, but still lively enough, "He must have a couple of bob, what with owning his own business, and I wouldn't kick him out of bed either!"

"Mam!" chastised Alex.

The girls started laughing,

"Well, I don't know what you two are laughing for, I wouldn't! he's a good-looking fella!" Answered Carole indignantly.

"And too young for you mam! You've already ended up in hospital once this year, if you go chasing men half your age you'll end up in there again!"

"What do you mean?" asked Carole.

"Well, you'll either give yourself a heart attack chasing them or you'll end up getting a slap off one of their girlfriends!" answered Alex seriously.

It was Carole's turn to laugh now, "Your face!" she said laughing at Alex's 'school marm' expression, "I'm only joking, he is a good catch though!"

Determined that the joke wouldn't be on her, Alex retaliated with, "Like Mario mam, he's a good catch!"

"Yes, he is" answered Carole determined not to rise to the challenge.

"I'm not sure if I'm keen on my father being talked about like this!" laughed Connie.

"Sorry Con, I keep forgetting, "Alex turned back to Carole, "but I don't know, you two down here cosying up in an apartment" She teased.

"Well, that's for us to know and you to find out!" replied Carole tartly.

"That's told you Al!" laughed Connie.

They had arrived at Carole and Mario's apartment block, Mario was still out with Ricardo,

"I hope that there's no bad heads in the morning!" said Carole.

"I expect you'll be there to make it better!" joked Alex.

"Ooh you!" laughed Carole.

The girls said their goodbyes to Carole and caught a taxi back to Alex's apartment, not relishing the climb back up from the port at ten o clock in the night!

Sofia mentioned starting a family" said Connie when the girls were getting ready for bed.

"I'm not surprised seeing how loved up they are, looks like we'll be looking for some new staff soon in Rivolli's because I remember Sofia saying before that if she ever had children that she would like to give up work, so unless she's changed her mind" answered Alex

"I'll have to give up work for a while too, I'm glad that I have Nicola and the new staff to rely on," said Connie.

"You could give up all together and come here and work part time in Rivolli's" said Alex, for the second time that day.

"Something's telling me that you'd like me to come and live here!" said Connie.

"It would be lovely though Con, especially if Mario comes to live here too."

"I think he's looking more towards Sienna, but I don't really know, I don't think he's sure himself"

"Worth you thinking about it?" asked Alex "Maybe" answered Connie, but didn't think it was possible, not really, "See you in the morning! Good night."

Chapter 28

The day of Sofia and Ricardo's wedding had arrived; the weather

was warm but not too hot for late September in Southern Italy.

"Looks like a beautiful day for Sofia and Ricardo's nuptials" said Alex

as she opened the curtains to let the sun stream through the

window.

"I'm so glad, and for us too, in our summer frocks!" answered

Connie.

Alex agreed, as she finished pressing her elegant Zara dress in

peach, hanging it back on the hanger along with its matching short,

boxy suit style jacket.

"That's gorgeous, Al" said Connie admiring Alex's suit, "and the

shoes and bag will look absolutely beautiful with it"

Alex had put her shoes and bag on the chair next to where the suit

was hanging; they were of a slightly darker coral colour and set the

suit off a treat.

"I thought I'd treat myself; I haven't bought anything new to wear

for ages, and it's not every day your boss and work mate get

hitched!"

"Good for you, I haven't bought anything new, I'm wearing my pink

bardot dress, it's the only nice dress that I have that still fits me, I

can't believe how much weight I've put on!" Connie said, as she put

her hands on her abdomen.

"Oh Con, it's so exciting, that's your baby growing in there, and you'll look beautiful in your pink dress and the gold pashmina you've brought will look really chic," said Alex.

"Hope I can walk on those gold heels too, mind you I think I'll take a pair of flip flops in my bag to change in case my feet start hurting" Connie laughed, she had never been one to be comfortable in heels and now she was pregnant her feet seemed to hurt even more than before.

"If you have room in your bag, take them, it could be a long day and you need to be comfortable" agreed Alex, suddenly wondering if her own feet would hold out in her new high heels!

The girls had a leisurely light breakfast, being warned not to eat too much by Mario, as the wedding receptions in Italy were notoriously plentiful with many, many, courses.

"To soak up all the wine most probably, as I've heard that it's free flowing throughout the day and into the night" said Alex, as she poured herself and Connie a fresh orange juice to accompany the omelettes she had made them.

The girls were being collected in a minibus provided by Ricardo, which would pick them up first and then collect others on the way to the cathedral, including Carole and Mario now too, who had been cordially invited as Carole's plus one! As neither Connie nor Alex had a plus one, they were happy to accompany each other. The transport arrived at 1.30pm and the girls clambered in as it drove towards the port area to collect Carole and Mario, and then on to collect Maria and Gabriella (Sofia's friends) who lived on the outskirts of Sorrento. As they drove along the Amalfi coast road, Connie marveled at the view of the aqua blue ocean below, watching the various boats and yachts as they bobbed on the ocean, bringing back memories of her first date to Capri with Wyatt on the 'Princess of Capri'.

"We're here!" announced Maria, as the minibus came to a halt, they all alighted and walked the short walk to Piazza Del Duomo, where the majestic Cathedral towered above them. It wasn't as hot as the last time Connie had visited here, where she had sheltering from the heat of the sun enjoying the local ice cream.

They ascended the steps of the cathedral, as they neared the top Connie didn't know if it was the steep climb of the sixty plus steps in the heat of the late September sun or the memories of admiring the magnificent cathedral last time in the company of Wyatt, but she suddenly felt lightheaded.

"Are you ok?" asked Alex concerned at Connie's wavering walk and pale complexion.

"Yes, I just came over a bit woosy, I'll be ok in a second" answered Connie smiling weakly to reassure Alex.

Mario was at her side, "Come on Connie, let's get you inside and sat down, are you sure that you are ok?" he looked at her as he took her arm, his big brown eyes full of concern.

"I'm fine, probably the bus journey and then these steps, I'll be alright after a sit down" she reassured him.

The big bronze doors were open to welcome in the wedding guests and Mario helped Connie into the magnificent cathedral and to a pew halfway down the aisle, accompanied by Alex and Carole. Connie felt better once inside, it was cool, and she felt relaxed by the sounds of music drifting from the cathedral organ.

"Better now?" asked Carole concerned too.

Connie nodded.

"It's nice and cool in here too" said Alex, she looked around her, the cathedral was filling up with guests, she recognised a few as Ricardo's and Sofia's families, even though she had lived just a few kilometres away she could count on both hands the times she had visited Amalfi and this was the first time she had actually been inside the grand Cathedral of St Andrew ,better known as Duomo di Amalfi, she marveled at the interior, the dozens of chandeliers that hung above the congregations heads, the intricate artwork that adorned the walls, pillars and ceilings, what an amazing place to get married, she thought. Her eye line wandered to the altar, Ricardo was standing there looking smart in is dark blue suit, he turned and smiled nervously at his guests and turned back to speak to Gianni, his best man standing next to him and looking as smart as Ricardo in their matching suits. Above the altar was a painting of the martyrdom of St Andrew, whom the Cathedral was named after, Gianni caught sight of the painting and shivered slightly at the graphic depiction of a crucifixion, he hadn't been in a church let alone a cathedral since he was a youngster, it always unnerved him a bit, all those paintings of martyrdom and religion, it wasn't for him, and neither was marriage he thought as he glanced at his unusually nervous looking big brother! He turned to look at the congregation, his mood suddenly feeling a lot lighter when he spotted some ladies he was yet acquainted with.

The organ music changed key, and everyone looked towards the back of the cathedral, Sofia and her father had arrived, and only fifteen minutes late! They began the walk up the aisle towards the altar, and Sofia becoming Mrs Rivolli!

Sofia looked absolutely stunning, dressed in a white lace dress edged with diamond droplets, she shimmered as she walked down the aisle smiling at all her guests from under her delicately embroidered veil, she held onto her proud father's arm as they glided down the aisle, followed by her two sisters Lucia and Isabella dressed in delicate pink and several smaller girls, nieces and cousins dressed in the same pink, all carrying posies of flowers in smaller versions of Sofia's lush bouquet.

After the ceremony Sofia and Ricardo had posed for photographs outside the cathedral, its mosaic facade with elements of Romanesque, byzantine, gothic and baroque style provided a breathtaking and romantic backdrop for stunning photos, then down on the beach for more photographs, with the climax being when Sofia tossed her bouquet into the excited group of single ladies that had gathered, only to be caught by Carole!

Alex looked at her mother's happy, flushed pink face, and Mario smiling broadly, and whispered to Connie, "See I told you, bet we'll be sisters by Christmas!"

Connie laughed and dug Alex in the ribs; she was feeling much better now, although she was glad, she had her flip flops tucked into her bag as she felt she would need to change her shoes before too long.

Two hours after watching Sofia and her father glide down the aisle, the wedding party arrived at Sofia's Auntie Francesca's restaurant to enjoy a sumptuous wedding breakfast.

A numerous course buffet had been arranged for the wedding breakfast and Francesca had her staff to set it out on tables inside the air-conditioned restaurant surrounding a magnificent wedding cake that was made with fresh cream and adorned with fresh fruit. Tables were set up both inside and outside the restaurant for guests, and also down onto the street outside too, to accommodate the close on 100 guests. Two of the restaurant staff was walking around with huge silver metal trays carrying glasses filled with prosecco and red and white wine as they weaved between the guests distributing the alcoholic refreshments.

Alex commandeered a table just inside the restaurant door, suggesting that if it got a bit chilly later on that they would be best inside, she carried 4 glasses to their table, three wines and fizzy water for Connie.

"What a beautiful wedding!" exclaimed Carole.

"Sofia looked gorgeous" Said Connie, they all agreed, "Like a princess!"

"Ricardo scrubbed up well too, not that he doesn't always wear a suit to work, but today he looked very smart!" said Alex

"I love a man in a suit!" agreed Carole.

Connie didn't know if it was her imagination, but Mario began adjusting his jacket and straightening his tie, preening like a peacock, she smiled to herself, perhaps Alex was right, that there was something going on between her father and Alex's mother.

Food was eaten, and speeches were made, and Ricardo announced that the live music was to begin shortly and that 'he and Mrs Rivolli' would be having their first dance, to an answer of cheers and applause from all of their wedding guests.

"Think I'll pass on the dancing" said Connie rubbing her feet as she changed her shoes into her comfy flip flops.

"Come on you two you don't want to miss the first dance!" said Carole getting up to go outside to where the live band had set up and an area had been cleared to make room for a dance floor, fairy lights adorned the trees that lined the dance area with the twinkling lights giving it a fairytale romantic like atmosphere.

They went outside to join the other guests to watch the new Mr and Mrs Rivolli dance their first dance, it was to an instrumental version, which Alex recognised as an Ed Sheeran song, other couples started to join them on the dance floor, including Carole and Mario, Alex noticed that Gianni had found himself a willing partner who was cosied up to him slow dancing, she smiled, saying to herself 'same old Gianni!'

"I'm going to get a drink!" said Alex to Connie, as she turned to walk back inside, glad to get away from all the cosy dancing couples

"I'll come with you, I could do with another sit down, what am I like, there's our parents whirling around the floor like professionals off 'strictly' and I'm ready for a sit down!"

Connie linked Alex's arm as they returned inside the restaurant

It was quieter inside as most of the guests were outside dancing or just sitting sipping their drinks, but the music outside could still be heard. The band changed from instrumental and now a male voice had joined them to sing, Alex had returned with a drink for them both, they sipped them as they chatted whilst listening to the outside music. Connie put her glass down suddenly as she listened to the song being played outside,

'My Celtic Girl, will you ever forgive me?'

'My Celtic Girl I wish that I had never left you'

'My Celtic Girl you mean the world to me'

"Al?" she looked at Alex questioningly.

"That's Wyatt Morgan's song, isn't it?" answered Alex as she was now also listening intently.

"That's not just his song Al, That's HIM!" Connie felt like the room was spinning around her, was she hearing things, it couldn't be him surely, could it?

Connie got up from her seat, steadying herself on the table, Alex was at her side, she took her arm as they went outside. There were people everywhere, the dance floor area where the band was playing was hidden from their view, Alex pushed through the throng of bodies, pulling Connie behind her, they finally got to the edge of the dance floor, couples were swaying and dancing, as Alex moved her head around to try and see the band, she pointed turning to Connie, "Look there Con, you can see the band through there!" she had to raise her voice to Connie, to be heard over the music. Connie moved position to see where Alex was pointing, Alex pressed her forward to the edge of the dance floor, Connie looked across the dance floor and as her eyes fixed on the singer's face, he spotted her, their eyes locked, she turned back to the crowd behind her, suddenly she felt claustrophobic, she had to get away, get some air, the singing stopped, the band stopped playing, "Connie, Connie Devereux!" a voice came over the sound system, the unmistakable sound of Wyatt Morgan's Black Country accent. Connie stopped and turned back towards the dance floor, the dancers stopped dancing, the guests went quiet, she looked at Alex, who was staring at her, everything seemed as if it was in slow motion, someone shone a stage light onto her, all eyes were on her now.

"Connie I'm sorry, please wait, I need to speak to you,"

Connie felt as if her feet were glued to the floor, she felt as if she couldn't move even if she had wanted to, she looked back in the direction that Wyatt's voice was coming from, temporarily blinded by the spotlight.

"Please Connie, I love you!"

The silence was replaced by whoops from the crowd, she felt Alex grab her hand, Wyatt had put down his guitar and was coming towards her, she felt she couldn't breathe, she caught sight of Mario also moving towards her, her head was spinning again, "Connie!" It was Alex voice now, but it sounded strange far away, Alex felt far away.

The next thing Connie knew she was back in the restaurant lying propped up on some chairs with a concerned looking Sofia holding a glass of water to her lips; she took a sip from the proffered glass "You frightened us!" Said Sofia.

"I'm sorry," answered Connie hoarsely, she looked around at the concerned faces of Alex, Carole, Mario, Ricardo and Wyatt Morgan "Trust you to upstage me on my wedding day!" said Sofia, happier to joke know she saw Connie had come to.

"I'm sorry" Connie repeated, she took another sip of water, "I'm only joking, we were so worried and it's all my fault!" said Sofia.

Connie frowned at this admission.

"No, it's my fault, I'm so sorry Connie I didn't mean to give you a turn!" it was Wyatt talking now, "I managed to get a flight here a couple of days ago and came down to Rivolli's to see if anyone would be able to help me get in touch with you."

Alex spoke now, "I didn't see you" she said sharply looking at Wyatt

"No, you were out with a client, Sofia was very cross with me when she saw me" he smiled slightly, glancing at Sofia, "I had a right ear bashing about not ringing you and all the crap in the press about me and Jayde Johnson!"

"You deserved it, I was very, very cross!" she answered sternly, nodding at Connie to show her how cross she had been.

"I know it's no excuse but basically Dolan had full control of me professionally, financially and personally in the states, I had no freedom and no phone, it all came to ahead and Jayde helped me as she could see what was happening and to cut a long story short I've had to get a lawyer and I'm hoping to be free of that bastard" he apologised for his language as he could see Mario bristle, "sorry, of Dolan, and as soon as I could leave I got on a plane and came here to the villa to get my head together and to find you, Connie."

"I hadn't heard anything from you and then all I read was about you and this Jayde Johnson being together, I thought that you had forgotten about me" Connie's voice sounded stronger now.

"Never Con, it was you and the thought of seeing you that kept me going, and Jayde has been a good friend, helped me release My Celtic Girl independent of Dolan, but Con there's nothing to worry about, she'd be more interested in you than in me, but you know management, making up some romance between the two of us, Dolan thought it'd be good for my image in the states!"

Connie smiled weakly, as Wyatt continued, holding her hand and crouching beside her.

"When I told Sofia that I wanted to see you, Ricardo said that you were coming here, to Italy for the wedding, and I asked if I could sing in the reception, I thought that if you heard me singing My Celtic Girl, you'd know how much I love you, you know that I wrote that song for you, don't you Con?" Wyatt looked like that little vulnerable boy again, as he looked at her pleadingly.

"Alex guessed and yes I thought it might be too" Connie answered

"Are you feeling alright Con, do you want to go back to the apartment?" Alex asked concerned.

"I'm ok, but I think I should go soon, I'm feeling tired" answered Connie.

"Will you consider coming back with me to the villa, I've got a car outside, it's just that I feel we've got so much catching up to do, and now that I've found you I don't want to let you go, but obviously that's up to you, I mean you might have moved on, and I wouldn't blame you, not hearing from me all these months, but if you will give me another chance, I swear I'll never let you down again!" It

325

was some speech, Mario and Carole exchanged glances, Sofia and
Ricardo knew how much he loved her and hoped shed say yes, and
Alex sat next to her protectively, but even she was secretly
impressed by Wyatt's declaration of love.

Connie sat up in the chair that she had been lounging on, she
looked at her friends and family expectant expressions,

"Please, Sofia, Ricardo, go back to your guests and enjoy your
beautiful wedding party, I am fine." they hesitated, "Honestly I am,
please go back and enjoy yourselves."

"Are you sure?" asked Ricardo.

"Yes" Answered Connie, "Go!" she waved her hand at them in a
shooing but friendly gesture.

"You too," she said to Alex, Mario and Carole, as Sofia and Ricardo
departed, Sofia blowing her an air kiss.

"But Connie..." started Mario.

"I'm fine now," she answered.

Mario frowned.

"Really, papa."

"Come on you two let's leave these youngsters alone, they have
lots to discuss" said Carole diplomatically, pulling on Mario's arm

"Papa?" asked Wyatt, remembering what Connie had told him
about her father "then you found him?"

"Yes, but it's a long story" answered Connie, smiling at her 'papa'
fondly.

Wyatt rose to his feet and offered his hand to Mario,

"I guess this is a strange way to meet, but I'm Wyatt Morgan and I love your daughter," Mario shook Wyatt's hand as he added, looking lovingly at Connie, "very much indeed sir."

Mario nodded, "I hear what you say Morgan and I hope you mean what you say, because Connie is a very special girl, and if you ever hurt her..." he trailed off as Connie glared at him and Carole tugged on his arm again.

"Papa, go and enjoy the party with Carole, please, I'm ok, you too Alex," said Connie.

"If you are sure, you know where I am if you need me" Alex kissed Connie on the cheek as the three of them went back outside to rejoin the party, albeit Mario going reluctantly.

Wyatt sat down next to Connie, "They are very protective of you, and I can't blame them, but will you give me a chance?" he asked looking deep into Connie's eyes, she felt her stomach do a somersault.

She swallowed hard and nodded.

Wyatt put his arms around her and held her to him, "Thank you Connie, I was so nervous about being here tonight, more nervous than playing in front of an audience of thousands, because I didn't know if you still wanted me."

"Of course, I did, I thought you didn't want me, and why would you? Being rich and famous, you could have anyone" answered Connie

returning his hug.

Wyatt pulled away from their embrace, "But I didn't want anyone else, we had a connection and a wonderful time together, I couldn't stop thinking about you when I went away, I just hoped that I could find you and that you wanted to be with me"

"It's not just me though," said Connie looking down at her growing bump.

Wyatt looked at her intently.

"I'm fourteen weeks pregnant Wyatt,"

His eyes widened and his mouth slackened, she went on, "You're going to be a father."

"Connie, oh my God, I can't believe it," he held her to him again "Oh Con!"

"Are you happy, because if you are not its tough because..." she didn't finish, his mouth found hers and he kissed her tenderly

"That's the most wonderful news I could have heard, apart from you saying that you'll give us a chance, I'm so sorry Con, you've been through all this alone, no wonder everyone was so concerned about you fainting, do you think we should get you seen by a doctor, you know just to make sure that everything is ok?"

"Don't you start fussing now too" joked Connie, then added "Come on let's go back to your villa, I think we've got a lot to talk about."

Chapter 29

Alex was back in work the next morning, Ricardo had said for her to take the day off, but she had told him that she had a few things that she needed to do and a client to ring and was happy to open up. He had conceded, Alex was in charge for the next week, so if she wanted to work, it was fine by him, he had more important things on his mind, things like getting married and going on a honeymoon.

Alex had left the wedding party the same time as Connie and Wyatt, accepting Wyatt's lift home. Connie had needed to collect some things from the apartment to stay at the villa with Wyatt and Alex had taken the opportunity to leave, everyone was so loved up, Sofia and Ricardo, Gianni and his latest lady friend, Connie and Wyatt and even her own mother and Mario! She felt that she had seen enough loved up couples for one day and couldn't wait to return to the solitude of her little apartment. Of course, she was happy for Connie and Wyatt, and didn't begrudge any of the others, not really, but she wasn't in the mood for any more PDAs (public displays of affection) She made her excuses and left. Wyatt had hired a car and drove carefully along the narrow winding coastal road, returning to the bright lights and wider roads of Sorrento. Between them, she and Wyatt had persuaded Connie to get checked out by a local doctor who Ricardo had recommended, and she felt happier as she kissed Connie goodbye, as she left to spend some time with Wyatt. The morning in Rivolli's had been quiet and as Alex had completed

all the tasks which she had gone in to do she decided to get on with the pile of filing which had accumulated over the past few weeks that they had all been putting off doing. She had just carried a pile of files to the filing unit situated in the back of the office, when she heard the office door open with a tinkling from the attached bell

"Un momento!" she called behind her as she struggled to get the files on top of the filing cabinet without dropping one, she succeeded, and turned around to see who had entered the office. There standing in front of her was the last person she had expected to see.

"Good morning, Alex" came the familiar voice.

"Jared!" Alex exclaimed, glad she had deposited the files first or she knew that she would have dropped them all in sheer shock!

"I was in the area, and we thought we'd drop in and say hello!" he said smiling that old familiar smile that made her heart flip

Alex had been so surprised to see him standing there in Rivolli's that she hadn't noticed the solemn faced little boy standing next to him holding his hand.

 "This is Theo, my son" announced Jared, "we were just passing, and I told him that daddies' old friend lived here, and we thought we'd pop in and say hello!"

He was so matter of fact, Alex was lost for words and smiled back weakly.

"I hope it's ok" said Jared, "it's just that when I last saw you, I had to

rush off and then I couldn't get hold of you."

Alex found her voice, albeit very quietly, and answered "Yes."

"When I told you that there was someone else that someone else is Theo, I wanted to explain everything to you, but then I had to leave and then you were gone!"

Alex found the edge of the desk behind her and gratefully sat down on it, Jared Jones here in Rivolli's, and with his son! She needed to sit down before she fell down!

Theo tugged on his daddy's hand, "Daddy can I play now?" he asked "There's a nice park just down the street" Alex smiled down at the little boy, a mini version of Jared with dark curly hair and big green eyes.

"Will you join us? Or are you busy?" Asked Jared.

"Er no, I've done what I came in to do, and I didn't really have to come in today, I wanted to ring a client, about a property that had just come available down by the port and Ricardo the boss, he's Ricardo Rivolli, got married yesterday to Sofia, she works here too, so I'm in charge" Alex didn't know why she was going in to such great detail, it was just that having Jared here in her office had completely thrown her off guard and she was now wittering away uncontrollably.

"Great," answered Jared, Theo smiled at Alex, "Come on" he said. Alex locked the office door behind them, she would come back later to finish the filing, this opportunity to speak to Jared was long overdue and something that she needed to do.

They crossed the street as she led them through a lemon grove, and onto the park.

"I can see how you love living here" said Jared as he breathed in the strong citrus smell of the lemons that were growing all around them on the numerous trees, "I remember that lemon smell!" he smiled at Alex, as Theo ran towards a little slide and began to climb.

"He is a lovely little boy, how old is he?" said Alex as they watched Theo play happily.

"He's just turned four" answered Jared.

"You didn't hang around then, you know, after you left me" Alex knew she sounded bitter, but she had barely dated anyone since Jared and here he was with a son that must have been conceived barely weeks after he had returned to Wales.

Jared caught Alex's hand closest to his and pulled her back towards him "I was a mess Al, when I returned home, I was drinking too much, my studies were suffering and yes I made some mistakes, Theo's mother Julia was a drunken one-night stand, I'm not proud of it, I behaved like an ass, but I don't regret Theo, he's my whole world."

Alex stopped walking away from him and they sat down on a bench together.

"So, you're not with his mother" said Alex hopefully.

Jared shook his head, "We were never together, we are friends, and

Julia is married now and has just had another baby, that's how I'm here, well sort of."

Alex listened, as Jared went on.

"I wanted to tell you all this when I came to your mother's apartment, but I didn't get chance."

Alex felt stupid now; if she hadn't ignored his calls and blocked his number, she would have had this conversation with him months ago.

"Julia and her husband Paulo are both doctors too, Paulo is Italian and had the opportunity to work on a project here in Naples, so they moved here to work just before the new baby was born, we share custody of Theo, so he was home in Llanelli with my parents when we met in the hospital and when I came to Carole's."

"I'm sorry that I didn't give you the chance to tell me this, I acted so childish" Alex felt ashamed, "mam had said, that on her last visit to the hospital that you weren't there, she was under the impression that you had moved away."

"I was here, I came over to help on the project that Paulo was working on, and to improve my Italian" he laughed, "it's coming on quite good now, anyway one thing led to another and I've been offered a job here in the hospital in Sorrento, I'm hoping to find somewhere for me to live here, and I thought who do I know in the real estate trade..." he smiled at Alex.

"Oh right, so you're looking for some help to find you somewhere to live" her hopes were dashed if she thought that Jared had come to see her and not for her house selling skills!

"Yes please, I saw one or two places that looked suitable on Rivolli's website."

"If you want to come back to the office with me, I can run through some details and arrange viewing" Alex was in her estate agent mode now, Jared Jones in Sorrento, how would she avoid him now? How would she feel about seeing him here in 'her' town?

"That would be great, but I tell you what, how about if I come in tomorrow, Theo will be back with his mum then and I can give you all my undivided attention" said Jared as he rushed off to catch Theo as he was just about to climb down from the top of the slide

"It's a date" said Alex, then suddenly realising what she'd said, blushing she added, "Sorry, you know what I mean, the date is fixed" she was bumbling again.

Jared returned carrying a wriggling laughing Theo, "A Date sounds good to me" he answered smiling that old familiar smile at Alex, Alex smiled back as her stomach did a somersault.

"I'm hungry!" announced Theo.

"Come on then let's go and get some lunch" said Jared as he put Theo down.

"And you too?" Theo smiled up at Alex.

"If I'm invited and daddy says it's ok then yes please" she answered smiling back at the little boy.

"Definitely" answered Jared, "where do you suggest?"

"Luca's" answered Alex, "I think you'll both like it there."

"Then Luca's it is" announced Jared, Theo held out his hand to Alex and she took it happily, as the three of them walked to Luca's for lunch.

"Signorina Alex welcome, and guests too!" said Luca as they entered the forecourt of his cafe,

"Buon pomeriggio Luca, table for three please!"

Luca showed them to a table in the corner and brought out menus and some crayons and paper for Theo to colour.

"Do you come here often?" Jared laughed realising what he had said, "Sorry, sounds like some cheesy chat up line."

"I don't mind," answered Alex looking at him shyly, adding, "Yes most days for an americano on my way to work, sometimes for lunch and a few times for tea too."

"On your own?" asked Jared suddenly feeling shy as he fiddled with the menu nervously.

"Mostly, unless Connie is over here, she's here at the moment" answered Alex.

"Oh great, I haven't seen Connie in years, is she living here now too?" he asked.

"No, well saying that I'm not so sure," answered Alex truthfully, she had spoken to Connie earlier that morning, and she had seen the doctor who had confirmed that everything was well with both

Connie and the baby, but had been told to rest as her blood pressure was on the high side, Connie was going to ring Nicola in Nice Ice to tell her that she wouldn't be returning home tomorrow as originally planned as she had to rest and that the doctor would see her again next week to see if he thought she needed further rest. She had told Alex that she and Wyatt had talked into the night and that when she would return to Porthcawl that he would be with her. She said that she hadn't ruled out splitting their time between Porthcawl and Sorrento, Connie had said that it had all been such a whirlwind meeting Wyatt again but had confirmed that they were both very much in love with each other and were going to take each day as it came, with the baby being their main priority.

"She's pregnant and the dad who is famous is sort of living in Sorrento, but Connie has just bought Nice Ice from Mario, who turned out to be her real father, so I don't think they know themselves yet where they are going to live!" Said Alex

"Whewwww!" exclaimed Jared, "That's one hell of a story; Mario from Nice Ice is Connie's dad?"

"Yes, she's only just found out, it's quite surreal isn't it?" Alex was enjoying talking to someone who knew all the same people that she knew from home, she felt that she was back in Porthcawl, gossiping with Jared and sharing secrets like the old days.

"And a famous fella," he dropped his voice, and asked conspiracy, "who? Or is it top secret?"

Alex burst out laughing, it was so good to be here with Jared chatting and laughing, even though they had been boy and girl friend they had also been good friends too, and she missed that, "Wyatt Morgan the musician!" she whispered back.

"What!!! Bloody hell, Al, think I need something stronger than this diet coke!" he exclaimed pointing to the drink Luca had just brought "How the hell did she get together with him, he's a huge star!"

"SSHHHH" laughed Alex, "well he was buying a villa from me and then I went home because mam had her accident, and Connie came over here to help out and the rest as they say is history!"

"Could have been you Al, if Carole hadn't had her accident, you could be Mrs Morgan wife of famous rock star!" said Jared

Alex looked into his green eyes, "No Jared, you know that there's only one man for me!"

Jared smiled and answered, "I'd hoped that you'd say that, because you know that there's only one girl for me too" he caught her hands across the table, it felt as if the world had stood still in that moment, until Theo's little voice piped up, "Daddy I need a wee!" They both laughed as Theo frowned at them, "Come on little man" said Jared as he got up from the table to take Theo to the toilet, Luca arrived with their orders just then and said, "A working lunch again Signorina Alex?"

"No, not today Luca," she answered smiling, "even though he's looking for somewhere to live, today's lunch is definitely something else!"

The End.

About the Author

Johanna Cogbill was born December 1972 in the Rhondda Valleys in South Wales. She is married, with two daughters and one granddaughter.

As a teenager Johanna loved to write and would often find herself asking her English teacher for essay writing for homework!

Work and homelife got in the way of any creativity for the next 30 years, but following a trip to Sorento during the summer of 2017, Johanna felt her creative urge reawaken and decided to write her fist ever book.

Ciao Cariad has been a working progress for five years now, but as a surprise for Johanna's 50th Birthday it has been proofread, edited and independently published!

We really hope that you enjoy reading Ciao Cariad, as much as Johanna has enjoyed writing it.

Printed in Great Britain
by Amazon